DEEP COVER JACK

JACK

by DIANE CAPRI

Published by: AugustBooks
http://www.AugustBooks.com

ISBN-13: 978-1-940768-70-0

Original cover design by Cory Clubb
Interior layout by Author E.M.S.

Published in the United States of America

Visit the author website:
http://www.DianeCapri.com

ALSO BY DIANE CAPRI

CAST OF PRIMARY CHARACTERS

Kim L. Otto
Carlos M. Gaspar

Charles Cooper
Lamont Finlay

Alex Branch
Susan Duffy
Theresa Justice
Terry Villanueva

Leo Abrams
Viktor Sokol

and
Jack Reacher

Thank you to some of the best readers in the world: Holly Hecker (Anneliese Miller), Mik Brown, and Michelle McQueen (Khalil), for participating in our character naming giveaways which make this book a bit more personal and fun for all of us.

Perpetually, for Lee Child, with unrelenting gratitude.

DEEP COVER
JACK

PERSUADER

by Lee Child

2003

"Not really. I don't really care about the little guy. I just hate the big guy. I hate big smug people who think they can get away with things."

"You produce the right results for the wrong reasons, then."

[Reacher] nodded. "But I try to do the right thing. I think the reasons don't really matter. Whatever, I like to see the right thing done."

CHAPTER ONE

Friday, November 19
Abbot, Maine
4:15 p.m. Eastern Time

THE DIPLOMAT'S COLLAR WAS flipped up against the raw
wind that blew across the compound from the frigid ocean
behind him. He pushed his gloved hands into his pockets and
ducked deeper into the wool coat he'd bought for city streets, not
for late November on the coast of Maine. Soon, darkness would
envelop the compound.

He moved awkwardly down the long, straight driveway from
the gray stone house toward the outbuilding closest to the gate,
losing his footing several times as his leather-soled shoes slid on
the slick pavement.

He sensed no threat or danger and expected none. The
property rested within a high, granite wall topped with coiled
razor wire. In the center of the wall was an iron gate. The gate
opened only on the Diplomat's orders when the man posted at
the gatehouse made it so. One way in. One way out. Entry by

invitation only. No unauthorized persons had entered since the Diplomat arrived two days ago.

He reached the gatehouse without falling on his ass, which was a minor miracle. When he was still attending the Russian Orthodox Church, he'd have offered thanks to God for safe passage. But that was a long time ago. He'd set aside the faith of his childhood and never looked back.

He reached up and dropped the heavy door knocker onto the thick oak door three times, then returned his gloved hand to his pocket and waited, stamping his feet against the cold.

The Diplomat was born in Siberia, so had known bone-chilling cold. He hadn't missed it.

He had chosen this house on the coast between Kennebunkport and Portland because it was vacant, renovated after some prior damage to the main dining room and the roof, and perfectly suited to his needs. Locals called the compound Abbot Cape because the rocky finger it occupied jutted into the ocean.

Long after he'd settled his organization here, after it was too late to relocate, he'd learned the troubling history of the place.

The new man opened the gatehouse door. He was tall. Maybe six feet, five inches. Big, too. Maybe two-sixty. Not an ounce of visible fat anywhere. His hands were as big as baseball mitts. He was dressed in a black T-shirt and black wool blazer that stretched taut across his hulking body. Black jeans rode low on his hips. The work boots on his feet were immense, yet seemed too small to support the rest of him.

The gateman nodded and said nothing. He stood aside and the Diplomat, not a small man himself, felt dwarfed when he stepped across the threshold into a room that was marginally warmer than the outdoors, even though the house featured an adequate heating system. Perhaps the new guy's body mass generated more heat than normal.

The Diplomat scanned the main living area's open floor plan. Small kitchen, table with four chairs, a fireplace surrounded by a sofa, two recliners, and a television. No one else was present. "What's your name again?"

"John Smith." He didn't smile.

The Diplomat shrugged. He could call himself Genghis Khan, as long as he did the job as required. "Where is she?"

"This way." Smith moved toward the back of the one-story gatehouse toward the bedrooms.

The Diplomat followed.

The last renovation here had tripled the gatehouse's size and added a private bath to each of the eight new bedrooms. Guests often preferred to entertain out here, away from the prying eyes and ears from the main house. Particularly if their desires were somewhat unsavory.

Tonight, the Diplomat was not entertaining guests. The extra bedrooms were empty.

At the end of the corridor was a doorway that led to a mudroom and beyond into an attached garage. Smith opened the door and stepped through, and the Diplomat followed.

The Diplomat shivered. He instinctively raised a gloved hand to cover his nose and filter the overwhelming stench of car exhaust.

One vehicle was idling here. A ten-year-old sedan, stolen from a shopping mall parking lot a hundred miles away. The sedan had spent its entire life driving snowy winter roads, wallowing in rock salt, and the rusted exhaust system had never been replaced. It vibrated loudly as if it might fall off its hangers.

The gasses made a chuffing noise as they passed from the engine and escaped before they reached the rear of the car.

The Diplomat nodded, and Smith pushed a button, and the double garage door rolled itself up along an overhead track. The open maw displayed the low cloud ceiling and the roiling Atlantic Ocean beyond like a giant theater screen, to majestic and chilling effect. Harsh wind blew into the garage and the ocean's roar collided with the running engine to combined ear-pounding decibel levels.

Smith pushed another button and ceiling fans whipped through the heavy air inside the garage at high speed, but the air was so thick it would take a while to clear it.

The setup was purposefully clumsy like a distraught woman bent on suicide had staged the scene herself. A flexible hose connected the tailpipe to the rear passenger window, which was open only wide enough to receive the hose. The interior of the car was obscured by smoky silver air as if the scene were a magician's trick.

The gas tank had been full when Smith started the engine, but it had to be almost empty now. The Diplomat estimated twenty-four hours run-time on a full tank. More than enough to do the job.

Smith opened the driver's door, reached in, and turned the engine off.

The Diplomat held his breath and pulled a linen handkerchief from his pocket. He covered his mouth and nose to filter the air. He walked closer to the sedan and peered through the window into the back seat.

She looked waifish lying there, stretched out on her back, as if she were enjoying the sleep of the just. In life, she'd looked angelic, almost. Tall, lean, pale skin and blonde hair. She had been the perfect type for his needs. Now, her skin was mottled and cherry red and hideous.

Still, she looked peaceful. Dressed in the outfit she'd been wearing when she arrived here. Black workout clothes. Gloves. A red hoodie. One neon running shoe on her left foot, the other resting on the roof of the sedan, waiting.

Her right shoe had been expertly repaired after the Diplomat's team took it apart and found the tracking device in the heel. She wasn't able to communicate using the device, but she could be tracked. The device had been returned to its hiding place. Let her team believe she was still on the premises. As long as they could pinpoint her location, perhaps they'd stay away, assuming her still on the job.

When he was ready to let them find her body, they'd find the device exactly where it should be. They'd be reassured, perhaps.

She'd carried nothing else with her the day she approached the iron gate and asked to come inside. She claimed she'd been running and turned her ankle. She had no cell phone. No ID. Nothing. The prior gateman had judged her harmless and admitted her. He'd paid for his mistake and so had she.

The Diplomat stepped away from the sedan and nodded. "You gave her the valium first?"

"I added it to her food. She was already sleeping when I put her in there." Smith's voice was medium pitch, a baritone not a bass. The words were clipped and somewhat Midwestern. Ordinary.

The Diplomat wondered briefly where Smith had come from and what his real name might be. He looked and sounded completely American, which was useful. Locals tended to accept Americans more readily than Russians. All of his hired muscle met those same standards. There seemed to be an endless pool of them. They were similar in size. They dressed alike. They were indistinguishable from one another, like a computer-generated army.

"Get her out of there."

The Diplomat stood aside while Smith made his way around the front of the sedan and opened the back door on the opposite side. He bent his heavy torso at the waist, slipped his big mitts under her arms, and pulled her out of the back seat.

"Check her pulse." She certainly looked dead, given the condition of her skin, but from experience, the Diplomat knew that some suicides took longer than others.

Cradling her easily in one arm, Smith laid two fingers the size of hot dogs alongside her neck. He moved his fingers a couple of times, trying to feel her carotid pulse. After a moment or two, he shrugged. "Probably. If not, she will be soon enough."

The Diplomat nodded. "Where's the freezer?"

"This way." Smith grabbed the neon running shoe off the roof of the sedan, set it upon the woman's belly, turned and marched toward a closed door in the far corner of the garage. The Diplomat followed. Smith opened the door, reached inside and flipped a light switch before he carried her over the threshold.

When The Diplomat reached the open doorway, Smith was sliding the woman into a body bag on the cement floor. Her eyes remained closed.

Smith zipped the bag closed. He lifted the lid on the twenty-cubic-foot white chest freezer, which was seventy-two inches wide and twenty-nine inches deep—large enough to hold a butchered cow, according to the sales data for this unit. He laid her flat inside the body bag, which would make her easier to transport and to thaw, then lowered the freezer's heavy lid and placed the shoe on top where it would be easy to find when they needed it.

The Diplomat handed him a padlock, which he passed through the freezer's hasp and clicked the shackle into place. Smith stood aside. The Diplomat yanked on the padlock. It was secure. The padlock opened with the key he kept on a chain around his neck.

The Diplomat looked around the room to confirm that everything was in order. He didn't expect to return to deal with her until after his business at the main house was concluded, probably not until next week or even the week after. Unfortunately. He'd prefer to return her thawed body to her personal vehicle waiting inside a garage in Houston now. Get her away from him and his operation. Knowing she was out here was an annoyance, felt like a loose end. But there was nothing for it.

Eventually, she would be found. No forensic evidence of freezing would exist.

Cause of death would be listed as carbon monoxide poisoning and manner of death would be suicide. Time of death would be established within appropriate recent parameters.

Her suicide would be lamented and mourned and not questioned. Her murder would go unnoticed and uninvestigated. The Diplomat and his business would remain off the radar.

But there was no time to ship the freezer to Houston. And while the woman remained missing, her agency colleagues might still come looking for her, which was less than ideal.

The Diplomat had considered all the reasonable alternatives. None was better than leaving her frozen until after his business was concluded. An imperfect solution that would have to suffice.

He turned and left the freezer room. John Smith followed. The Diplomat handed over another padlock. Smith used it to secure the room's only entrance. Once again, he stepped aside to allow The Diplomat to check his work. After several hard yanks, he nodded at Smith and waved a gloved hand toward the sedan.

The Diplomat walked through the open garage door and made his way to the main house, leaving Smith to dismantle and dispose of the sedan as instructed.

CHAPTER TWO

Wednesday, November 24
Houston, Texas
11:06 a.m. Central Time

THE ASSIGNMENT FILE FBI Special Agent Kim Otto
received had dispatched them to Houston, Texas. Which was just
fine with her. Houston was one of her favorite cities, particularly
as late fall moved closer to early winter. Houston could be
counted on for moderate weather. Kim hated the cold.

Her partner, FBI Special Agent Carlos Gaspar, parked the
rental in the lot at the Houston Field Division of the Bureau of
Alcohol, Tobacco, Firearms and Explosives off North Sam
Houston Parkway. It was a typical modern office building in
what developers would call Class A office space in northwest
Houston.

Three similar rectangular, multi-story granite buildings
forming a U shape opening upon a retention pond, with a
sidewalk around the site's perimeter and a perpetual fountain in
the middle. At the open end of the U, beyond the retention pond

and opposite the building that housed the ATF office, was a carpet of green space showcasing a panoramic view of downtown Houston in the distance.

"Give me a minute." Gaspar opened the sedan's door and swung his left leg out. "I need to check in." He was already placing the call as he stepped out of the vehicle.

They had been working the Reacher case off the books for twenty-three days. Kim had come to appreciate her new partner and accept his limitations. But she missed the Detroit field office where she was permanently posted.

She wondered what her supervisor had been told about her special assignment and where he thought she was. She hadn't spoken to him since that first morning when the Boss had called her out at 4:00 a.m. and sent her to Margrave, Georgia, allegedly to complete a background check on a ghost.

The assignment had taken on a life of its own since then, and the search for Jack Reacher's history had changed her at the molecular level. She was exceptionally good at chasing crime, but hunting intel on a man who deliberately stayed so far off the grid was a deadly pursuit far from her training.

She'd never return to what she now thought of as her previous self. The jury was still out on whether the new Kim Otto was better than the old.

Gaspar was pacing, talking to his wife on the phone a few feet away from the car, limping on his right leg as he usually did after a period of inactivity. He reached into his pocket for another Tylenol. Probably thought she wasn't watching.

She'd never asked him about the Tylenol or the limping. He'd made it plain that the questions were intrusive and unwelcome. But she would ask him. When the time was right. Or when she was forced to. Respect for boundaries was something she appreciated and demanded. Gaspar was good on both counts. So was she.

Kim waited inside the car, reviewing the subject's files again, giving Gaspar a bit of privacy. She had a large extended family, but no husband, no boyfriend, no children and no pets. Her work was her life, and she wanted it that way. Gaspar was fine, but she wasn't used to being Velcroed to another human being 24/7. Every now and then, she needed some breathing room, too.

But Gaspar lived in a totally different world. He rarely had privacy of any kind. His wife, Marie, was very pregnant and due to deliver at any moment. In Miami. He'd been back to check on her twice since their assignment began.

Marie was managing the late stages of pregnancy, and parenting four daughters alone at the same time, much more effectively than Kim would have. Gaspar was worried about his family, and he wanted to get home.

Which made total sense to Kim, even though dealing with kids made her itchy. Four kids constantly underfoot would make her break out in hives worse than the time she ate five pounds of strawberries.

Unlike her, Gaspar's worldview was not influenced by unbridled ambition and unquenchable desire to succeed.

Kim returned her attention to the assignment files. Photos of their interview subject, ATF Special Agent in Charge, Hector Alvarez, were included. Her first brief pass through the documents showed no mention of Reacher or any clues about why the Boss had sent them here. Which was annoyingly normal for this assignment.

Gaspar rapped hard on the side window, sending Kim jumping high enough into the air that she hit her head on the sedan's roof. She could hear him laughing through the glass and tossed him a vicious scowl.

Trying with no success to hide his amusement, he opened her door and bowed like an old-fashioned limo driver. "A thousand pardons, Madame Butterfly, but I have completed my call. How may I be of service to you?"

"Very funny, Cheech. You should take that act on the road." She shoved the files into her bag, got out of the car and steamed off toward the front of the building, rubbing the rising knot on her head and leaving Gaspar to keep up as best he could. "Come on," she called back. "We've got work to do."

She heard him press the electronic door locks and chuckle again behind her.

She'd left her electronics in the car except for the cell phones. With each new set of orders, the Boss delivered new disposable cell phones to each of them, and they spent too much time attempting to evade oversight. Not today. There was no point in attempting to thwart his constant tracking. The effort would be futile. Every government building in the country was completely submerged in surveillance.

When Gaspar caught up, he still looked awfully pleased with himself.

"You know it occurs to me," she said, "you get all this entertainment value from me, and I get nothing for it."

He grinned. "You're right. Next time, black coffee's on me."

"You are such a prince." But she smiled. He was totally likable, even if he was also maddening. "Everything okay at home?"

Once Gaspar worked out the tightness in his muscles, he easily kept up with her. "Marie is doing okay. I'd like to get back for Thanksgiving tomorrow, but it's not crucial. The doc says the baby could be two weeks late."

"You believe him?"

"Our other kids were late, so he might be right." His tone put an end to the conversation about his family. Maybe he was worried or maybe he just wanted to get on with things and get home.

She nodded and changed the subject. "So the file we got on Alvarez is sparse. I'm sure there's more to it."

"There always is." He was wearing aviator sunglasses that shielded his eyes, but she recognized the tone. She was not an optimist, but he was a cynic. Which was not the same as being wrong. The Boss had been withholding information from them since this assignment began. Of course, the materials he supplied for the Alvarez interview wouldn't be any more complete than the others.

Gaspar's long legs carried him at her pace without too much struggle. "You read the file and I didn't. Give me the highlights. What do I need to know before the interview?"

"Not much to tell. Alvarez has been with ATF his entire career. He's an Army vet. One way or another, he's been employed by Uncle Sam forever." She shook her head before he had a chance to ask. "Not likely he knew Reacher when they were both soldiers, but possible."

He glanced toward the buildings and scanned the area. There were a few other pedestrians on the sidewalk around the pond and a few more in the parking lot. It was midday. Office workers headed to and from lunch, probably.

Kim wasn't worried about being watched at the moment. The Reacher assignment was off the books, but she wasn't undercover. No need for covert ops out here in the open. There were several cameras visible from the sidewalk, and she noted the locations, just in case. She never worried about things she could see. It was the unseen, unexpected, unrecognized things that made her nervous. "One curious thing, though."

"What's that?"

"Looks like he might be Susan Duffy's boss."

Gaspar's right eyebrow popped up in the comical way that meant he was surprised.

"The timing, as far as we know it, is right. Her paper trail says she's assigned to this field office."

"We've been trying to find Susan Duffy for days. You think it's likely we'll just show up and see her walking the halls? Surprise her at work?"

Kim shook her head. "As usual, I think the Boss is up to something. Keep your eyes open and your wits about you."

Duffy would be easy to spot. Pale. Slender. Attractive. Taller than her formal headshot suggested. Fit and capable, of course. They'd dealt with her twice in the past twenty-three days. They knew precisely what she looked like.

Gaspar had shoved both hands in his pockets and loped along as if he was an accountant or a banker returning from lunch. "Alvarez have anything to do with Reacher?"

"As usual, there's not a single mention of Reacher in Alvarez's file. But I'd say Reacher involvement is a solid guess since the Boss has us standing here, wouldn't you?"

When they reached the building that housed the ATF offices, they walked through the security checkpoint easily. Only their badges were inspected. The Boss had greased the process.

Inside the elevator, Gaspar said, "Say we find her, wandering the halls. Duffy hasn't been very helpful before."

"I'm hoping things will go better this time." Kim shrugged.

It was Gaspar's all-purpose gesture, and she'd come to find it useful.

Gaspar ran a hand through his hair and blew a long stream of pent-up frustration through his lips. "An optimist. Unusual for a lawyer or a cop, and you're both."

"Our luck can change." Her voice sounded sanctimonious in her own ears.

"Yeah? I wouldn't bet the Otto family farm. Your mother would not be pleased." The elevator dinged, and the doors opened, and they stepped into the lobby. A woman was waiting.

"Agents Otto and Gaspar?" She said Kim's name first. Which meant she knew Otto was the agent in charge, and Gaspar was number two. Which implied their visit was adequately foretold. Unusual. The Boss generally preferred to toss them into a situation without any preamble.

Kim nodded. "We're here to see Assistant Special Agent in Charge Hector Alvarez."

"He's expecting you. Come with me." The woman smiled. She led the way down a long corridor.

Kim met Gaspar's gaze and smirked as if to say, "I told you so."

CHAPTER THREE

THEY FOLLOWED THE WOMAN down a long corridor to a spacious office framed on one side by a wall of windows facing east. She stepped inside and immediately announced, "FBI Special Agents Kim Otto and Carlos Gaspar, sir." She turned to face them and said, "Assistant Special Agent in Charge, Hector Alvarez." After that, she left the room and closed the door.

Kim stepped forward. Alvarez shook hands with her first and then with Gaspar before turning his attention back to Kim. He knew she was the lead agent, too. Someone had briefed him, and she wondered whether it was Duffy.

"Thank you for seeing us on short notice so close to a holiday," Kim said. Alvarez nodded, waved toward a couple of chairs and Kim began with her usual opening. "We are assigned to the FBI Special Personnel Task Force. We're completing a background check on a civilian being considered for a special assignment."

"Happy to help, if I can. Who is the civilian?" He was polite. He seemed to be willing. Also unusual. Their interview subjects had been hostile from the outset.

Kim took a chance that at least one of the subjects they'd been assigned to interview might actually be willing to do his job and cooperate. "Major Jack Reacher. U.S. Army, retired."

Alvarez didn't react at all. No surprise, anger, or any emotion they'd run into from Reacher's friends and enemies before. He cocked his head and seemed to be thinking about the question. As if he were searching his internal hard drive for data.

Finally, he shook his head slowly. "I'm drawing a blank here. I don't know the name."

Kim reached into her pocket and pulled out her phone. She found Reacher's last official headshot from his Army file. It was fifteen years old, but it was the only photograph she had. She passed the phone across the desk.

Alvarez studied it a few moments and returned the phone. "I'm sorry. He looks like a lot of other Army officers I've known over the years. But otherwise, I don't recognize him. How am I supposed to have come into contact with him?"

Gaspar leaned forward in his chair. "We were sent here by the Director to collect background from you about Reacher. He was in the 110th Special Investigations Unit. An MP. For thirteen years. Graduated West Point. Retired fifteen years ago."

"I'm happy to help, of course, but you're barking up the wrong tree." Alvarez's blank look and slow head-shaking greeted each of Gaspar's reminders. "None of that rings any bells with me. I didn't attend West Point. When I was in the Army, it was Armored Division, not MP. My record was clean. No activity that might have flagged me to MPs so that I'd have had dealings with him. Seems like your man Reacher may have already been retired when I served, anyway."

The slim file the Boss had provided for Alvarez provided no clues about his connection to Reacher or why the Boss thought he might have useful knowledge about Reacher's life since he left the Army.

Kim changed her approach. "Sometimes, unfortunately, veterans get into trouble when they leave the military. Is there any chance that you've run into Reacher professionally? Has he been the subject of an ATF investigation, perhaps?"

"Anything's possible, I guess." Alvarez's blank look didn't waver. "I don't recognize his name, and I don't recall him being involved in our cases. Have you checked our files?"

Kim shook her head. "Would you do that for us now?"

"Of course. I'll ask my assistant, Anneliese, to conduct a quick search. That should turn up anything of significance." He pushed away from the desk and walked into the hallway, closing the office door behind him.

Gaspar looked at her. "Now what?"

"You think he's lying?"

"No."

She didn't think so, either. Which raised the danger level several notches on Kim's personal threat scale. The Boss only sent them into disaster, and so far, contact with Alvarez had been pretty tame.

All of which meant the Boss had sent them here for another reason.

"So we can keep shooting in the dark," Gaspar said.

Kim nodded. "Or we can get on with it and ask him about Duffy."

If the Boss had meant them to find Duffy here, he would have told them as much.

He knew they'd had two encounters with her in the past twenty-three days, one in DC and one in Virginia. Both times, Kim suspected that Reacher had been with Duffy. Which meant she'd had contact with Reacher at least twice in the past twenty-three days alone. After the second encounter, Gaspar had quietly contacted his sources attempting to find Duffy, while Kim had maintained radio silence. No one they'd asked had been able to pinpoint her location.

Kim suspected that the Boss had located Duffy and sent them here. But why not simply say so? Why the misdirection with Alvarez? Experience said the answer to that question wasn't benign. Frissons of electricity ran along Kim's body.

What kind of deadly game was the Boss playing here?

Alvarez returned, shaking his head. "Unfortunately, it seems you've made the trip for nothing." He settled behind his desk. "We can find nothing on Reacher as a suspect or an informant or any capacity in our investigations going back twenty years."

Kim put a smile in her voice. "Thank you for checking. We will report that you can neither recommend nor disqualify Reacher, then."

"I'm sorry." Alvarez nodded. When they didn't immediately stand to leave, he cocked his head again. "Was there something else you wanted?"

Kim cleared her throat before she told the lie. "We have also been asked to interview one of your agents while we're here."

"Oh?" He frowned. No lawman likes surprises and protocol required that he be given notice before his personnel was questioned, formally or informally.

"Agent Susan Duffy is assigned to the Houston Field Office. We'd like to see her."

A flush crept up his neck from his collar all the way to his receding hairline, but he said nothing.

"Where is Agent Duffy?"

Alvarez glanced down at the desk, then met her eye. "I can give you her home address. You may find her there."

Kim and Gaspar remained seated. "What's going on here, Agent Alvarez?" Kim asked. "Is Duffy sick today?"

"Not exactly." His features settled into a hard stare. "Look, I wouldn't ordinarily disclose this, but I will since you're here at the Director's request. The truth is, Agent Duffy's on leave."

"What kind of leave?" Kim suspected Duffy had been in trouble before. The files Gaspar's sources had been able to find showed that nine years ago, Susan Duffy was at DEA. Spent her whole career there. On the fast track and going all the way to the top, some said. Until Duffy got in trouble on her last assignment. She wasn't asked to leave, but things were headed in that direction. Something must have pushed her out.

She'd landed on her feet. The transfer from DEA had been at her own request, but it was odd all the same. Like she'd left the DEA before they could kick her out. Was she doing the same thing now?

"I suggested she take a vacation. Wait for the usual procedures to iron things out." Alvarez nodded, decisively, as if he'd made the only correct choice. "I don't know where she is right at the moment."

Gaspar's right eyebrow arched. "What did she do?"

Alvarez cleared his throat again. "The matter is under investigation, Agent Gaspar. I wasn't involved, and I don't know all the facts. I'm sure the Director can get that information for you if you need it."

Kim was sure the Director had that information, too. Question was, why didn't the Boss know all about Duffy being on leave before he sent them here? The answer was that he *had* known. Of course, he had. What was he playing at?

"We'll take Duffy's home address," Kim said, frostily.

"We can get that for you, of course." His tone was as frosty as hers. "I'm sorry I don't have any more to share with you at the moment," he went on, sounding not the least bit sorry. His change in demeanor was decidedly odd.

Kim paused a moment. "Since Duffy's not here, we'll settle for an interview with her partner. He can probably answer our questions."

Alvarez shook his head, a woeful expression on his face. "Agent Duffy is between partners at the moment. Her last partner left the agency."

Gaspar stared at him. "What do you mean he 'left'?"

"Neither Duffy nor her partner reported directly to me." Alvarez shrugged as if he didn't much care what had happened to either of them. "I heard he quit."

"He *quit*?" Gaspar said. "He's been with us for a decade at least, right? Why would he quit?" He sounded as if he couldn't comprehend the concept of quitting an agency job. In truth, he probably couldn't. He'd been employed by Uncle Sam one way or another for his entire working life.

Kim was more worldly. She knew no one was chained to the desk. Still, the timing was beyond suspicious. "What is the former partner's name?"

"Special Agent Alex Branch."

"We'll need a home address for him as well."

"We can get that for you, too." He made no move to make good on the promise. She nodded toward the phone on his desk. He frowned before he picked it up and buzzed the intercom. "Ms. Miller, please find a residence address and phone number for Agents Duffy and Branch and bring it in."

"I'd like to see Duffy's office while we're waiting." Kim

stood aside and waited until Alvarez left his desk and led the way. She and Gaspar followed him about six doors down to another closed door on the same side of the hallway. Special Agent Susan Duffy's name was engraved on the plate on the door.

Alvarez turned the handle and pushed the door open, allowing Kim and Gaspar to enter, but he remained standing stiffly in the hallway.

Duffy's small office was furnished with standard government-issue furniture. Nothing special about it. The usual official photos hung on the wall. An American flag stood on a pole in the corner. The room was anonymous and androgynous. Nothing suggested it had ever been occupied by any particular agent with a defined gender.

There was nothing to be gleaned here about Duffy or her whereabouts or her relationship to Reacher.

Gaspar approached the desk and its drawers and the credenza. "These have been cleaned out. Nothing in here except a few office supplies and a phonebook. Looks like Duffy isn't expected back."

Kim looked out the windows. Duffy's view across the retention pond toward Houston was similar to Alvarez's, but her window wall was narrower because her office was smaller. There was nothing to see. Nothing to find. They were wasting their time here.

She pulled out a business card and handed it to Alvarez. "We need to speak to Duffy. Ask her to call me."

He didn't take the card, and he didn't promise.

She looked down at the cheap gray carpet for a moment, struggling for patience. When she looked up again, she infused her words with menace. "We're all aware that you don't report to the Director of the FBI. Don't think that means he can't reach out and touch you."

Alvarez smirked in the way of weasels everywhere. "You misunderstand me, Agent Otto. We are more than happy to assist the FBI anytime. If I knew where Agent Duffy was, I would tell you." He squared his shoulders and buttoned his suit coat. "She's on leave and under investigation. That's all I'm authorized to say. Indeed, it's all I know about the matter. You can pick up the home address and phone number for Duffy and Branch from my assistant on your way out. What you do with that information is up to you. Good day."

He turned and strode back to his office. Kim heard the door slam at the opposite end of the hall.

"That went well." Gaspar shrugged. "You do have a way with men, don't you Susie Wong?"

"Let's go." She stood aside and allowed him to precede her along the corridor toward the exit. She stopped at the desk outside Alvarez's office and Anneliese Miller, the woman who had escorted them earlier, handed over two business cards, one with Agent Duffy's contact information on the back and the other for Agent Branch. Kim slipped both into her pocket.

When they reached the elevator, Kim said, "We'll check out Duffy's residence, then Branch's."

"And then what?" Gaspar pushed the elevator call button.

"We'll figure that out when we get there."

They rode the elevator down and walked through the lobby and outside to the rental without speaking. Gaspar might have been thinking about his family. Kim ran through the contents of the Duffy file in her head.

The file they had been able to cobble together on Duffy so far was thin. Too thin. They couldn't find the exact nature of

Duffy's DEA trouble nine years ago, but it had something to do with unauthorized activity and death of another agent. She'd ended up here at ATF, where she'd been since. Nothing in the file to warrant putting Duffy on administrative leave, either.

Exactly how the Boss made the decision to send them to particular subjects was unknown. Kim's working theory was that he believed Reacher would show up to help his friends out of trouble.

Particularly his female friends.

Reacher had spent thirteen years in the army at a time when the military was overwhelmingly male. Yet, the Boss's focus on the men Reacher knew seemed like an afterthought. Even though each woman Kim had met was more than capable of taking care of herself, Reacher's female companions were at the center of this investigation.

The question was, since Reacher was so far off the grid that no one could find him, how did the Boss know which friends needed Reacher's help?

Kim's guess on that score was that the Boss was monitoring Reacher's old contacts illegally. When he thought Reacher might show up, he sent Otto and Gaspar into the situation, hoping for an intercept.

She hadn't worked out what the Boss thought they should do if they found Reacher when they got there. And she hadn't discussed any of these conclusions with Gaspar. Yet.

Right now, she wanted to know where the hell Susan Duffy was and what had the Boss sent them here to find?

CHAPTER FOUR

ACCORDING TO THE GPS on the rental's dashboard, Duffy lived in a condo in the tony West University area of Houston between Westpark Drive and Bissonnet Street, twenty miles south of the ATF offices. Branch's address was a single family house in Fort Bend, ten miles further south.

"Unless she's dead, she won't be home." Gaspar pulled the sedan onto the highway while Kim secured an alligator clamp on the seatbelt at the retractor to avoid being beheaded. He grinned. "And if Duffy's dead, there's no point in trying to interview her."

"Probably get as much out of Duffy either way."

Gaspar laughed. "You're catching on, Sunshine."

But she felt her brow knitting itself into a frown. Gaspar could relieve his tension with gallows humor, but hers never left her. She reached into her pocket for an antacid and chewed thoughtfully while Gaspar drove.

"Stands to reason Duffy's in trouble," Kim said. "She stepped way out of bounds on that kidnapping case two weeks ago."

"Maybe." Gaspar glanced at her. "But the victim was the Vice-President's grandson, which means the whole thing was hushed up afterward like it never happened. Nobody's going to tell anybody anything about her involvement in that case."

"Whether anybody can get their hands on the truth or not, Duffy will get more than a hand slap for that one. She shouldn't have been involved at all. Kidnappings aren't ATF's responsibility or expertise. She didn't have any authority to order and organize that rescue." Kim was talking aloud, working things through in her head, because she didn't have all of the facts. "Let's assume Duffy wasn't authorized, but thanks to her the ATF took down the kidnappers and rescued the kid, with one of the kidnappers killed. The brass would not have been happy."

"Heads were bound to roll. Duffy's should have been the first." Gaspar frowned as he changed lanes to pass a slow-moving truck. "If all those assumptions are correct, then ATF is doing the right thing putting her on leave, and she'll probably be phased out, one way or another."

Kim took a deep breath. "Not to mention that she did it all to help cover up Reacher's involvement."

"Even if that's true, and we don't know it was Reacher for sure…" Gaspar glanced across the bench seat and watched her a moment. He raised his right eyebrow. "Who knows that besides us, the Boss, Duffy, and Reacher?"

"Somebody does." Kim shook her head. This case was always more questions than answers. "Somebody with enough juice to get her benched without making a public splash."

Gaspar made no further argument. He was probably thinking the same things she was. That there were quite a few bosses higher up the ladder who had a lot more juice than that. Hell, the Vice-President himself could have ordered things hushed up.

About twenty minutes later, Kim realized the car was slowing along the exit ramp, leaving the Interstate.

Gaspar glanced her way. "How about a coffee stop before we reach Duffy's place?"

Whatever trance-like state she'd been in was slow to clear. Her brain felt thick and foggy. "Coffee's always a good idea."

"Coming right up." He turned right at the bottom of the ramp. A few blocks down the road, he turned right, into a fast food joint's parking lot. He parked under a shade tree near the back. "Getting out? Breathe some fresh air? Get your gray cells going?"

"Absolutely." She shook her head to dislodge the cobwebs and took a few deeper breaths and put some energy that she didn't feel into her voice. Maybe she was coming down with a cold or something. *Great. That's all I need.*

Gaspar pulled out his cell. "I'll meet you inside."

"Perfect." She left the car and walked toward the building. Inside, she went to the restroom and took care of business. She washed her hands and splashed cool water on her face. She didn't wear much makeup, so there was no danger of washing it off. She looked at her face in the mirror and was relieved to see that she didn't look as spacey as she felt.

By the time she reached the line to order, she was feeling better. Several customers were stacked up ahead of her. The cashier seemed to be in training or something. He was spending an inordinate amount of time finding the right buttons on the register. The line moved slowly and grew longer behind her. The smell of fried grease permeated the place.

Gaspar joined her when she was almost to the register.

"Want anything besides coffee?" He was always ravenous, so she wasn't surprised when he nodded. She ordered a large black coffee and stepped aside. He ordered almost every item on the menu.

She grinned and moved away while he paid. She filled her cup at the self-service coffee pot and found a table. From experience, she knew she didn't want him eating fast food in the car. They'd be smothered in old-grease-stench for the rest of the trip.

He joined her with his tray, which was piled so high two of the sandwiches fell onto the floor. He picked them up and laid them aside. He had plenty more.

"What's going on here, Sunshine?" He unwrapped some of his food and began to consume it like a vacuum cleaner, barely pausing to chew. "Let's wrap this up and go home for Thanksgiving tomorrow. Whaddaya say?"

"That would make my mother happy. Missing the Otto family Thanksgiving is a federal crime as far as she's concerned." Kim grinned and removed the lid from her black coffee. "First issue is Duffy. The Boss sent us to her office knowing she wasn't there. Why?"

"Maybe he expected us to find her there." Gaspar shrugged. "It's possible he didn't know she'd been put on leave."

"You believe that?"

"No. But it is possible. He's not God, you know." He'd already consumed one small pack of fries and reached for another.

"So you keep saying. But she's been on leave for days. Maybe even since the kidnapping mess in Virginia. When she helped the guy we think was Reacher get away. After he made damn sure that kidnapper died." She tried to sip the coffee but burned the hair off her tongue with the first sip. It was scalding hot.

"Maybe the Boss wanted us to meet Duffy's partner. Sounds like Branch quit after she was put on leave. Maybe that happened just this morning. While we were on our way here."

"Possible." She tapped her index finger on the table, absently.

"Well, we couldn't have been here to interview that toady Alvarez. The Boss would know how useless a conversation with that guy was likely to be." He wadded up the paper from the hamburger he'd just consumed and opened another.

"True." She cocked her head and narrowed her eyes. "So what's he up to?"

"We could keep speculating about it." Gaspar finished off the second hamburger. "Or we could just ask him."

"Like he'd tell us the truth, even if we asked." She wrinkled her nose and tried to sip again. Still too hot.

"There is that." He finished off the last of his fries and turned to the coffee. He'd added what looked like half-a-cup of heavy cream and a pound of sugar to the dark brew. "Or we could just head over to Duffy's place and figure it out for ourselves."

"My plan precisely. Let's go." She stopped at the soda machine and grabbed an ice cube to melt on her tongue. She plopped another one into her coffee and replaced the lid. A few minutes later they were back on the road.

Kim turned on the GPS audio and allowed the disembodied voice to relay directions. The coffee was finally cool enough to drink. "The Boss knows."

Gaspar glanced at her and scowled. "Of course he knows."

"He knows before he sends us into these situations that there's going to be a problem."

Gaspar nodded. "And he thinks Reacher will come to solve it."

"And he wants us to be there when Reacher shows up."

"I agree." Gaspar glanced at her again. "No other explanation makes sense."

"So far, it's working. Not the way he expects it to. But every time we get there, trouble happens. And before things are over, Reacher shows up."

"You're guessing. Maybe he shows up, and maybe not," Gaspar said. "We haven't actually seen the whites of his eyes."

"Yeah, and hopefully we won't." Kim drank her coffee, and they rode the rest of the way in silence.

Gaspar followed the orders from the GPS. When they pulled up to Duffy's condo building, he parked out front and turned off the ignition. He turned to face her.

"You know we're not going to find Duffy inside there, right?"

She nodded. "The Boss knew Duffy was in trouble, and he knew why. He knew she wouldn't be in that office when he sent us there. But I'm betting he didn't know Duffy's partner had quit."

"Makes sense." Gaspar nodded slowly. "And if that's true, then we might find Branch, and he might lead us to Duffy. Should we head over there?"

This was the thing she'd been mulling over in her head. Was there something in Duffy's home that she needed to find before she approached Branch? Would she have time to find it before Branch bugged out if that's what he was going to do? Or were they already too late? Was Branch with Duffy?

"You think Duffy's dead?" She glanced up toward Duffy's building.

"I meant that as a joke, Sunshine." Gaspar's eyes were hidden behind the aviators. "Why the hell would she be dead?"

"Wouldn't be the first time one of Reacher's friends ended up dead before we arrived." Kim shrugged. "If she's not dead, then where is she?"

"Hell, Susie Wong, haven't you been listening to me? I don't know. Maybe she took Alvarez's advice. Went to a spa or something. She's on paid leave until they sort out whatever mess she's in. What would you do if you were in her shoes?"

"That's what worries me." She squared her shoulders and took a deep breath. She drained the last of her coffee. "Because what I'd do is try to clear my name, at the very least."

"And how would you do that?"

"In a normal world?" She paused a couple of beats. "I'd call Jack Reacher. He got Duffy in this mess. He can get her out."

Gaspar blinked. "And how the hell would she do that?"

She understood what he meant, and he was right. They weren't operating in the normal world. Duffy couldn't call Reacher. As far as they'd seen, no one had been able to contact him in more than fifteen years. If Reacher could be found, the Boss would have already found him.

Kim craned her neck to look up at the condo building again. Duffy's home was a unit on the fifth floor. There were no lights on in the entire floor, and all but a couple of the drapes were closed. "Unless her place faces the back of the building, Duffy's not here. Reacher's sure as hell not here. But we are. Let's take a quick look inside and get back on the road. Maybe we can still find Branch today. And get home for Thanksgiving dinner tomorrow."

"Whatever you say, Dragon Boss Lady." He was already halfway out of the car when he cocked his head and asked, "You coming or not?"

CHAPTER FIVE

THE WEST UNIVERSITY AREA of Houston was upscale.
Kim was surprised that Duffy could afford to live here, and she
made a mental note to check out Duffy's finances. Although she
didn't seem like the type, Duffy wouldn't be the first agent to
stick her fingers in the illegal cash she came into constant
contact with on the job.

The condo building was relatively new. Maybe built in the
last ten years. According to the file, Duffy lived alone. Kim
didn't believe she was the kind of person who would be sulking
alone in her condo unless she was sick or maimed or something.

Gaspar was right. Duffy wasn't here.

Gaspar led the way to the front door. He pressed the doorbell
for Duffy's apartment, 5A. After a few seconds, when no one
answered, he pushed the button for another unit on Duffy's floor.
There were four units, and he tried them in order. On the third
try, 5D, they were rewarded with a response.

"Yes?" The voice was tinny but sounded male and young. A
teenager, probably.

"We've got a package for Susan Duffy. She doesn't seem to

be answering her bell, and I hate to leave it out here on the sidewalk. Any chance we could bring it up and get you to sign for her?" An old ruse, but still effective. People liked to help their neighbors.

"Yeah. We sign for her stuff all the time. Come on up." He buzzed the release on the front door. Gaspar entered first, and Kim followed.

Gaspar's leg wasn't great on stairs, so they took the elevator. At the fifth floor elevator lobby, they ignored the kid in 5D and made their way down the short hallway to Duffy's unit. Gaspar made quick work of the locked entry door, and they slipped inside.

The interior of Duffy's condo was not impressive. It did have an unused fireplace, which was the only original feature Kim saw. The rest of the place had been renovated, maybe within the last couple of years. The furniture and decor were expensive but minimalist. Everything spare. Lots of white walls and empty space. No warmth to the place at all.

A quick survey of the five small rooms confirmed that Duffy was not here. Kim picked up the cordless handset for the landline and scrolled through the caller ID.

The last phone call Duffy had answered was five days ago. She scrolled back a few more days and saw the same number repeated several times in the past couple of weeks.

She replaced the handset on its charger as Gaspar returned from the back rooms. "Well? Find anything?"

He was already shaking his head before he answered. "Not a thing. You?"

She pointed her chin toward the phone. "An anxious caller. There's about seven calls from the same phone number in the past two weeks."

"A robo call? Looking for a donation or a survey or something? Most real people are not that insistent."

"Could be. There's no call duration listed on the log and robo calls are short, usually. Since she'd answered one five days ago, if they weren't put off by her response I'd expect to see more calls right up until today, too. Those robo calls are notorious for perseverance."

"Did you try calling back?"

"We need to get moving." Kim took one more quick pass through the condo. This time, she looked in the closets, drawers, and the medicine chest. Clothes were neatly organized. Nothing but over-the-counter drugstore items in the medicine cabinet.

She found a wall safe in the back of the master bedroom closet, similar to the one she had in her own apartment back in Detroit. For more than a few seconds, she considered breaking into the safe before she reminded herself that she was FBI, not KGB. She'd already breached Duffy's privacy simply by being here, and she was uncomfortable about that. Breaking into Duffy's safe seemed a bridge too far.

The whole place seemed unnaturally sterile. The vibe was off, but Kim couldn't name the feeling precisely. Duffy could be germ-phobic, or she could have allergies. She might be paranoid, even. But the feel of the place was like Duffy had bugged out and didn't expect to return.

"That kid in 5D is going to be wondering where we are." Gaspar seemed to be getting a little antsy himself. He shifted his weight from one foot to the other, but maybe his leg was hurting more than usual.

"You think Duffy's coming back here?" Kim asked.

Gaspar shrugged.

Kim shook her head. "I don't think so either. It's like she

doesn't expect things to work out with the ATF. Like she's already moved on. Maybe she quit, too."

"Or maybe she's on some kind of suicide mission," Gaspar said, frowning. "Don't look at me like that. Stranger things have happened since we've been looking into Reacher, and you know it."

When Kim and Gaspar returned to the front room, Kim was a few steps in the lead. She stopped walking abruptly. Gaspar moved into the room and stood beside her.

An average-looking man, maybe six feet tall, blocked the condo's front door, feet braced shoulder width apart. Brown hair, hazel eyes, unshaven. He was fit enough, but not overly muscled. He wore indigo jeans and a black T-shirt and boots. No jacket to cover his shoulder holster and the Glock 17 resting within it. He wore a coolly appraising expression.

Kim recognized him immediately from his ATF headshot. "Alex Branch, right?"

"Anneliese told me you were on your way here. She's always been fond of me." Branch grinned briefly before settling back into his watchful, slightly skeptical attitude.

His natural expression, Kim imagined.

"Where's Duffy?" Branch said.

"If we knew that, we wouldn't be standing here messing around with you, now would we?" Gaspar's frown covered his entire face. He was generally agreeable and willing to take direction. But he didn't appreciate surprises any more than Kim did.

Branch moved away from the door, toward the kitchen table. "Let's sit. Maybe we can help each other out. But I need to know why you're here first. For real. I've already heard the phony story. From Anneliese."

He pulled one of the chairs away from the table and sat down, which brought his face about eye-level with Kim's. She was not quite five feet tall. Males over the age of ten were rarely at her eye level, even the average-sized ones. She pulled a chair out and sat across from him.

"I'll stand, thanks." Gaspar moved into the kitchen and leaned against the counter.

"Anneliese must have told you why we're here," Kim said. "FBI Special Personnel Task Force. Conducting a routine background check on a civilian being considered for government work."

"Who's the civilian?"

His tone was too demanding for Kim's taste. "Sorry. That information is need-to-know."

"I see." He backed off the attitude. The guy was a quick learner. "Why do you want to talk to Duffy?"

"Duffy is familiar with the civilian," Gaspar said.

"Sounds like something you could've obtained with a phone call or an email."

He was suspicious, but then, most cops were suspicious by nature. On personality tests, good ones scored high in skepticism. A healthy trait that Kim shared and felt comfortable around. Which didn't mean she was going to answer his questions.

"It's standard SPTF protocol to conduct these interviews in person," she said. "We asked to interview Duffy at work. We found out she wasn't there. Alvarez suggested we check Duffy's home. End of story." She held his gaze and let him process the information for a moment. "What about you? Why are you here?"

"I don't see how that concerns you," Branch said.

"We heard you quit the ATF." Gaspar put a little extra emphasis on the word quit. "Why?"

"I don't see how that concerns you, either." Branch's tone wasn't belligerent, exactly, but Kim could tell he was stubborn. Another trait she shared, though she called hers tenacity.

"Looks like we can't help each other out after all." Kim pushed back from the table and stood. "We'll be on our way. Let's go, Gaspar."

"I know you're working for Charles Cooper. Duffy knows that, too. The man's a snake. Not to be trusted." Branch remained seated, hands folded on the table. "Duffy told me not to trust you, either."

Kim absorbed the information, but she didn't stop to worry about it. "She mentioned us by name?"

Branch nodded. "She was quite specific about it."

"No problem." Kim turned and continued toward the front door. Gaspar pushed himself away from the sink. She heard his footfalls behind her.

"I resigned because Duffy was put on leave," Branch said as they neared the door. They stopped and turned to him. "It's political bullshit. You met Alvarez. Did he seem like a standup guy to you? The agent in charge is worse." Branch ran his hands through his hair. "Messing with Duffy was the last straw for me. I had a long-standing offer from BlueRiver, and I took it."

"BlueRiver? The paramilitary outfit?" Gaspar asked. "Contractors assigned to patrol the border and deal with the Mexican gangs and cartels?"

Branch nodded. "After ten years with ATF, I'm more than qualified to deal with armed outlaws." Branch turned his gaze directly to Kim. "Your turn. Why are you looking for Duffy?"

"I told you. We're doing a background check." Kim turned

to the door, reached for the handle, but didn't open it. She looked back at him. "Duffy knew our subject. We need information from her. About him."

"What kind of information?"

"The usual kind. Whether he's capable and fit for the job."

"What kind of capabilities and fitness?"

"Full range. Physical, mental, emotional, and financial fitness. General and special qualifications, if any."

Branch pressed his lips into a thin line and seemed to consider what she'd said, but he offered no reply.

Kim said, "Where is Duffy? You can protect her while we interview her if you like. Maybe that's your new assignment with BlueRiver. Maybe that's why you're here. Take care of Duffy? All we need are answers to our background questions. After that, we're on our way."

Branch rubbed the back of his neck. He took a deep breath and looked directly into Kim's eyes. "I don't know where she is."

"When did you see her last?"

"The day Alvarez put her on leave. Thirteen days ago." He dipped his chin slightly. "I've been on assignment for BlueRiver. I just got back this morning and found out she was gone. Same as you."

"Okay." Kim nodded and turned to Gaspar. "Let's go." She opened the door and walked out.

Gaspar closed Duffy's door behind him and followed Kim to the elevator. "You figure Branch does know where she is?"

"Maybe. Maybe not." She shrugged. "Either way, talking to him was a waste of time."

"What do you think he's doing in there now? Calling Duffy?"

Kim shrugged. She felt the Boss's cell phone vibrating in her pocket, indicating a text message. She read the message and dropped the phone back into her pocket as the elevator arrived.

On the way down, Gaspar leaned against the wall. He nodded toward the phone. "What does he want?"

After three weeks of this assignment, neither of them was surprised that the Boss's timing was always perfect. He kept them on a short leash, and he made no pretext about it. Now and then, he was actually helpful.

"He says forget about going to Branch's residence. He says Branch isn't there."

Gaspar grinned. "I told you. He's not God. He doesn't know everything."

"And he's slow to share what he does know." She cocked her head and looked up at him. "He also says we have a flight in two hours."

"A flight to where?"

"I'll tell you, but you won't like it."

"So what else is new?" Gaspar shrugged, but she heard the edge in his voice. He was concerned about increasing his distance from his family in Miami.

Kim didn't like it, either. And not merely because the trip required another dangerous plane flight. One of the things she missed about working out of the Detroit Field Office was driving everywhere, keeping her feet firmly on the ground. Where she had a fighting chance.

CHAPTER SIX

Wednesday, November 24
Houston, Texas
1:45 p.m. Central Time

BRANCH REMAINED SEATED AT the table for a few
moments after Otto and Gaspar closed the door. He shook his
head. For FBI agents, this duo was entirely too touchy. Which
likely meant they had something to hide. He wondered what that
could be and whether it had anything to do with Duffy's
disappearance. He figured the two were probably related, but
how?

He stood and stretched and wandered around Duffy's home,
trying to get a better feel for the situation. He'd been here several
times before. Duffy's style had always been sterile, but the place
looked a little more abandoned to him today. It was as if she
expected people to come into her home and she didn't want them
to find out anything about her. *Mission accomplished.*

He walked through the small condo. Every room looked like
it had been vacuumed for evidence. The sinks and tub and toilet

had been cleaned. There wasn't as much as a stray hair on any of the floors. The bed was made with the type of sharp precision required for a drill sergeant's approval. Duffy had never served in the military, and he wondered where she'd picked up the habit.

She was a clothes hound. Her closet looked like an expert sales clerk had stocked and organized it. The second bedroom had a big closet and it, too, was full of her evening dresses, shoes, and other female stuff. But nothing was a quarter inch out of place.

He shook his head and grinned. If they were roommates, they'd drive each other crazy. Most of his clothes were piled on the floor and chairs—every flat surface. He never looked pressed or polished. Duffy would probably shoot him the first time he tossed dirty socks into the corner.

He went straight to the thing he was looking for—her safe in the back of her bedroom closet. He'd helped her decide which one to buy. When she had it installed years ago, he had teased her that her bedroom closet was an obvious place to have a safe and if she really wanted to hide something, she definitely should not put it there. She'd flashed him one of those frowns that meant he should mind his own business.

He reached to try the handle. The safe was locked, and he didn't have the combination to open it. Which had never stopped him before. This one looked a bit more secure than some, though it wasn't.

He opened the safe in less than two minutes.

Inside, he found Duffy's service weapon. Her Glock 19 was cleaned and loaded. It rested neatly in its polished shoulder holster. The extra ammo was there, too. Snuggled beside the holster was her ATF badge in the wallet.

And next to that, her cell phone. Which explained why she hadn't answered his recent calls. He grabbed the phone and powered it up. The list of recent calls included several from him in the past three days. And a couple of voice mails, also from him in the same timeframe.

But he found no outgoing calls since Duffy was put on leave two weeks ago. He remembered the date precisely because he quit the ATF the same day. November 11.

He held the phone and tapped it absently against his thigh as if its secrets might fall out. They didn't.

She might have left the cell phone here to avoid being traced. Carrying a cell phone was like wearing a tracking beacon on your body. If she wanted privacy, or to get away from Alvarez, or even just a bit of peace, leaving the cell phone here made sense. He could rationalize that decision.

But she wouldn't have gone anywhere important without her badge and her gun. Duffy was always armed. She carried a weapon everywhere. And her badge promised instant access to any place she wanted to go. Why would she leave these essentials behind?

Which might mean she'd taken Alvarez's stupid suggestion to go on vacation or something. But the idea didn't sit right with him.

There were several pieces of fine gold jewelry in the safe. One necklace was larger and heavier than anything he'd seen Duffy wearing. He didn't know much about jewelry, but he assumed the pieces were valuable. Otherwise, why put them in a safe?

The last item was a small package of gold coins.

He took the coins out and examined them. Five coins, one of each type. The ornate Turkey gold 100 Kurush was on the top of the pile. A generic one from South Africa was second, and the third was a Krugerrand. The fourth was a Chinese Panda, and the last one was an Indian Gold coin. All five were official gold coins issued by the governments of those countries.

He didn't remember Duffy mentioning any particular interest in gold coins. She wasn't a collector because she'd have told him about that. Like him, she didn't really have any hobbies. They both worked too much.

Branch had done a short stint at Treasury before his years with ATF. Both agencies had made him something of an expert on various ways that criminals preferred to get paid. Gold was an old-fashioned and cumbersome method of exchange, but a tried-and-true one.

The coins seemed genuine, but they could have been fakes. Had Duffy stumbled on a counterfeit ring? She hadn't mentioned anything like that to him.

He saw nothing to indicate where Duffy might've gone, and that was all he was interested in at the moment. He put everything back in the safe and locked it again.

He walked back to the kitchen and glanced around. Again, the room was as clean as any abandoned home could possibly be. No pictures or notes on the fridge. No bulletin boards or spoons in the sink. Nothing for a forensic team to find.

His gaze fell upon her landline phone. He picked up the handset and scrolled through the call log. He didn't remember Duffy having a landline. She was rarely home, and a landline was practically obsolete for a lot of people these days. Now, with Duffy missing, a new landline seemed ominous somehow. He pulled up an online database on his phone. A quick check confirmed that Duffy's phone number was unlisted, and the account was not in her name. Which was odd but not necessarily sinister.

She could have kept the landline's existence off the radar easily enough because she knew how to hide things. Nobody knew better than Duffy that everything was monitored by someone these days. The problem was usually separating the haystack from the needle with so much data collected every hour.

Unless Duffy was some kind of specific investigative target. Was she?

He thought things through for a minute. Plausible. He nodded decisively.

He pulled the phone number off the landline from the handset and made a note of it. He scrolled through the list of calls. Several calls from a phone number with a 207 area code. One had been answered five days ago. The log listed no other incoming calls for the past two weeks. No outgoing calls were listed, either.

Why would Duffy install a separate landline to receive incoming calls from one specific number? The only thing Branch could think of was that she wanted the voice recordings to be available in case anyone ever checked. But why would she want to create an evidence trail like that? What the hell was she up to?

He pushed "call back" for the last incoming call and the number redialed. The phone rang five times. Six. And then a three-toned, piercing-beep alert. A mechanical voice said the number was no longer in service.

Branch pulled out his cell phone. His source answered promptly. "I've got a number here I need you to trace for me," he said. "No longer in service, but it was working five days ago."

"Okay. Shoot."

He relayed the number. He heard keyboard keys clacking.

"Okay. Got it. You're right. Number's out of service. No

activity on this number at all since—let me see—Friday morning."

"Do you have a location?"

"The two-oh-seven is Portland, Maine. To get an address or an account holder, I'll have to dig a little."

"Let me know when you have it." Branch waited for a few seconds, then he asked, "Can you let me hear the last conversation?"

Most Americans didn't know that the communications companies recorded everything. Texts, emails, phone calls. Everything. The problem was finding any particular call in a sea of worthless conversations. When one had the exact phone numbers, dates, and times, the search was simple, and almost anything could be located.

"Depends. I'll check." She clacked a few more keys. "I can give you the last call because it was only five days ago, but if you want anything older than that, I'll have to dig for that, too."

"Just give me the last one for now." He heard more clacking. She said, "Here you go."

A moment later, the recording began. He turned up the speaker volume on his phone.

"I'm worried. I think this line may be monitored now." A female's whisper. A voice he recognized but couldn't place. Where had he heard that woman's voice before? He might have identified her if she hadn't sounded completely freaked out. "I was right. Everything is exactly as I suspected. I'm in serious trouble. I need help."

"I see." That was Duffy in reply. He'd been her partner for nine years. Her voice was easily recognizable to him. He heard the worry in her tone. She definitely sounded shaken by the other woman's news. "I-I'm in some trouble here, too," she went on.

"I've been put on leave. I don't have access to resources. I can get a team out to Abbot, but I'll need to call in some favors. It might take me a while. Hang tight."

Nothing but silence on the line for a beat too long.

"I'll do it right now," Duffy's voice became urgent. "Call me back in two hours. I should have something lined up by then."

"Hurry. Please hurry."

Branch thought he heard a sob as the line went dead. What was that all about?

Branch asked his source to play the recording twice more. He closed his eyes to eliminate distractions and listened carefully, but he still couldn't place the caller's identity from the near-hysterical whispers.

He swiped his open palm over his face and sighed. He'd tried, but he knew he wouldn't get any more from the recording, no matter how many times he listened to it. "Send me a copy of that call. And then pull up the records on this two-oh-seven number and find all the other calls, in and out, and send those to me. Can you do that?"

"Depends on how far back the calls were made. It'll take a little research and some cooperation from the phone company." She paused, and he waited while she searched around. He heard more rapid clacking noises. "Looks like I should be able to dig up everything going back about a month or so. After that, I'd have to get a court order to pry things out."

He stretched his neck and shoulder muscles, which had begun to cramp with his focused attention. "We don't want to get an order quite yet. Do what you can."

"Will do," she said. "I'll send you whatever I manage to find in the next couple of hours."

"Great. Thanks. And get everything you can on this number,

too. Account holder, billing history, everything." He gave her Duffy's landline number.

"Will do. Hang on." She clacked a few more strokes. "Uh, that one's going to be a little tougher."

He didn't argue. If Duffy wanted to hide the paper trail on this landline, she knew how to do it. "Soon as you can."

"You got it." She disconnected.

Branch leaned against the cool granite countertop and scrolled through Duffy's handset again, to be sure. The setup menu confirmed that incoming and outgoing calls should have been saved in the handset's memory. But there were no outgoing calls listed for the past two weeks. Not one. And the incoming calls were received once or twice a day, all from the two-oh-seven number. No calls at all were listed since last Thursday when she'd answered that last call.

What the hell had Duffy gotten herself involved with? And why the hell hadn't she told him about it?

Only one way to find out. He'd have to find her and keep asking until she provided the answers. He ignored the nagging suspicion that he was already too late.

Branch returned the handset to its cradle and pulled his cell phone out of his pocket again. He found the number for Texas Airlines and made the call on his way out. He locked Duffy's door and dropped her key into his pocket. He hustled down the stairs as he made plane reservations to Boston and booked a rental for the ninety-five-mile drive to Portland, Maine.

He unlocked his SUV with the key fob before he reached the driver's door. He glanced into the back seat to confirm that he'd tossed his packed bag inside when left his home a couple of hours ago. He slid behind the wheel and raced the engine.

The more he thought through the facts, the worse they

seemed. His gut said that with every passing moment, Duffy's situation deteriorated. Who was that woman on the phone?

Something else was bugging him, too. Why hadn't Duffy asked him to help? He was her partner. Duffy needed help. Help is what partners do. She had trusted him with her life many times. She knew he'd quit ATF because of her. Why hadn't she called him?

Those two FBI agents. How were they involved in this? It was no coincidence that they showed up today. His churning gut told him that much.

He slammed his palm down on the center of the steering wheel in frustration. "Where the hell are you, Duffy? And what have you gotten us all into?"

CHAPTER SEVEN

AFTER THEY HAD SETTLED into the rental sedan again and headed toward Bush International Airport, Kim said, "Our flight departs for Portland, Maine. But we're headed south of Portland. A few miles from a small town called Abbot, near the coast."

"Abbot, Maine? Never heard of it. What the hell is up there?"

"Working on that now." Kim pulled out her laptop and connected to the Boss's server via the secure satellite. She downloaded the files from the Boss and saved them to her hard drive. She opened the first file and scanned it quickly.

Gaspar drove in silence while she read. When he pulled into the rental return and parked, he asked, "Well? What's this about? Are we abandoning Duffy?"

"No." Kim closed up her laptop and slipped it into her bag. "I haven't read everything yet, but it looks like the Boss thinks Duffy is there. He traced the calls to her landline when he heard us talking about it back at her condo. The calls came from Abbot."

They collected their belongings and headed into the terminal.

"We're going to need coats," Gaspar said. "Boots and gloves too. It's cold up there."

Kim's body began to shake as if the cold were already upon them. The flight was due to depart in forty minutes, which meant no time for shopping. "Come on. We've gotta hustle. The Boss said to clear security through the TSA Precheck line. Look for a guy named Khalil. He'll pass us through quickly."

Kim's flights into and out of Houston almost never arrived or departed on time, and they spent way too many minutes on the runway to suit her. Houston's George Bush Intercontinental Airport was the tenth busiest in the country, last time she checked. It was also one of the fastest growing U.S. airports so it might have surpassed those numbers. It had five terminals and served as the hub for two major airlines.

All of this should have meant they could fly non-stop to Abbot, Maine.

No such luck. Abbot, it turned out, was one of those places you couldn't get to from anywhere by commercial jet. The nearest commercial airport was Portland, ninety-five miles north of Boston. There were no non-stop flights to Portland from Houston, either. Of course.

Which meant two flights, two takeoffs, and two landings, the most dangerous parts of any flight. She always breathed easier when she heard the landing gear lock firmly into the plane's belly after takeoff and when the pilot lowered and locked it for landing on the other end.

The Boss had booked them through New York's John F. Kennedy airport. Total air travel time to Portland, including the one stop, was listed as six hours and twenty-eight minutes. They would arrive in Portland, with luck, about midnight.

After that, the drive to Abbot was twenty miles south, not

too far north of Kennebunkport. According to the maps, drive time was thirty minutes from the Portland airport, give or take.

After they had cleared security, Gaspar led the way through the busy airport toward their gate. Kim's blood hummed in her ears as she hustled along behind him.

Every departing plane must have been filled to capacity, with long standby lists, for the holiday weekend. She stayed close as Gaspar dodged slow-moving wheelchairs, kids in strollers, and bobbed around arriving business travelers with briefcases and rolling bags. Harried gate agents announced the boarding ritual at every gate as soon as the arriving plane was cleaned and ready. It seemed like every man, woman, and child in Houston was on their way out of town to make room for the arriving hordes.

Kim's first thought was how the place would make the perfect target for a mass-casualty terrorist attack. Her gaze swept the terminal for U.S. Air Marshals, Houston PD, and TSA security officers. She felt her gun snugged against her side and kept her personal threat level shoved hard on high alert.

When they reached the gate area, Kim glanced at the television monitors in the gate area for the weather report. The National Weather Service had issued a winter storm warning for the northeast. The big white swath on the weather map scooped across the entire area from south of Boston to Canada, showing heavy snow moving up the East Coast. Forecast to hit Portland, Maine, from 10:00 a.m. Thursday until 7:00 a.m. Friday.

The meteorologist smiled as she said, "The window of heaviest snowfall looks to be from six p.m. until after midnight on Turkey Day, folks. Power outages are expected due to heavy snowfall on the trees. Accumulations of eight to twelve inches are expected, with six to ten inches along the coast. So cook your turkey early and break out your parkas to take the kids on a toboggan ride after that big Thanksgiving dinner."

She looked at Gaspar. A frown creased his features, and his mouth was a firm, straight line.

CHAPTER EIGHT

Wednesday, November 24
Abbot, Maine
4:45 p.m. Eastern Time

THE DIPLOMAT WATCHED, TRYING to observe everything with fresh eyes, as would his companion and the seven other cautious and suspicious visitors yet to arrive. Each visitor and his bodyguards would be on edge. He'd chosen the grandly named Abbot Cape house because it was isolated and secure, as his business demanded. It was imperative that his visitors feel invisible to the constant monitoring they found difficult to escape.

His passenger had said little from the seat across the aisle during the flight. The Diplomat had realized the bumpy flight was making the man uncomfortable twenty minutes ago when he'd pursed his lips and turned a bit green through a particularly rough patch during initial descent.

Brisbee Airfield nestled among the trees, its runway barely identifiable beneath three inches of accumulated snowfall. The late November winds buffeted the Gulfstream 450, rocking the plane as the pilot approached for landing with a confidence borne of experience. The Diplomat quietly moved his knee away from the path of any unfortunate vomiting that might occur from the man across the aisle.

The snow-cover was the least of his pilot's flight challenges tonight. Gale force winds and unseasonably cold temperatures were more dangerous. The pilot had made the three-hundred mile trip from New York many times under worse weather conditions and had never crashed. The visitors had been appropriately warned.

The pilot executed a perfect if bumpy landing and taxied to a stop at the end of the runway, where the black limousine waited. The Diplomat released his restraints and deplaned ahead of the other passenger to give him time to compose himself. When they reconnected at the bottom of the flight stairs, the passenger seemed slightly wobbly and unable to speak.

"This way," the Diplomat said.

The passenger nodded and followed.

The limo driver, Nathan, was a large, well-muscled, bald man who had been employed at the Abbot Cape compound for two years. He'd proven himself reliable. He greeted the two men with a quiet nod and all three traveled the entire distance to the house without speaking. Which suited the Diplomat perfectly. He had no interest in small talk. The driver's tasks were to serve as chauffeur and bodyguard. No more.

The Diplomat was impatient to complete preparations for the weekend's business, but face-time spent at the embassy was necessary to maintain his clandestine operations. His absence would be noticed by enemies who watched him. Which was one of the reasons he'd scheduled this meeting during Thanksgiving weekend. The embassy would be quiet until Monday. He'd told the embassy staff that he was taking a long weekend in the mountains. He'd said authorities had approved his travel. He'd said he'd be out of cell range. He'd promised to call in periodically.

None of this was true.

His supervisors at the embassy were puppets. They dared not question his movements. He took direction only from the rulers of his country, instructions to which his supervisors were not privy. The staff knew better than to ask questions of him or the supervisors. His excuses were misdirection for his enemies, nothing more.

About twenty miles south of Portland, Nathan left the expressway and turned onto a narrow road heading east. They drove fifteen miles through dark wooded areas and then across granite headlands toward the Atlantic. Heavy gray clouds overhead blocked any trace of moonlight. The rough landscape was bathed in darkness, but he knew it was mostly trees stunted by salt winds and exposed rock where storm tides had long ago scoured the dirt away.

Farther on, the road pushed past inlets on both sides and gritty sand beaches, which the Diplomat couldn't see tonight. Finally, the road curved left and right and rose up onto a headland shaped like the palm of his hand that narrowed into a single finger jutting out into the roiling ocean. He could feel the harsh wind buffeting the limo as if it were a child's toy.

The road ended at the dead center of the familiar high granite wall, with its massive iron gate firmly attached to the thick stone. On the other side of the gate, the long, straight driveway led to the front of the house.

The Abbot Cape compound was a fortress. That's why he'd

chosen it. He saw his passenger's eyes widen with appreciation.

Nathan pulled up to the gate. A surveillance camera on the gatepost tilted and panned. He had called from the airfield and pulled up to the gate exactly at the appointed time. The Diplomat watched as John Smith exited the gatehouse and strode through buffeting winds, punched the code to unlock the gate, and stood aside as it swung slowly open.

The limo moved into the compound and stopped when the Diplomat asked Nathan to do so. The Diplomat lowered his window.

"Good evening, Smith. Any unusual activity during my absence?" The Diplomat already knew the answer. But he remained unsure about Smith even after the extensive background check. Smith had followed orders so far. But he was new, and the deal was too important to risk.

Smith nodded. "Earle found a woman jogging along the entrance road yesterday."

"Who is she?" Another government agent, the Diplomat suspected, but he didn't want to alarm his passenger. The less said in his presence, the better.

Smith shrugged. "Earle handled her. I handled the vehicle."

The Diplomat nodded. Smith's caution was well-placed. He could easily meet the same fate as his predecessor. He seemed like the sort who would keep that possibility at the top of his mind.

Smith said, "The housekeeper has been preparing for Thanksgiving."

"Excellent."

Smith had not been briefed on the weekend's activities. He'd been permanently assigned to the gatehouse. His job was simply to identify visitors and request permission before admitting them to the compound. The Diplomat pressed the button and raised his window.

He watched as Smith closed the gate and returned to the gatehouse. "Let's go."

Nathan pulled into the carriage circle at the entrance and stopped once more.

The sprawling three-story stone house showcased intricate features like cornices, beadings, and folds. The builder had stopped short of gargoyles, but had he also featured them, they would have seemed appropriate. The roofline was complicated, which made the house loom even larger. From this vantage point, Abbot Cape seemed an appropriately grandiose moniker for the place. His passenger nodded as if he were properly impressed.

The front door was huge. Oak darkened by the weather and time. Banded and studded with iron. His passenger appeared to notice, too. At any rate, he nodded again, almost imperceptibly.

So far, so good.

The Diplomat and his guest left the limo, turned and watched until the limo disappeared halfway down the driveway, moving on toward the main garage which was quite a distance from the house. Long ago, the garage had been a carriage house complete with stables, he'd been told. These days, it housed his vehicles and several guest rooms he could put to good use when needed.

Standing outside the big oak front door was Harvey Walter Earle, head of security. The Diplomat thought Earle looked the part. Six-five, two-fifty, fit. He'd been a detective at the Chicago P.D. before he joined U.S. government service for a while. He was indicted for some kind of corruption and went to prison, but that had only improved his qualifications as far as the Diplomat was concerned. He required that his head of security be loyal, competent, knowledgeable, and disaffected from law enforcement. Earle was all that.

"This is Earle." The Diplomat tilted his head.

The visitor spoke for the first time since they left New York. He extended his hand, and Earle did the same. "Abrams."

Quietly, for Earle's ears only, the Diplomat said, "Where's the jogger?"

"Downstairs." Earle looked tired. As if he had been working around the clock, which was as it should be. "We've never had joggers here before. We get two in less than seven days?"

The Diplomat understood. Both women were sent here. The threat to his plans was real. But it was too late to abort. More and tighter security was essential. Collateral damage likely. He didn't want to discuss the situation in front of Abrams. "Is dinner prepared?"

Earle shrugged. "The housekeeper says twenty minutes."

The Diplomat looked around the compound again. Everything appeared in order. His visitors should be reassured by Abbot Cape's remote location. Isolated. Surrounded by the ocean at the bottom of the cliff on the north side and the impenetrable wall on the south side. "The additional security staff has arrived?"

"Delayed by weather."

The Diplomat frowned and flashed a fiery glance toward him.

Earle looked down briefly. "Should arrive in the next hour."

The Diplomat nodded, still wearing the fierce expression. "The women are on schedule?"

Earle nodded. "Helipad's ready. They arrive tomorrow to get settled. Depart after the others leave on Sunday."

Abrams nodded approvingly. He didn't smile.

The Diplomat extended his hand, palm out, toward the big oak door. Abrams walked toward the entrance.

Behind his back, the Diplomat returned his gaze to his security man and spoke so that only he could hear. "Bring our jogger to me after our guest retires for the evening."

Earle nodded and moved ahead of the visitor. "Let me open the door. That handle is tricky."

The Diplomat entered first. The house was warm, like a sauna after the frigid winds outside.

When Abrams walked through, the metal detector, recessed into the doorjamb, alarmed. Abrams appeared unsurprised and unconcerned; of course, he'd be armed. As expected. Earle followed and the metal detector alarmed again. Now, all three were aware.

"Earle will show you to your rooms," the Diplomat said. "Dinner will be ready soon. We'll talk afterward. I have something you'll want to see."

"Right this way," Earle said, leading Abrams up the stairs to the nicest of the second-floor guest rooms.

The Diplomat went directly to his office where he watched yesterday's news report again. The video had been spliced with quick cuts to the relevant action. First, the fireball exploded the target in midair. Total destruction of the transport plane. Prideful responsibility quickly claimed by militants in the region. Only twelve lives lost.

He shrugged. Casualties of war. These demonstrations were tiresome. But they served a useful purpose. Abrams was a sophisticated man. He would appreciate the implications.

The Diplomat cut the power to the screen and joined Earle in the dining room to review the weekend plans once again before Abrams joined them for drinks before dinner.

CHAPTER NINE

Wednesday, November 24
Houston, Texas
5:30 p.m. Central Time

WHILE BRANCH WAITED AT the gate to board his flight to
Boston, he made a call. The gate area was crowded and noisy.
He looked around for a quiet corner. The only place he saw to
escape the crowds was in the small corridor behind the wall
behind the gate agent's desk. He walked around the partition,
leaned close to the wall, and blocked his other ear with his palm
to muffle the cacophony, at least a little.

His source finally picked up on the third ring. "Sent
your files out thirty minutes ago. You should have them
already. But—" She paused. Maybe she could hear all
the noise and wanted to be sure Branch comprehended her
words.

He leaned closer to the wall and pressed his palm more
firmly to his ear. "What?"

"Someone else downloaded the data on that old Abbot ATF

raid earlier today." Her voice was husky, like a torch singer's. "I'm trying to track down the requesting party."

Interesting news. "Okay."

She coughed and sipped something and cleared her throat. "And the info on the two FBI agents is all standard. No other searches on that stuff in the last seventy-two hours."

"I'll call you after I've looked at everything if I need follow-up." Branch ended the call.

His flight was called for boarding. He joined the long line of passengers waiting their turn and thought about the call. Both pieces of intel were mildly reassuring. If others were looking for data on the old ATF raid, that probably meant he was on the right track. There'd be no reason to access those old files unless something was active, or about to be.

And whoever was searching for the old files would be involved in the current situation. Whatever it was.

As for the intel on Otto and Gaspar, they were FBI. Their files should be routine. He wanted the information simply for background. If no one else was interested in Otto and Gaspar at the moment, their activities could be as routine as they claimed. Or they could be engaged in well-covered classified activities. Either way, the background data was available, and now he possessed a copy. All good progress.

The first class passengers were invited aboard. Branch covered the jetway to the Boeing 737, settled into his first class seat, and downloaded the remaining files. He closed the laptop and relaxed for takeoff. He'd be on the ground in Boston in less than four hours.

When they reached cruising altitude, the flight attendant brought the whiskey he'd requested. There was a storm crossing north of the flight path into Boston, the captain said. He had turned off the seatbelt sign, though, with a warning about bumpy air ahead.

Branch opened his laptop and found the files. He was no longer employed by the ATF, but he still had quite a few friends inside. He also retained his security clearances because of his work with BlueRiver. He expected the files to be complete and unredacted, which they were.

He ran through Otto and Gaspar's confidential bios first. Both FBI Special Agents. Otto, early thirties, assigned to the Detroit Field Office and on the fast track to high places. Gaspar was a decade older. Posted to the Miami Field Office, where his career had peaked a couple of years ago. He was marking time, Branch figured.

This was their first assignment as partners, which could have accounted for some of the odd vibes he'd felt when he met them. It usually took a while to settle into a solid working relationship with a new partner. He'd spent more than six months getting comfortable with Duffy after she came over to AFT from DEA nine years ago. He understood how it was to be partnered with someone new.

Deeper into the data, he saw that Otto was more than a rising star at FBI. Strong credentials, too. Double degrees. JD and MBA. She'd worked in forensic accounting before she was recruited by the bureau. Qualifications in marksmanship, covert ops, and a few other areas. Multilingual. Damned impressive. She was tiny but fierce according to those who had evaluated her performance.

Branch grinned as he studied her official photo and the covert photos of her family that were not a part of her official file, but his source had somehow located. Otto looked like a typical Asian over-achiever, which she wasn't, exactly. She wasn't one-hundred percent Asian.

Her father was blonde, blue-eyed; American of German ancestry. Vietnam War vet. Army. Worked as an engineer.

Had Kim Otto been adopted?

The next batch of photos answered that question. Mother was a Vietnamese war bride. That explained a few things.

Four siblings. Three brothers, all older, all of whom looked more like their dad. And one sister, younger, who also looked like their mother.

FBI Special Agent Kim Louisa Otto must have felt like a fish out of water her entire life. German but not, Vietnamese but not. No wonder she was so ambitious. She had something to prove to herself and everyone else. Branch recognized those signs, too.

Carlos Gaspar was another matter. Longer service with the FBI. Also, multicultural and multilingual, Spanish and English. Cuban-American. His career was sidelined a few years back by a drug bust that went bad. Not many details in the file, but he'd been shot. Injuries were downplayed in the official report, but they must have been devastating. He'd spent several months in rehab after discharge from the hospital.

Gaspar was still on the job. Which was nothing short of a miracle. Or just plain stupid. Hard to say without more intel.

The guy had four kids and a pregnant wife to support. He'd be chained to the desk forever. Poor bastard.

Branch closed the bios and sipped the whiskey, thinking about Otto and Gaspar for a few moments. The files were routine. They listed the facts. But the words didn't convey much about them as people. Maybe his path would not cross theirs again. Maybe he'd never need to know more. He shrugged.

He'd initially assumed Duffy left Houston to avoid Otto and Gaspar. At this point, he thought Duffy had traveled to Abbot for a reason that had nothing to do with them. One he didn't yet comprehend.

He turned to the old files on the raid in Abbot, Maine. He hadn't known about the bust at the time, but he saw the usual ATF procedures had been in place. Looked like two ATF teams involved. Started out as Duffy's DEA project because they'd believed the situation was a drug cartel. Turned out to be something entirely different.

The DEA operation was shut down when Duffy screwed up a major piece of evidence involving photographs illegally obtained on private property. The DOJ rightly pulled the plug. Duffy, being Duffy, kept going. Off the books. Until she closed the whole operation down.

Severe casualties resulted. Not good.

Branch shook his head. That was just like Duffy. She had a habit of failing to follow orders. She got great results, but it was no wonder she'd landed in hot water. Hell, based on the contents of that file, she'd been lucky ATF accepted her. Probably based on factors not disclosed in these file documents, and he wondered what those factors were.

He used the plane's onboard Wi-Fi to find roadmaps and get directions. The closest hotel to Abbot, Maine, was a rundown place about ten miles from the site of the old raid. The family-owned and operated motel boasted its thirtieth year. Even the photos used to attract guests made the place look about ten years past its prime. He booked a room and put the address into his cell phone.

He reclined his seat and closed his eyes until the flight had been cleared for landing at Boston Logan International Airport. The airport was closed by the time he deplaned. No food, no coffee, no nothing. He collected his rental and hit the road. He found an open burger joint a few miles north and picked up food at the drive-through. Then he pointed the SUV due north via I-95, eighty-one miles to the motel.

He'd catch a few hours' sleep and then search for Duffy tomorrow. He knew her well. Understood her as few people did. In a small town like Abbot, Maine, population 5,352 according to recent census data, a blonde beauty with a stubborn streak like Duffy shouldn't be hard to find.

CHAPTER TEN

Wednesday, November 24
Portland, Maine
11:35 p.m.

KIM HAD TIGHTENED HER seatbelt and hung onto the armrests until her fingers ached. Rough weather bounced the Boeing 727 like driving a Jeep over lava rock on the flight from New York to Portland. Buffeting winds pushed and lifted and dropped the plane with nauseating frequency, which the pilot described to passengers as "light to moderate turbulence." He claimed the bad weather was still on the way, and the plane was ahead of the storm.

Across the aisle, legs stretched out, hands folded across his torso, Gaspar was snoring.

The pilot had aborted the first approach. Due to a dangerous microburst wind shear recognized by the jet's detection system, probably. He'd circled the airport only to abort his second attempt.

Kim pushed everything she knew about deadly weather and a dozen passenger jet crashes caused by wind gradient out of her mind. Only about one commercial flight every ten years had crashed due to wind shear since the detection systems became mandatory two decades ago. Should not be a serious problem tonight.

If the crew was on their toes.

But crew members were people.

With problems.

Subject to distractions.

Like all people.

No mechanical device could completely shield passengers from human error.

Sleet pelted the windows on both sides of the first class cabin as the plane continued its descent.

When, on the third attempt, wings still wagging side-to-side, the pilot finally landed on the tarmac, the passengers broke into wild cheers like fans at a rock concert.

The noise stirred Gaspar from his nap. He sat up and glanced at Kim. She must have looked as green as she felt. He yawned and grinned. "And the crowd goes wild," he said. "Bad flight, Sunshine?"

"Not at all, Chico." She pried her claws from the armrest. Her throat was parched. Her voice sounded husky in her ears. "Some big celebrity has been performing for us. One of your favorites, I think."

The plane taxied up to the terminal.

"Sorry I missed the excitement." He shrugged and stood to stretch his cramped muscles and wait for the flight attendant to hand his bag down from overhead. He pretended the bag service was a perk of traveling first class, but the truth was that he couldn't lift the bag into the overhead bin. One more thing they never discussed.

After taking a few stabilizing breaths, Kim pulled her bags from under the seat and wrestled the fluffy down parka she'd hurriedly acquired at JFK during their layover into temporary submission, then followed Gaspar on rubbery legs through the bulkhead exit door and along the jetway into the terminal.

She'd never been to Portland, Maine, before, but one airport terminal looked much like another. Gates, walkways, seats. All deserted at this time of night.

"The Boss reserved our rental," she said. "No Crown Vics here, Chico. Sorry." She grinned when he frowned. He claimed the old Crown Vic was the best cop car ever. Many police departments agreed with him. But the heavy vehicle was no longer in production, and even the Boss couldn't dig one up for them in the smaller cities.

She glanced out through the terminal windows into the darkness as they walked. She saw light snow falling, but nothing like what it would be in a few hours' time. Kim was no stranger to snow. She'd grown up in Michigan and lived there most of her life. She knew what to expect from twelve inches of snowfall. Gaspar, on the other hand, had probably never seen that much snow. Certainly, not as a regular part of his Miami winters.

On the long walk to the ground transportation area, they split up at the first set of restrooms. Kim splashed water on her face and washed airplane germs from her hands and chewed an antacid to settle her still queasy stomach.

She was in no rush. Gaspar was probably calling home again to check on his wife and kids.

Kim had called her dad from New York and explained that she wouldn't make it home for Thanksgiving dinner tomorrow. He hadn't complained. He understood. He'd been forced to work too many holidays himself. He'd insisted that she call back when her mother was there, which she'd promised to do.

She could put off the other call no longer, so she found her personal phone, took a deep breath, and dialed the number. The phone rang twice. Her mother might be asleep, exhausted from the preparations for the big family Thanksgiving. After four rings, voice mail picked up and Kim fist-pumped the air. She left a message. She'd call again in the morning, but she had a reprieve from her mother's disapproval for the moment.

She slipped her phone into her pocket, gathered her belongings, and met up with Gaspar again in the terminal.

"When we're outside of monitoring ranges around the airport," she said, "I'll download the rest of those files from the Boss." She'd stacked her laptop bag on top of her rolling suitcase and pulled them along. The parka was lightweight but so bulky it could only be tamed for a few minutes before it popped out of whatever hold she'd placed it under. "He said he'd send the ATF report from that raid in Abbot nine years ago. Should have more intel than what I found online."

"Be good to know why we're here," Gaspar said darkly.

She glanced over to see a matching frown on his face. If something in his phone call home had gone amiss, he didn't say so.

The entire airport was closed. Kim searched for a coffee stand to grab a caffeine fix, but no luck. Steel gates were pulled down to cover the entrance at every shop and eatery.

She put a couple of bucks into the last vending machine she found before they reached the down escalator. She bought a Diet Dr. Pepper for her and the full sugar version for Gaspar. He bought dinner out of another vending machine. Peanuts for her, peanut butter cups for him.

"Let's find a hotel for the night." She juggled the bags and the soda and the parka, along with her bags, on the way down. "I'll read the files, figure out what's what. And we can drive on to Abbot in the daylight. The big snow isn't predicted to start until tomorrow afternoon. We've got a little breathing room."

"I'd rather push on. Do whatever it is we came here for as quickly as we can. Maybe get out of here sometime tomorrow." She'd just taken a breath to argue when he shook his head. "Relax, Sunshine. You're the boss. We can do it your way." He sighed. "Based on those internet photos you pulled earlier, we probably can't find the place in the dark anyway. And there's nowhere to stay out there, most likely. Closer to Portland for the night is a better strategy."

Five minutes later, they'd found the terminal exit leading to the rental vehicles and hunched into their jackets against the cold wind as they walked across from the terminal to the garage. She was missing Houston's warmth already.

The big board at the rental office directed them to parking slot H-22. Gaspar led the way. The wind whipped through the covered parking garage, lashing every inch of her exposed skin. Next time, she'd slip into the parka and gloves before they left any building.

Sitting in H-22 was a full-sized SUV bigger than her first apartment after college. Black and boxy. It looked like a hearse. Which was bad enough. Worse was the bulky-looking man leaning against the trunk, arms folded across his chest, waiting for them.

CHAPTER ELEVEN

Wednesday, November 24
Abbot, Maine
11:55 p.m.

THE HOUR WAS LATE in Abbot, Maine, but early morning in the target areas. The Diplomat and Abrams had enjoyed a relaxing dinner. They were seated at a long table in his office and connected by video conference to each of the seven observers.

A tactician narrated. The Diplomat placed the speaker on the table and barely listened as the tactician's voice droned on for the benefit of the others who were hearing the plan for the first time.

The Diplomat sipped brandy and watched the images on his screens. Abrams craned his neck to view them, too.

Four screens lined the wall opposite the Diplomat's table. The first screen displayed the same images everyone else saw on the video conference feed. A series of slides explaining the weapon, deployment mechanisms, trajectories, terrain, expected casualties, and other variables.

Video feeds at the train station on the other side of the world produced a perfect signal, but sporadic images were being fed from the field, where signals were not as strong.

The second screen showed raw footage captured at the village train station. The train was due at 07.40 hours local time. The platform was busy. The town was far inland, and the train was its only lifeline to the nearest cities.

The third screen was a panoramic satellite view of the approaching train from the city. The image revealed acres of brown, flat land. The train tracks were equally flat and ran straight from the city to the village and beyond to the next village and the next and then another city, which he could not see. Nor could he see the launch location, which was as it should be. One of his product's many advantages was the distance it could travel and still hit the target accurately.

The fourth screen was focused on the target area. As the demonstration took place, his systems would have accurately captured and recorded the relevant images for effective use with future clients.

The narrator's voice recited the dry facts. "The train is eighty-seven miles away from the target zone, traveling steadily through open plains at seventy miles an hour."

No one asked questions.

In late November, the Diplomat noticed, the caramel-colored fields were dry and barren.

"The engineer will be growing bored. Watching for signs of civilization ahead or animals on the track," the narrator explained. "He's been operating this route for two decades. He's no doubt expecting the same mind-numbing experience today."

Indeed. For the first time since the Diplomat met the man, Abrams seemed amused. The corners of Abrams' mouth lifted in a small smile. He was delighted by the coming destruction. He knew what the weapon could do. The Diplomat had shown him before he agreed to procure the weekend's customers.

"Two passenger cars, each half-full of workers returning from night-shift jobs in the city, snakes behind the engine." The voice sounded like narration for a documentary film. "Behind the passenger cars are five cargo cars. Seven in all today because Thursday is the day the train hauls four gasoline tankers from the city to the towns and villages on its route. Normally, when the train arrives in the town, car number seven would be decoupled and left to fuel vehicles and farm equipment for the day. Normally, the engineer would recouple the empty car on the return trip to the city, to be refilled for next week's delivery."

The narrator did not say that today was not a normal Thursday. He didn't mention that this would be the train's last trip.

The observers were experienced in the methods of war. At least one had admitted to failed attempts to bomb trains before. The Diplomat expected him to be more impressed than the others, who were less worldly. Unfortunately, the Diplomat had no video cameras inside their offices. He couldn't see their reactions or judge their responses. He had firsthand access only to Abrams, which would have to be enough.

The Diplomat's customers were sophisticated warriors who would recognize the difficulty and be awed, he felt sure. But *their* customers were street fighters. They were only interested in destruction. The new weapons would not disappoint them, either.

The Diplomat smiled.

The grandfather clock standing in the corner chimed once to mark the half-hour.

"Ten minutes until launch," the narrator said.

The Diplomat pointed to the third screen. Abrams looked to

see the train steadily closing on the target area. He nodded. "Yes."

"The precision timing for the strike was determined by the train's schedule." The narrator explained such rudimentary details because they were most likely to be used by the Diplomat's customers in the field. "A volunteer on the train confirmed departure from the city and has reported continued steady speed toward the target site. The missile will be fired from a significant distance. The train cannot be recognized visually by the launch team."

This was the only significant potential for error at this point. A two-minute margin was built into the timing. Two minutes should be plenty. The engineer was not likely to alter his speed because he had no reason to do so.

For a brief moment, the Diplomat considered the passengers again. Thursday was the lightest passenger travel day of the week, which was why he'd chosen it. According to the volunteer who had counted them as they boarded the train, only twenty-six passengers would be sacrificed. Including the engineer and the volunteer, the total collateral damage was expected to be twenty-six souls. Regrettable, but unavoidable.

At five minutes out, he turned up the volume on his speaker to hear the narrator. Now, the video feed to the first screen and the fourth screen were identical. In the unlikely event of an error, the first screen's images would be diverted to a pre-recorded video of a prior successful hit.

The Diplomat would not allow human error today to abort his carefully constructed plans for the weekend.

The fourth screen continued to depict events as they occurred on the ground. The countdown clock in the lower left corner of the screen continued its relentless march.

His finger was poised to switch screen one to pre-recorded video if necessary.

In the final thirty seconds, the Diplomat glanced at the third screen to confirm the train's steady approach and then kept his focus glued to screen number four while the narrator's monotone droned the final countdown in his ear.

The narration stopped.

The Diplomat, Abrams, and the distant observers watched the silent progress on screen four.

The train entered the target zone.

The engine, both passenger cars, and two cargo cars moved left of the target zone's center. Cars four through seven were the gasoline tankers.

The missile was fired as the tankers entered the bulls-eye. When two tankers were on each side of dead center, the missile hit car number five, and both exploded.

Almost instantly, cars four and six exploded. Followed by three and seven.

Passenger cars one and two flew into the air and landed in the raging fire.

The train's engine exploded last, and the Diplomat's breath returned to its normal rhythm.

He removed his finger from the button and flexed the stiffness from his joints as each of the train cars sent flames and dark smoke into the sky.

The noise on the ground must have been deafening. The only things the Diplomat could hear were the cheers from Abrams and his far-flung audience through the speaker.

CHAPTER TWELVE

Thursday, November 25
Abbot, Maine
12:15 a.m. Eastern Time

THE MAN LEANING AGAINST Kim's rental had a faint
Spanish appearance. Or maybe he was Black Irish. Dark hair and
weary blue eyes. He looked like a retired plainclothes detective
from a big, rust-belt city cop shop. Cleveland or Pittsburgh or
someplace like that.

He held himself like a stubborn old-timer, too. He was wide
and barrel-chested and wore a plain dark suit of thick wool and
an old, wrinkled raincoat he might have bought at the start of his
career. He was tall but stooped, which made him seem like an
older man.

But if he'd retired from a big department, he was probably in
his late fifties, early sixties, maybe. Mandatory retirement age
for the FBI was fifty-seven. Most big city departments were
similar. The work could have aged him more than the passing
years like it does a lot of cops. Either way, he looked like a man

who had seen his share of trouble and somehow managed to make it through.

Gaspar halted about twenty feet from the rental. Kim placed her bags on the concrete and freed both hands, just in case.

"You look exactly like the headshots Agent Duffy sent me." The old guy's voice was gravelly. He nodded toward them. "You're Otto, and you're Gaspar."

Kim said, "And you are?"

"Detective Tony Villanueva, Boston P.D., retired. Friend of Duffy's."

"Where is she?"

"Great question. I'm hoping you'll help me find that out."

Gaspar said, "We got a tip that she was here. That's why we came."

"She was here. She's disappeared." He pushed himself away from the SUV and raised the hatch. "Let's get your gear stowed and find somewhere warmer and more private to talk. Everything we say and do here is too public."

They tossed their bags into the open black maw of the SUV. Villanueva lobbed the keys to Gaspar, which was telling. He knew Kim was lead, and Gaspar was number two. Number two always drives. Or maybe he was an old-fashioned chauvinist. Either way, he'd guessed the right driver.

"There's an all-night pancake house couple miles down the road. I'll meet you there." He clambered into an old Town Car parked across the lane from H-22.

Inside the SUV, Gaspar used the pushbutton start and fired up the engine. Kim fastened her seat belt, pulled the alligator clamp out of her pocket, and placed it at the retractor. She rubbed her hands together to warm them, wishing she'd grabbed the wool gloves from the pockets of her new parka.

"Well, Susie Wong? Follow the old guy? Find out what he knows?"

"Sure. Why not? I'm hungry anyway. Aren't you?" She retrieved her laptop as soon as the SUV crossed the outer perimeter of the airport's automatic surveillance. She fired it up.

The Boss had sent several thick files through private, secure channels. She downloaded and unencrypted them quickly and scanned through for highlights.

"Anything interesting?" Gaspar had stopped at a red light behind Villanueva. The SUV's engine had heated up enough to chase the cold from the cabin. Strong winds slammed against the outside of the vehicle, but the big storm was still several hours away.

"Mostly the same facts we found online earlier. But Duffy was involved in the old bust somehow. Puzzling, since she was DEA at the time."

Gaspar raised his right eyebrow. "Joint ATF/DEA operation?"

Kim was still scanning the files. "Looks like legitimate rug importers up to no good of some kind."

"Since it was an ATF bust, they were probably smuggling firearms. Maybe shipping them out in the containers that brought the rugs in?" The light changed, and he rolled the SUV forward again, close enough behind Villanueva's taillights.

"Duffy is mentioned. And five more DEA agents. One was her partner. Two more males in addition to Villanueva. And a woman named Teresa Justice. Name mean anything to you?" She rushed through the paragraphs she'd spend more time with later.

"Besides being a great name for a federal agent, you mean? No. Any info on Villanueva?"

"Not yet. But there's a lot of stuff here, and I'm just skimming through."

"No mention of Reacher, either, I guess." He glanced her way for a response.

She flashed him a look that said *Oh, Please,* like a teenager disrespecting her parents.

He laughed. "Okay. I deserved that one."

Two miles later, he pulled into the parking lot and parked next to Villanueva's sedan. They walked inside without speaking.

The Pancake Palace looked like a cross between a diner and a shoebox. A long, narrow building. A single aisle ran its width. A counter with stools on the left. A row of booths on the right. Lots of plastic laminate and vinyl everywhere. The decor wasn't an effort to be retro. This place had probably been here since the Nixon administration, at least.

Villanueva chose a booth in the back with a view of the parking lot. He took the bench seat facing the door. Gaspar's jaw tightened. Two alphas sparring for the back-to-the-wall position. Kim shrugged.

To give Gaspar the aisle, she slid across the bench and snugged up against the window, which effectively pinned her against the wall. She had a good view of the big mirror mounted above Villanueva's head. She could see the door behind her and every person in the place from this angle.

Only one booth was occupied at the opposite end of the building. Three college-aged guys. A lone waitress stood behind the counter, and a cook moved around behind the window to the kitchen.

The waitress picked up three plastic-coated menus and three plastic coffee mugs and a pot of coffee and followed Gaspar to their booth. She said she'd give them a minute with the menus, poured the coffee, and left the insulated pot on the table. Kim liked her already.

When the waitress walked away, Villanueva leaned in. "Tell me why you're looking for Duffy."

Kim gave him the SPFT cover story she'd offered so many times she could recite it in her sleep. She knew how lame it sounded. She'd read his name in the file, but she asked for confirmation. "What's your connection to Duffy?"

He leaned his forearms on the table and held his coffee mug between his palms. "She's a friend. I've known her a long time. I'm worried about her."

"She seems like the kind of woman who can take care of herself," Kim said, holding the warm coffee mug between her hands and inhaling its delicious aroma. "What are you worried about, specifically?"

"Where she is right this minute, for starters."

"When did you see her last?" Gaspar asked.

Villanueva glanced at his watch. It was well after midnight. Thanksgiving had officially begun. "I guess it's two days ago. Tuesday afternoon. I was supposed to meet up with her again Wednesday morning. She didn't show."

Which meant that Duffy hadn't been in Houston this week at all. The Boss had to have known as much when he sent Kim and Gaspar there. So that made it all the more certain that the Boss had sent them to Houston to encounter Branch. But why?

"Maybe you'd better give us a little history here," Kim said. "What's going on with you two?"

Villanueva glanced up and pushed back into his seat. Kim looked into the big mirror and saw the waitress approaching with her order pad. They ordered breakfast food. A waffle for her. Eggs and toast for Gaspar. Villanueva ordered a short stack of pancakes with an egg on top, which sounded disgusting. Why put an egg on top of perfectly good pancakes?

The waitress noted their orders on an old-fashioned pad, set another pot of coffee on the table without being asked, and went to put the orders in.

Villanueva leaned forward again. "Duffy called me last week. She asked me to meet up with her. She said she needed help."

"Help with what?" Gaspar asked.

"Look, I've checked you out. I'm trying to decide whether or not to trust you. You're probably making the same assessment about me." Villanueva looked down at the table for a moment before he focused his gaze on Kim. "But I have information you want, and I'm not giving it to you until I'm satisfied. So you first. Why are you hunting Duffy?"

"What is it you think we want?" Gaspar asked.

Villanueva smiled. "You want to find Duffy. I'm the last person sitting in this booth to have seen her."

Kim studied him closely like she was interested in every word he said. Ninety percent of successful interrogation is listening to the answers. Villanueva had been a detective with Boston P.D. He knew every interrogation technique there was. But so did she.

"We're FBI agents, Villanueva," she said. "We're cops, just like you were. We're all on the same side here."

"Are we? I'm on Duffy's side." He cocked his head. "Can you honestly say that?" When she didn't reply, he said, "I thought not."

Gaspar asked, "Who knows that Duffy was here? Who

knows she's disappeared? Who knows why she's involved with whatever it is she's doing?"

"Just me and Duffy. And soon, you." He glanced toward the front again. "Hold up. Food's coming."

Kim held her breath. Villanueva was wrong. He and Duffy were not the only people who knew she was here or what she was involved in. The Boss knew. Stood to reason others knew, too.

When the waitress had delivered their breakfast and left again, Kim said, "Tell us about what's going on between you and Duffy."

"She called me. We met up on Sunday." Villanueva squirted ketchup all over everything on his plate. "She was in trouble at work, as you probably know. She knew you were looking for her, and she figured you were related to her problems. She said she had to handle this particular situation fast. She said she needed a big score before the ATF fired her, or indicted her, or worse."

"Because she used ATF resources without authorization and way outside of her jurisdiction when the Vice President's son was kidnapped," Kim said as if these were known facts.

"I'm retired." Villanueva shrugged. "I spend most of my time these days buying and selling gold and collecting gold coins, so I was game for some excitement."

"Gold?" Gaspar asked.

"It's not insane. Lots of people do it. Gold investing's not just for billionaires and crazy survivalists, you know." He smiled briefly before his eyes narrowed and he became serious again. "So we did a little recon, figured out a few things on Monday. We split up on Tuesday to take care of separate issues. We were to meet at the motel again on Wednesday morning. She never showed up."

"And this particular situation you two are working on wouldn't have anything to do with the ATF raid that went down in Abbot, Maine, nine years ago would it?" Gaspar asked.

"Not exactly." Villanueva had finished his food. He'd made quick work of the meal. He poured more coffee into his cup and offered more to Kim. She pushed her mug closer to the pot.

Gaspar shook his head. He frowned. "What do you mean, not exactly?"

Villanueva waved for the checks. "Are you on board or not?"

"We'll do what we can to help. We need to find Duffy and interview her, anyway," Kim replied.

Villanueva narrowed his eyes and looked at Gaspar first, and then turned his steady gaze to Kim. "Duffy got a tip that somebody is using Abbot Cape, the compound where the prior raid took place, for human trafficking. Makes sense. Someone is living there, and it's a perfect spot for criminal activity. Remote. Protected on all sides. Hard to get into. Harder still to get out. Duffy's got personal reasons for wanting to bust it open." He shrugged his heavy shoulders as though he had some reservations about those reasons or Duffy's plan.

"But?" Kim asked.

Another shrug, and then he drained the last of his coffee. "But say she's right. It's another case that isn't ATF jurisdiction. Kidnapping and human trafficking are FBI."

"What personal reasons does she have for doing this thing?" Gaspar wiped his palm across his face. He looked exhausted, and he probably was.

"Besides getting herself back on track with the ATF? One of her friends has been kidnapped by these creeps," Villanueva said. "Duffy thinks her friend is inside that compound."

"Duffy works for ATF. She should report hostages to the FBI," Gaspar said. "That's how she got herself into trouble before, and she's doing it again."

Villanueva shrugged.

Kim might have asked more questions about Duffy's actions and motives, but there was nothing she could do about the situation tonight. That issue could wait until morning. They ate in silence while she thought things through.

"We need to get up to speed. And we need sleep," Kim said. "We're going to find a hotel room, and we'll reconnect with you tomorrow."

"I've booked two rooms for you out at the Abbot Motel. It's a good location. Fairly close to Abbot Cape." Villanueva tossed two twenties on the table. "We can talk more in the morning."

Kim considered the proposal for a moment and shrugged. She didn't have a better plan. Not so far, anyway. "Lead on."

Gaspar followed Villanueva along I-95 south until they reached an exit twenty-five miles south and west of Abbot. They followed the surface streets until they ended up on the west side of U.S. Route 1 about a hundred yards south of the Kennebunk River.

Villanueva pulled into a potholed parking lot at the Abbot Motel. In the daylight, it might have been a cheerful place. Under the yellow-wash of the parking lot floodlights, it looked like a dingy and worn string of New England saltboxes.

The place was almost deserted, which wasn't surprising. It was a holiday weekend, and nothing anywhere near here was likely to draw tourists as far as Kim could see. Only one vehicle was in the parking lot. Another big, black SUV.

Villanueva parked in front of the end unit and Gaspar parked in front of the room next door. The SUV's dashboard clock read two-seventeen a.m. They unloaded their bags, and Villanueva handed them each a key for the two rooms. "Meet in my room at seven a.m. I'll get coffee and donuts. We can talk."

Kim nodded. Gaspar scowled.

Villanueva said, "See you in a few hours and we'll get to work."

CHAPTER THIRTEEN

Thursday, November 25
Abbot, Maine
4:12 a.m.

KIM HAD PORED OVER the files the Boss had sent until she was bleary-eyed and exhausted. He'd included satellite photos taken a few weeks ago of the house and the area surrounding it on the rocky point at the end of the wooded road where the old ATF raid had occurred. The compound, called Abbot Cape, seemed to be occupied again. Not surprising. It had been nine years since the raid, and the compound was a desirable property, even if it was remote and lonely and more than a little creepy.

It would make a terrific location for one of those old, gothic romances like *Wuthering Heights* or *Rebecca,* or a horror movie, perhaps. She imagined yet another remake of *Dracula* on the premises.

Abbot Cape was a fortress surrounded by an eight-foot stone wall topped with barbed wire on one side and looming cliffs high above the Atlantic Ocean on the other. An iron gate in the middle of the wall was the only entry point for any ground vehicle. There were open spaces inside the stone wall large enough to accommodate a helicopter, assuming an exceptionally skilled pilot and halfway reasonable weather conditions.

The Boss had included more photos shot yesterday, before nightfall at 4:40 p.m. She and Gaspar had only learned about Duffy's connection to Abbot Cape an hour or so before dusk. The timestamps on the photos said 15:43 hours, or 3:43 p.m. Which meant that the Boss had located satellite video and pulled still frames from the feed. The full video was not included.

She had zoomed in on the compound.

The ground was covered with snow, which had been falling off and on for the past twenty-four hours. The Boss had access to satellites that could penetrate through many types of cloud cover, technology that had been developed for military use and wasn't available commercially.

Smoke wafted from the chimneys of both the main house, the smaller house at the entrance gate, and in the dormer rooms above the main garage. Lights were on inside both houses, too.

Eventually, she fell across the bed with her clothes on, closed her gritty eyes, and surrendered to sleep.

What felt like seconds later, her phone rang. She fumbled around on the bed until she found it lying near her right knee. She glanced briefly at the screen. It was 6:45 a.m. Two whole hours of sleep. She closed her eyes again and pressed the button to accept the call.

The Boss said, "Are you awake?"

"No. What do you want?"

"I can't send you any help."

"Did I ask you to?"

He chuckled a dry, humorless sound. "Did you see the pictures?"

"The old ones or the new ones?"

"Both."

She said nothing more. He was calling for a reason. She wished he'd get to it. She rolled over and off the bed and caught a glimpse of herself in the mirror hanging over the dresser. She looked like she'd been mauled by a slimy creature from a Stephen King novel. She closed her eyes again and plopped heavily onto the end of the bed, waiting.

"Where's Duffy?" he finally asked.

"That seems to be the question of the moment. Villanueva says Duffy was here two days ago, and now she's not." She didn't bother explaining. Villanueva's name was included in the old files. The Boss already knew who he was. "My guess is she's inside that compound. You can probably find the point of entry on the old video. Pull it up and look."

He didn't reply to her suggestion. "There's no way the three of you can get in there and get out without somebody getting hurt. Understand me? No way."

"You can't help, and I can't do it on my own. What do you suggest? Give up? Move on? Find another witness to interview about Reacher?"

There was another long pause on the other end of the line and she'd almost gone back to sleep when he said, "I'm sure you'll figure something out."

"Send me the rest of those old ATF files and I will. Otherwise, my mother is expecting me for Thanksgiving dinner." She hung up and tossed the phone onto the bed. It was an empty threat. She wasn't going home, and he knew it. But she wanted the rest of those old files. Her churning gut confirmed that what she didn't know could get them all killed.

She rubbed her eyes with the heels of her hands. Another hour's sleep would have helped. But instead, she took a deep breath and pushed her feet to move toward the bathroom. She turned the hot water on full blast, grabbed her toothbrush and slogged into the rain room.

The effort to reinvigorate herself didn't work. After twenty minutes, she gave up the effort. She dressed and found the parka, slipped her arms into what felt like pillows instead of sleeves and made her look like the Stay Puft marshmallow man. She grabbed her key and left the room in search of caffeine, and lots of it.

It was still darker than it should be. Sunrise was half an hour ago, but with the worsening storm, there might never be much daylight today. The northeast wind was still blowing hard, and the snowfall was light but had intensified. She pulled her parka closer and crossed her arms over her torso as if she could hold onto her body heat. The other SUV she'd seen parked in the lot last night was still there along with Villanueva's Town Car and her rental, but there were no new vehicles in the lot.

Two rooms down, the door to Villanueva's room had been left ajar. What drew her in was the overpowering aroma of freshly brewed coffee. Her feet moved toward it automatically.

Gaspar was already there. He was eating donuts and seemed chipper. "Good morning, Sunshine." He'd probably slept five or six hours last night in addition to his long nap on the plane.

She frowned at him, and he put a cup of hot, black java in her hand. She breathed the heavenly aroma deep into her lungs. After the first couple of sips, she blinked hard a few times to clear her vision and glanced around.

Villanueva's cheap motel room was exactly like hers. There was a small desk and one straight chair hugging close to it. She pulled out the chair and sat down. Villanueva sat on the end of the bed and Gaspar sat at the head, feet propped up on the mattress. No one wanted to sit on the floor. The carpet looked like it had been used to sop all manner of foul liquids over the years.

"You look like crap," Gaspar said.

"How kind of you to notice." She scowled at him and drank more of the coffee, which was having the intended effect of making her feel almost human.

"Did you sleep at all?"

"I spent the night reading files on that old ATF bust. You were involved, weren't you, Villanueva?"

He took a deep breath and nodded. "It's where I first worked closely with Duffy."

"So she's like a daughter to you or what?" Gaspar asked.

"She's tough and smart, and the Feds could use more like her." Villanueva's tone bordered on belligerence. "Not that they act like they know that."

"Why did she come back here?" Kim glanced around again. "What are you two doing in this place?"

"I told you that last night."

"We need a lot more than what you told us. You said Duffy got a tip that there was human trafficking going on, presumably involving that compound out there on the ocean. And you said one of her friends was taken. Who's the friend? Why doesn't Duffy turn the situation over to the FBI?"

Villanueva looked distinctly uncomfortable. He stood and shoved his hands in his pockets and began shuffling around the room.

"The woman's name is Teresa Justice. Nine years ago, she was a DEA agent. Reported to Duffy. She was held captive in that house, and that's why we were here back then. Duffy needed to get her out. We did." Villanueva plopped himself onto the bed again. He looked defeated.

Gaspar said, "So what happened after that?"

"The experience changed Teresa. She wanted to move over to the FBI where she could work undercover on human trafficking cases. Didn't work out so she joined the NYPD." He took a deep breath. "But she was a crusader. Erratic. She risked herself and her team too many times."

"What finally happened?" Gaspar asked.

"One of her partners was killed." Villanueva looked down into his cup. "Finally, she was, let's say *encouraged* to move on."

"Where did she move on to?" Kim asked. "I mean, it's been nine years. How'd she end up back here if she's not on the job anymore?"

Villanueva cleared his throat. "Yeah, well, she, uh, started working as a private investigator with a small team."

"Doing what?"

"She went deep undercover. She found human trafficking rings and her team busted them up." His voice was quiet. He seemed saddened by the story, Kim thought.

"Sounds dangerous," Gaspar said.

He took another deep breath and blew a long stream of air between his lips. "It was. She was hurt. She was hospitalized. More than once. She's a mess."

"So, it's not surprising that she's gotten herself in a mess again, is it?" Gaspar drained his coffee and looked around for more. "Can't save every puppy in the pound. You're old enough to know that."

"Duffy feels responsible. Hell, so do I." He raised his

shoulders and stood up straight. "Duffy sent her in there nine years ago and, well, the aftermath hasn't been pretty. So Duffy needs to get her out. Not just out of that house. But out of that life."

"That's what this is about?" Kim asked. She was surprised. She'd expected Duffy to be hot on the trail of a big crime ring or something.

Villanueva nodded. "She thinks she can get Teresa out of there, and Teresa can testify about the human trafficking."

"Duffy figures she'll get herself out of the hot water she's in with the ATF, too, I suppose. Some kind of big score has helped her out of trouble before. She thinks she can repeat the trick." Gaspar's tone was laden with sarcasm.

"Exactly." Villanueva nodded again, decisively. "Everybody wins."

"Let's say we help you with this project," Kim said, nodding to Gaspar, who had located more coffee somewhere in the room and handed her another cup. "What do we get in return?"

"I can help you. With your assignment."

Gaspar stretched his legs out on the bed. "What do you know about our assignment?" His tone was easy, but Kim's internal radar had gone up a couple of notches, and his probably had, too.

"I know your target is Jack Reacher. Duffy told me."

Kim didn't flinch. "Assuming Duffy's right, so what?"

He paused and glanced at both of them, maybe to be sure they were paying attention. "I know the guy. Worked with him." His voice was quiet. "You help me with Duffy and Teresa, and I'll tell you what I know about Reacher. Help you build your file."

Of all the things she'd expected Villanueva to say, she hadn't considered that he might volunteer intel on Reacher.

Neither she nor Gaspar had mentioned Reacher to him before.
And she'd found no reason to believe he knew Reacher at all. If
the Boss knew about it, he'd conveniently failed to mention
anything.

"We've been through Reacher's files with a microscope."
Gaspar's tone was full of exasperation. "You're not mentioned
anywhere. Not even once."

"No shock there." Villanueva stared directly at Gaspar. "The
case we worked on together was way off the books. Neither one
of us was interested in putting anything in writing at the time."

"Reacher was Army Military Police. An officer. With wide
latitude, which he often overstepped and usually got away with,"
Gaspar said. "Why would he work off the books? And why
would he work with you?"

"It was after he left the Army." Villanueva glanced toward
Kim.

She said nothing, but her heartbeat quickened. This was the
first time any witness had confirmed that Reacher stayed active
in any kind of cases after he left the Army. Was Reacher an
intelligence asset after all? Working deep undercover? Was that
why there was no mention of him in any government files after
his discharge?

She'd considered the possibility that Reacher might be
undercover many times. And it made sense. In fact, it made more
sense than anything else she'd come up with. But the Boss had
denied it. And even undercover operatives had files and bosses
and teammates. Reacher seemed to have none of those.

Kim said, "What proof do you have that Reacher worked
with you in this off-the-books assignment? We'll need to verify."

"Figured you might say that." Villanueva nodded. "Find the
old Army file on a corruption investigation from twenty years

ago. One Reacher handled back in the day. Suspect killed a couple of Reacher's team members. The suspect died. His name was Francis Xavier Quinn."

She was instantly alert. She recognized the name. Her stomach did a couple of backflips. Francis Xavier Quinn had died during the old Abbot Cape raid, nine years ago. The cause of death was a spike shoved into the back of his skull. Somehow, killing a guy like that didn't seem consistent with Villanueva's style. Duffy wouldn't have had the strength to pull it off. None of the other agents on the scene had taken credit for it. Reacher, though? She could see him doing it like she could see herself shoving a thumbtack into a wall with the heel of her hand, putting her weight behind the hard push.

She chewed another antacid and sipped more of the black coffee. One probably canceled out the other, but she didn't care. "Why is that old Quinn file relevant?"

"Quinn's the guy Reacher and I were chasing in the case we worked together."

"You said Quinn died," Gaspar said between donut bites.

"He did." Villanueva smirked, picking up his cup. "But it took a while."

Gaspar said, "How did Reacher get involved in your case?"

Villanueva narrowed his eyes and stared through to Kim's conscience. "Will you help me with Duffy or not?"

She swallowed her coffee and considered the question.

He offered a sweetener. "Back then, when I worked with Reacher, I pulled every file on the guy that I could find. Interesting reading. I still have them."

"You'll give those files to us in exchange for what?"

"Duffy's working off the books here. Just like you are. It won't help her if she gets deeper into trouble over all of this and

I can't go in there and get her out on my own." He paused. "When we're done, when we've found Duffy and Teresa Justice and this is over, I'll give you my Reacher files. And I'll tell you everything I know about him." Kim didn't commit immediately, and Villanueva took another deep breath and exhaled. "And I'll tell you how to find him."

Still, she hesitated.

"You can't possibly have a better offer," Villanueva said. "If you did, you wouldn't be sitting here at all. What's it going to be?"

CHAPTER FOURTEEN

Thursday, November 25
Abbot, Maine
7:15 a.m.

"WE NEED MORE INFO from you. I've been through some
of the old files on the ATF bust here. It's an interesting report,
but there are a lot of holes. The kind of holes that can get us
all killed. So you need to tell us what you know." Kim paused.
"And then we'll decide whether we're on board for this or
not."

Villanueva resumed his seat at the end of the bed. "It's a
long story."

"Just give us the highlights," Gaspar said. "We don't need
War and Peace. It's Thanksgiving. I'd like to get home
sometime today."

Villanueva shook his head as if Gaspar might as well be
looking for a genie in a bottle to grant that wish. "The crime
back then was thought to be drug smuggling. Duffy and I were
with DEA at the time. We were chasing a drug dealer from LA."

"Turned out not to be drugs, I take it, if ATF got involved," Gaspar said.

Villanueva nodded. "Duffy ended up working off the books, and that's how she got Reacher involved. I'm not sure what she said to persuade him."

"How did they know each other before that assignment?" Kim asked.

"I had the impression theirs was a new team for both of them." Villanueva shrugged. "Anyway, Reacher helped us solve the problem, and he was actually the one to rescue Teresa Justice for us."

"All's well that ends well," Gaspar said.

Kim looked at Gaspar and Gaspar stared back.

"What's in these files you say you have on Reacher?" Gaspar wanted to know.

"The usual stuff. Personnel matters, mostly. He had been Army MP, but he worked freelance when I knew him," Villanueva said. "He had some useful contacts within the Army, and we exploited those during the case."

Gaspar cocked his head and narrowed his eyes. "That's just bullshit we already know, Villanueva. If you've got more, spill it already."

Villanueva shrugged again. "We all know that old and cold cases are often solved in unexpected ways, don't we?"

It was a fact. All detectives familiar with old cases knew they had to keep their eyes open and their ears to the ground. Serial killers had been brought down by unpaid parking tickets. Missing girls stolen from their homes showed up fifteen years later in somebody's backyard or basement. When something turned up, experienced cops were ready to make the arrest.

"I don't know, Tony." Kim stretched and squared her

shoulders. Her body ached, and her eyelids felt like sandpaper when they scraped her corneas. "If you know how to contact Reacher, why haven't you already done that? Based on what we know about the guy, his skill set would definitely be helpful to you and Duffy right about now."

"I made that suggestion two days ago. Duffy asked me not to contact him."

Kim searched Villanueva's face for truth and, after a bit, she found it. "You don't actually know how to contact Reacher, do you? You don't have any of his files. And you wouldn't tell us anything important about Reacher regardless, even if you could."

Villanueva shrugged again. "I guess you'll just have to trust me on that, won't you?"

Kim stood and looked around for more coffee. All gone. She looked at Gaspar. He nodded. She said, "We have to find Duffy anyway. We might as well have some help."

"She feels sorry for you, Villanueva. You're old. And you won't give up. And you're not up to the job by yourself, so you'll just get hurt or killed unless we help you," Gaspar said. "But Otto's more trusting than I am. I don't believe you. You need to give me something as a show of good faith."

"I already did. Pull the old Army file on Francis Xavier Quinn, like I said."

"It's Thanksgiving. Do you think anybody's gonna be working on non-essential documents today?"

"The Army is a 24/7/365 operation. You were a soldier, weren't you? Surely you know somebody you can call."

Gaspar pushed off the bed and walked outside, pulling his phone out of his pocket on the way.

Kim stood. "Where'd you get that coffee? I need another gallon."

Villanueva said, "Across the street. Convenience store. I'll get more."

She tapped Gaspar on the shoulder as she walked past him on the sidewalk toward her room and tilted her head toward her room. He nodded. They needed to talk. Alone.

CHAPTER FIFTEEN

Thursday, November 25
Abbot, Maine
7:35 a.m.

WHILE SHE WAITED IN her room, Kim opened her laptop and found the additional files from the Boss on the previous ATF case. She scanned the material quickly. No autopsy on Francis Xavier Quinn, but the cause of death seemed obvious enough. A chisel spiked to the skull behind the ear and into the brain doesn't leave a lot of room for misdiagnosis.

But there was no mention of Reacher in any of the narrative reports or witness statements or even the evidence collection lists. Not that she hadn't come to expect the absence of Reacher references in every file she searched. Didn't mean he wasn't there.

Now that they knew what to ask for, she expected Gaspar would find the old Army file Villanueva had sent him after, and that it would show Reacher's connection to Quinn. Somehow, Quinn must have been the one that got away for Reacher. Until Abbot.

One of the things she'd learned about Reacher in the past three weeks was that he never let a grudge wither away or die a natural death. Whatever Quinn had done, Reacher would have chased him to the ends of the earth to make him pay for it.

How the old Quinn case connected to the old Abbot case and then connected to Duffy and Reacher was not likely to be a straight line. But it would be enough verification of Villanueva's bona fides. Not that she disbelieved him. But it was always wise to confirm.

The challenge would be to get him to tell her what he knew about Reacher. Could she trust him to do that? Or not?

The addendum to the files on the Abbot raid showed that the owner of that house on the rocky point nine years ago was a guy named Richard Beck. Beck went to prison and died there a couple of years later in some sort of prison fight. Beck's wife and kid disappeared after the raid. The files didn't mention where they might be. Probably witness protection or something like that, if Kim had to guess. Otherwise, they'd be dead by now, too.

Several other bodies were found inside and outside the compound back then. Some were law enforcement, which might have had something to do with Duffy's move over to ATF and Teresa Justice's early exit from the DEA.

Villanueva was saying that Reacher had been there. Kim was willing to believe him. Stood to reason Reacher was involved in some way.

Gaspar knocked on the door and let himself in. "We'll have Reacher's old Quinn file in about an hour."

Kim nodded. She glanced at the clock. It was only seven forty-five, but she felt like the day had already lasted its full twenty-four hours. She gave Gaspar a quick rundown of the materials she'd just reviewed.

"So what are we going to do, Susie Wong? We came here for Duffy, and she's not here. What's the point of hanging around? All we have is Villanueva's hunch that she's still in the area. She could be anywhere."

Kim nodded and said, "I checked the flight schedules. Assuming the storm isn't as bad as they're forecasting, or if we can get ahead of it, we can get out of Boston Logan tonight and be home in time to see our families for Thanksgiving, at least technically. We can dig the leftovers out of the fridge and see everybody before they head to bed."

"So how about we help Villanueva until time to leave for Boston about, say, one o'clock? If we find Duffy, we stay here and get whatever we can out of her and then go." Gaspar paused. "If we don't find her, we fly home tonight and get back to hunting Reacher info again after the holiday on Monday."

"The Boss won't like it, but that works for me. Duffy's not essential to anything we're doing, as far as I can see. No guarantee she'll tell us anything, even if we find her." She took a deep breath and stretched the fatigue from her shoulders. "Reacher's been missing for fifteen years. Another couple of days can't matter that much."

She pulled up the Boss's files on her laptop. "Here. Take a look at these photos. Say Duffy *is* inside Abbot Cape. I don't see how we can get her out before we head to Boston, even if we wanted to. Getting into that compound won't be a walk in the park unless you've acquired pole-vaulting skills."

CHAPTER SIXTEEN

Thursday, November 25
Abbot, Maine
8:05 a.m.

BRANCH WOKE UP HUNGRY and caffeine deprived, as always. He left the warmth of his bed and looked around, but there was no coffee pot in the room. He'd driven through a small town a few miles back last night. Maybe he could get coffee there, even on Thanksgiving. He took a quick shower and dressed and went outside.

Last night's snow had accumulated about two inches and was still falling. The wind was bitingly cold. On the way to his SUV, out of habit, he scanned the area. There was another SUV parked in the lot in front of the third room from the end of the row. Must have come in really late.

He glanced in the opposite direction. The motel office was closed, as the clerk had told him it would be. Across the street was a gas station with a convenience store that might have coffee. He needed gas anyway. He'd try that place first.

He started his SUV and watched while an old guy pulled out of the gas station in an old Town Car and drove across the road. He parked near the end of the lot next to the other SUV. The old guy loaded up both arms with a trio of huge Styrofoam cups and struggled out of the driver's seat. After pushing the heavy door closed with his foot, he shuffled toward one of the rooms and punched the door with his elbow, nearly losing control of the enormous cups in the process.

Branch sat up straight when Agent Gaspar opened the door and relieved the old guy of his burden.

"What are they doing here?"

Gaspar and the old guy exchanged a few words that Branch couldn't hear as the old guy entered the room. They must have been talking about him because a couple of seconds later, Agent Otto stepped through the open doorway and looked his way.

He considered ignoring her. But they seemed to be dug in here. Maybe they'd found Duffy. He'd make sure she was okay and then he'd turn around and head back to Houston before the blizzard made escape impossible.

He tried calling Duffy's cell again. Duffy might even have returned to Houston. Voice mail picked up after a dozen rings. He left another message, even though he figured only the cell phone he'd found in the safe in her bedroom would hear him, then hauled himself out from behind the wheel and trudged toward their motel room.

Otto had left the door propped open. Branch stepped inside, made a quick assessment of the situation, and then closed the door behind him.

The room was exactly like his. Cheap. Cramped.

Otto was seated on the room's only chair. Neither Otto nor Gaspar greeted him.

"Alex Branch." He extended his hand to the old guy. "Got any coffee?"

"Tony Villanueva." He nodded toward the big Styrofoam cups he'd plopped onto the small desk. "Let me refill my old one, and you can have what's left." Villanueva didn't ask for ID, so Otto must have explained his relationship to Duffy.

"Thanks," Branch said as the man handed him the big cup, now only half-full. He recognized Villanueva's name from the old ATF file. He'd been involved in the case back then. He'd been at DEA with Duffy. "Good to meet you. We have Duffy in common, I guess." He turned his gaze to Otto. "You haven't found Duffy yet?"

She shook her head. "You haven't found her, either."

Branch ignored Otto's belligerence "I'm worried about her. She's still not answering my calls."

"Join the crowd," Villanueva said.

Branch widened his stance and settled his weight. "Can you catch me up?"

"What do you already know?" Villanueva asked.

"I've reviewed the ATF files from the raid out here nine years ago." Branch took a big swig of the hot coffee. It burned his throat going down, and he coughed. When he had control of his voice box again, he said, "Duffy's been getting phone calls from an Abbot number over the past couple of weeks."

Otto and Gaspar remained silent.

He figured a show of good faith was required to warm Otto up a bit. He fished out his phone and found the recorded call he'd pulled from Duffy's landline. He turned up the volume and played the call through the phone's speaker.

When the recording finished, Otto said, "Play it again."

He complied.

"I recognize Duffy's voice." She turned to Villanueva. "Is the other one Teresa Justice?"

"Maybe. Play it one more time," Villanueva said.

Once again, Branch complied. He nodded as the message replayed. Was the whispering caller Teresa Justice? He knew her. She worked at ATF once. A friend of Duffy's. He hadn't spoken to her in at least seven years. But he had a good ear for voices. The whispering made it harder to say for sure, but it sounded like her.

"It's been a long time." Villanueva cocked his head as he listened to the end of the call. "It's got to be her, though. Duffy told me Teresa had called her several times. Who else could it be?"

Otto's spine straightened, and Branch wondered what she was pissed off about.

"Take a look at these photos." Otto moved away from the laptop to give Villanueva and Branch an unobstructed view of the screen. She explained the images as she ran through them. "This is the house on that rocky finger that juts into the ocean just east of here. The compound and everything in it is called Abbot Cape. And a few different shots taken this morning of the people we believe are the current occupants."

Villanueva sat heavily in the chair, and Branch stood behind him. Villanueva hit the trackpad on Otto's laptop to cycle through the half dozen photos again.

The first two were shots from a satellite encompassing the entire compound. The photos had been taken a few weeks ago. No snow on the ground. Fall leaves still attached to the trees.

Branch had studied similar photos in the old file. The house itself looked pretty much the same way it had nine years ago, but it had been springtime then. The house and the compound would look the same nine years hence, he figured. It was that kind of place. Mostly rock and ocean and not enough people living there to destroy things through regular use.

The house was probably built a hundred years ago. But he noticed several changes to the other structures. The gatehouse had been enlarged and almost doubled in size. The old stable had already been converted to a garage back then, but it, too, had been expanded. Another story was added, and all the new rooms had windows.

The granite wall that protected the compound from intruders was high, thick, and imposing. The barbed wire on the top made it look like a prison enclosure. The heavy iron gate looked the same as the old pictures, but newer somehow. This one might be a replica of the old one. Maybe the original was damaged at some point.

And he could see surveillance cameras mounted around all of the buildings. In the photos from nine years ago, he'd noted cameras at the gate, but not inside the wall. He'd figured they wanted privacy inside the compound back then. Maybe this was a place, like so many others around the world, where security trumped privacy.

The next four photos had been shot closer to ground level from four different angles. Perhaps a micro-drone with a camera had made these. Or maybe the security cameras inside the compound had been hacked briefly.

These shots focused on entrances, exits, and the people who came and went. Two smallish women wrapped in thick coats disappeared into a back entrance where a modernized kitchen could be glimpsed through a large window.

Four extremely large men and two slightly smaller men had been photographed in various locations around the property. The larger men were similar enough that they might have been clones. Upon close examination, he identified visible differences. But from afar, they looked tall, wide, and dangerous.

The last photo was of a well-dressed, dark-haired man standing at the front door.

Branch said, "Can you go back to photo number five?"

Villanueva hit the back button.

"Can we zoom in on that guy right there?" He pointed to a two-man photo including a huge man standing near the big iron gate secured to that granite wall. Six-five or so, maybe two-fifty. A chiseled block of stone almost as hard as the granite boulders used to build the place. Hand-to-hand combat with that one should definitely be avoided.

Villanueva hit the zoom until the big man's profile filled most of the laptop's small screen. Branch leaned in and examined the photo. He was dark complected. His hair and eyes were dark brown. Eyebrows thick as caterpillars. Nose looked like it had been broken a few times. Wide at the bridge, slightly narrower at the nostrils.

Branch pointed to the slightly smaller fellow standing next to the giant. The second man's head was turned, exposing a fleshy right ear. "Can you zoom that in a bit more?"

Villanueva did so.

Now, the dark brown birthmark that covered the smaller man's neck behind and slightly below his right earlobe was unmistakable.

Otto said, "What did you recognize?"

Branch tapped the laptop screen with his forefinger. "I know that guy."

"Who is he?" Gaspar asked.

"Name's Leo Abramovich. Shortened to Abrams. Not related to the Russian billionaire as far as we know. He's on the

ATF's most wanted list." Branch leaned in to study the birthmark again. "Abrams is a Russian mobster. He's into a variety of illegal activities. Human trafficking, drugs, guns, murder, kidnapping for ransom. We've got a long list. He was based in Mexico for a long time, but lately, he seems to have relocated to Europe or the Middle East, we think. We're not sure where. ATF's been chasing him for years."

Gaspar swiped his palm over his hair. "That's just what we need." His tone made it clear he thought the news was far from ideal.

Branch nodded slowly as he straightened his back to stand. "Exactly."

"Who knows how long he'll be there?" Otto had been leaning against the wall, one of the huge Styrofoam cups clasped in both small hands. "Get some help out here from ATF's Boston field office and bring him in."

"I'm not ATF anymore, but I need to do exactly that. And I don't see how I can." Branch shook his head. "Not until we figure out where Duffy is and whether she's okay. She's already in trouble without adding another layer to her problems."

Otto said nothing.

Villanueva nodded approvingly and continued to flip through the photos on the screen. "I've been there, you know. Inside the compound and inside the house. Some of the furniture and decorating is probably different from back then. But the footprint of the main house is the same."

"That may help, if we have to go inside before ATF gets on scene," Branch said.

"These people are all new. None of them were there nine years ago." Villanueva continued to rotate through the photos as if they might change or morph into something different. They didn't.

"What are you looking for?" Branch asked.

"I thought maybe the kid, the one we used to get inside last time, had inherited the house or something." Villanueva flipped through the photos several times, peering at the screen. Otto watched him more carefully than Branch thought Villanueva's actions required. "But I don't see him. These guys are all way too big to be that scrawny kid."

Gaspar said, "Sometimes scrawny kids bulk up."

"Sometimes they do." Villanueva nodded. "But this particular scrawny kid was missing his left ear. All of these hulking dudes have both their ears."

"He could be inside but not included in these photos," Branch suggested.

"True." Villanueva turned to Otto. "Your boss say there's anyone else in the compound?"

She shook her head. "We don't have eyes inside all the buildings yet, but as far as we can tell, these are all of the people on site this morning. We've done a sweep of the garage and the gatehouse. The main house has thick stone walls and not many windows."

"Don't suppose your boss elaborated on how he did that, exactly?" Villanueva asked.

"I could guess." Otto frowned. "Doesn't really matter how we know, does it?"

Villanueva shrugged. "I might like to see more, that's all."

"So the suggestion is that Duffy's not inside. Which means we should be looking somewhere else." Branch drank his coffee. "We need to know whether Duffy's there. And if she is, we need to get her out. And then I can call ATF and get a team out here to pick up Abrams."

No one said anything. No one agreed. But no one walked out, either.

CHAPTER SEVENTEEN

KIM RAN THROUGH THE logic in her head. The timeline was tight, but all the pieces fit together like a puzzle. She had been called out to hunt for intel on Reacher twenty-four days ago. She'd seen Duffy in D.C. on day seven, and again in Virginia on day ten. After that, she'd had no contact with Duffy for the past two weeks.

During those fourteen days, Duffy must have been handling two things simultaneously. She was somehow in touch with Teresa Justice, and that situation turned south on day nineteen. And she'd also been fighting for her career after the Vice-President's son was kidnapped and returned. Kim believed Duffy's troubles on that score were courtesy of Jack Reacher, but for timing purposes, whether Reacher was involved or not probably didn't matter.

In many ways, she and Duffy were a lot alike. Dedicated careerists. Focused on the job, first and foremost, sure. But not exclusively and not to the exclusion of everything else.

Kim would have multi-tasked to handle both goals: take care of her friends and save her career. She wouldn't have prioritized one above the other. Duffy had probably done the same.

Kim believed Duffy was with Reacher when Kim saw them both in D.C. and again in Virginia. Duffy was already working with Teresa then, too. If Teresa and Duffy were both in trouble, would she have told Reacher about her problems? Would he have shrugged it off? Or would he have tried to help her, especially after she'd put her career on the line for him?

Branch had been talking, but Kim had tuned him out. He must have noticed because he cleared his throat and raised his voice. "We need to see for ourselves. But the problem is, how do we get in there?"

Kim sipped her coffee and tried to pay attention.

Villanueva said, "That was always the issue back then, too. The road leading to that gate is about fifteen miles of nothing between the interstate and the house."

Gaspar said, "Dense woods on both sides until you get closer, which is okay. But then the woods stop where the beaches begin, leaving anybody trying to approach that gate exposed for too long."

Villanueva nodded. "Nine years ago, there was no surveillance on the road. But here I see cameras deployed in the trees at regular intervals." He poked the laptop screen with a finger, showing the cameras he'd identified. "Whoever is in charge these days is even more paranoid than David Beck was."

Branch drained the last of his coffee. He stuffed his hands into the back pockets of his jeans and leaned his shoulder against the wall. "If your boss has the ability to hack into their internal surveillance systems, that means I can probably do it, too. But surveillance can only do so much. We need to get inside the compound and take a close look."

"Running through those trees on foot would be rough going, even before the blizzard began. Fifteen miles of road is a long stretch," Gaspar pointed out. There was no way Gaspar could run a single mile on a track, much less fifteen through a forest. He was probably thinking about that, too. "We could try disabling the cameras along the road, but that's a longer-term play and might be beyond our tech capabilities."

Kim asked about the thing that had been nagging her for a while. "Where's Duffy's car?"

"No idea." Villanueva shook his head. "The last time I saw it was here at the motel, in the parking lot, before she disappeared."

"Was it a rental?"

Villanueva nodded. "Small SUV. Rav 4, white. She complained about how many miles it had on it. She said it drove like it had been through a war zone or something."

"We rented in Portland last night," Kim said. "There's only three rental companies on site at that airport." She looked at Branch. "You rented in Boston. I assume you had all of the usual rental options there?"

"But Duffy would have done what I did," Branch replied. "Chose an off brand, one that isn't usually used by ATF. Harder to trace my activities that way."

"Meaning what?" Gaspar asked. "She'd have used StellarCar like you did?"

Branch nodded again. "Probably."

Kim said, "StellarCar has GPS in those vehicles, I assume? Can you get on the phone and have someone trace her Rav 4? Get her full travel history. Find out where she went and where that Rav 4 is. Could help." Unless they found her body inside the vehicle, too. But Kim wouldn't think about that yet. If Duffy was already dead, there was nothing Kim could do about it.

"Roger that." Branch nodded. "I'm on it. What else?"

"If it's got a dash cam or any kind of interior video, get that, too," Kim replied. "Once we know the travel history, I can get satellite video. Maybe we can get eyes on her activities for the past few days."

There was silence in the room for a few seconds. Kim's mind felt foggy, still. She needed sleep, but she wasn't going to get any for a while.

"No way could she have overpowered that guy," Gaspar said as if he was thinking out loud. "If Duffy went all the way to the house by way of that road, she'd have used a subterfuge of some sort to get through the gate."

"Like what? A lost tourist would have turned around and gone back out again," Villanueva said. "No one would have driven down that twelve miles of road unless they knew that house was on the point."

"Duffy's a jogger. She runs about ten miles a day, every day, in all kinds of weather," Branch said. "She could have run all the way from the closest intersection there on Route 1. Twelve miles. Not a problem."

"They would have seen her coming. Because of the cameras," Gaspar pointed out.

"Which is probably how she got picked up," Villanueva said.

"Which might've been fine with her," Kim said. "Pretend she's a lost runner. Talk her way inside."

No one responded. Something about that creepy old place caused Kim's stomach to churn like a cement mixer. She wasn't going in there unless and until she knew for sure that Duffy was inside.

"Can your boss get the video feed for the morning Duffy disappeared?" Branch asked Kim. "Along the road and at the gate? Maybe we can start there."

"I'll make the request." Not that she'd have to ask. There were a dozen ways he could be watching and listening to everything going on in the room anyway. "How about you, Branch? You're working for BlueRiver. They have access to all kinds of things."

He nodded. "What else?"

Kim sensed his impatience. Branch was an old-fashioned man of action, she guessed. A charter member of the act-now-and-plan-later brigade. She figured he'd die young. Maybe he was counting on it.

Villanueva pulled up another photo. The well-dressed man standing at the front door of the main house. "Who's this guy?"

"I'm running him through facial recognition, along with the others," Kim replied. "I'm guessing he's the man in charge or maybe the owner. Do you recognize him?"

Branch said, "I don't."

Kim studied the picture again. The man looked Eastern European, she thought. He was well groomed. Handsomely Slavic. Dark hair, dark eyes. His casual clothes fit him perfectly. Probably bespoke.

Kim stretched to get her circulation going. "Okay, to recap. As far as we know, we have four burly security guys, Abrams, the guy we'll call the owner, and two women, let's call them the cook and the maid. No one else shows up on any of these photos."

"There's a thousand hiding places in that compound. There's a basement. Teresa was held prisoner there for weeks last time," Villanueva said. "Who knows how many people are in there where we can't see them?"

Kim felt the Boss's cell phone vibrate, indicating an incoming text message. She fished the phone out of her pocket and read the one-word text. "Incoming."

"Let's see what's going on." Kim opened her Internet connection to her secure server and found the appropriate satellite to observe the compound on a live feed. She couldn't get an unobstructed view of the entire area. The gray clouds and continuing snowfall obscured the images on the feed. But the general area was visible enough.

There were lights on inside the main house and inside the gatehouse. The garage had no light showing through windows. No one was walking around outside. No vehicles were approaching or visible anywhere inside the compound.

"What are we looking for?" Branch asked.

"I'm not sure yet. Be patient," Kim replied.

They had watched for a couple of minutes before a full-size Airbus EC145 helicopter came into view, approaching from the north. The video feed had no sound, but Kim imagined the big helicopter's rotor noise to be as deafening as those birds always were. The helo had no identifying marks that she could see from this angle.

The helicopter's rotors swirled the snow on the ground into a mini tornado as it struggled to land, hovering above and then setting down between the main house and the gatehouse. When it settled on its wheels atop the snow, four burly security men hurried outside from the gatehouse, bent at the waist to escape the rotor wash and snow pelting their bodies.

The helicopter's flight stairs were lowered, and the men waited on the pavement.

One after another, seven tall, slight, blonde women wearing white gowns appeared at the helicopter's exit door and seemed to float down the stairs. The effect was ethereal as if a bevy of angels descended from a modern day chariot.

They gathered at the bottom of the stairs, surrounded by the security team, and then appeared to float into the main house. A man inside the EC145 raised the helo's steps and closed the door.

Once the women and their escorts were inside the big house, the helicopter spooled up and battled the wind to lift away, returning north and disappearing into the low clouds.

Kim sat back in the chair and all three men, who had formed a semicircle behind her to view the small laptop screen, continued to watch in silence.

After twenty minutes, when they spotted no further movement, Kim turned in her chair to face them. "We didn't have a great view from this distance and the live feed was running under less than optimal conditions, but could anybody tell whether any of those women was Susan Duffy or Teresa Justice?"

Villanueva shook his head. "They all looked so similar. Any one of them could have been Duffy. Or Teresa. They're similar body types, I guess, although I never thought about that before, really."

Kim looked at Branch. He shrugged. Shook his head. "Maybe if we had seen close-ups of their faces."

"I couldn't tell, either," Gaspar said. "You've seen Duffy twice before and spent enough time with those old files. Do you think she was in that group?"

Kim drank more of her coffee, thinking about the question. She closed her eyes and replayed her memories of Susan Duffy and compared them to the angels descending from the helicopter, but it didn't help. She opened her eyes and shook her head. "I don't know."

Out of the corner of her eye, Kim noticed the images on the laptop's screen. The ground snow inside the compound began to swirl again. She zoomed out to get a wider view.

The earlier scene was repeated, almost as if she had rewound and replayed a recording. The same helicopter hovered into view and landed again. The door opened and the steps lowered. Four security guys came out of the house and escorted seven tall, slight, blonde, females dressed in white gowns through the front entrance of the big house.

The helicopter buttoned up and lifted off again. But this time, it flew south instead of north.

They continued watching as this process was repeated twice more. A total of four deliveries. Each time, the cargo was the same. Seven tall, slender, blonde women dressed in white. Twenty-eight women in all. Why? Why not twenty-five or thirty? Why twenty-eight? Where did they find them all? And perhaps most importantly, what plans had been made for them?

After the fourth delivery, the helicopter lifted off and flew north and did not return. The entire process had consumed two hours.

Kim stood and stretched. She glanced at her Seiko. It was possible to drive back to Boston and make flights to Detroit or Miami, maybe. But they'd come this far. Should they stay or go? Her gaze met Gaspar's. He shrugged.

"Anybody interested in food?" Villanueva asked. "We can drive toward Boston and find a restaurant and a decent table where we can talk and make a plan."

"I'll drive," Branch said. "Meet at my SUV in ten?"

Villanueva and Branch left Kim's room, and Gaspar lumbered off the bed. "I've got to make a call."

"Say hello to Marie for me." Kim glanced at her Seiko. The Boss should be there. She reached for the dedicated cell phone. He picked up on the first ring. "We need help."

"I've got the videos of those women. We're working on that. Doesn't look like Duffy."

"Are you sure we're watching the same scene?" If he'd been in the room, she'd have gaped at him. "They *all* look like Duffy."

"Duffy's type. But not Duffy. Confirmed."

Kim took a breath and swiped her palm over her hair to the low ponytail at the back of her neck. "Then where is she? Inside the house? Villanueva says there's a basement."

"Maybe. More likely one of the outbuildings. I'm looking at the video footage along that road on the day she disappeared. All I'm seeing is a lot of empty road in the shadows so far."

"Branch says she's a runner. That she might have parked her rental, a white Rav 4, and jogged the rest of the way to the gate. It's a StellarCar. Probably out of Boston. Can you run down the GPS on it?"

"I'm already on it, but with the holiday, it'll take a while." He seemed distracted, irritable. He was probably expected somewhere else. "I'm going to be tied up most of the day."

Figures. She had one more thing on her wish list. "What about the well-dressed guy standing in the doorway? Have you identified him yet?"

"Working on it. Go do something useful." He disconnected the call.

She looked into the camera on her laptop and flipped him the bird.

She pulled out another burner phone and dialed a number she had memorized.

Lamont Finlay picked up on the second ring. "How can I help you, Otto?" His voice was deep and melodious, his tone patient. As always.

"How did you know it was me?"

"You're the only one who has this number. What do you need?"

"We're looking to find an ATF agent, a woman we know was associated with Reacher during activities that led to an ATF raid in Abbot, Maine, nine years ago."

"Uh, huh." She heard shuffling in the background. He was probably at some holiday event, too.

"As far as Reacher's concerned, it looks like that old business was a pure revenge play."

"Uh, huh."

"The woman who was involved in that event has returned to the same location."

"Uh, huh."

"She's missing."

"Missing persons are local jurisdiction. How does this involve me?"

"We've seen her with Reacher twice since we received this assignment. The first time, in D.C. The second time, in Virginia. She's in trouble."

"Good thing you're there to help, then."

"I think Reacher is on his way here."

"You've been chasing his past for more than three weeks. Now you believe he's coming straight at you. Why are you telling me instead of Cooper?"

"You're not interested? I must have misunderstood. Sorry to bother you." She waited a moment.

He breathed loudly into the phone. "What's her name?"

"Susan Duffy. Most recently, ATF. Nine years ago, DEA."

"I'll call you back." He disconnected and once again she was listening to dead air.

"Doesn't anybody ever say goodbye anymore?"

CHAPTER EIGHTEEN

BRANCH WALKED TO HIS room without looking back. He opened a secure email from his contact. "Call me," was all it said. He dialed the number. "Branch," he said when the call was answered.

The guy didn't beat around the bush. "There are no files on Jack Reacher."

"That's not even possible. We monitor everything. A five-year-old goes to the potty, and we know about it."

A long sigh blew through the receiver. "We have Reacher in the files prior to 1997. Army files, mostly. But that's it. Nothing else."

"Where did you look?" Branch squeezed his eyes shut while he concentrated on the possible options. "Homeland Security? TSA? CIA? FBI? Civilian records?"

"All of that and then some. Reacher has been erased." His tone was quiet but firm. "Any references to him have been thoroughly removed from anywhere and everywhere."

"Erased?" Branch's eyes popped open. "You're sure?"

"I know what to look for."

Branch shook his head and wiped his palm over his face. "Why would someone go to all that trouble?"

"Damned if I know."

Branch stopped arguing because there was no point to it. He paced the room and rolled his shoulders to loosen up. "Let's assume you're right."

"I am right. No assumption required." Keyboard clicking sounds. "He's got a passport, but the address and contact info on it is phony. No way to trace him using what we have, so don't ask."

All of which meant that Otto and Gaspar's inquiry was probably legitimate. If his source could find nothing on Reacher, then there was nothing to be found. Completing a background check would be the logical thing to do, assuming Reacher was being considered for a special assignment, as they claimed.

"Talk me through this," Branch said. "The guy needs money. Where does he get his cash? And don't say from the bank."

"He has an Army pension. Deposited into the same bank every month for fifteen years. And from time to time, he makes ATM withdrawals in cash, but even that hasn't happened for a while." His tone said it all. That was the end of the money trail.

"Got any video of those transactions?"

"Still checking, but going back for the past year, no. Not even one. He's careful not to be recorded when he collects his money."

"Is he dead?"

"Possibly. But we've got no record of his death."

"Witness protection?"

"Again, possibly. But no records there, either."

"He was military police. Back in the day. Has he gone over

to the dark side? It's easy enough to do." Branch warmed to the idea as he talked it out. "A guy has some success solving problems with force. Finds himself hanging around on the outside looking in. Might have no patience for the vagaries of civilian life."

"Once more, possibly. But—"

"Yeah, I know. No records. No proof." Branch dashed through the facts he knew. Nothing popped. "It's just not possible that every single mention of this guy that should be recorded somewhere has been erased."

"It *is* possible because it's happened. I've checked and double-checked."

"Come on. You know Uncle Sam. If nothing else, we're not that competent. Somebody trying to erase the guy must have made at least one mistake. Find it."

"I'll keep looking, but I know my business." He paused a couple of beats. "And Branch?"

"Yeah?"

"Watch your back. Whoever erased every mention of Reacher from the files is somebody to be careful of."

"No kidding." A guy with that much power was a man who could erase them all without flinching and make it look like they'd never existed at all. Branch heard a sharp rap of knuckles on his door. The door opened.

Otto filled the doorway, cocooned in a quilted down parka. "You coming?"

"Yeah. Be right there." When she walked away, he returned to his contact. "I'll check with you in a few hours. Dig deeper. There's got to be something on Reacher. Take a look at connections to Charles Cooper."

"Cooper? You think he's behind this?"

"Possible."

His contact whistled. "I didn't sign on to get sideways with Cooper."

"Yeah. Me neither." Branch grabbed his coat and stepped outside, trying not to think about how impossible his life would become with Charles Cooper as an enemy.

"Check something else for me," Branch said. "Duffy rented a Rav 4 from StellarCar at Boston Logan last Sunday. Find the GPS history on that vehicle. And see if you can ping it for me. I want to know where it's located."

"Duffy's missing?"

"That's what we're trying to find out." Branch disconnected and slid behind the wheel of the rented SUV. Everyone else was already belted into their seats.

Branch drove south toward Boston. He watched for Duffy's disabled Rav 4 along the shoulder, just in case. But he didn't find it. The snow accumulation was more than four inches, but the all-wheel drive SUV had no trouble moving through.

About five miles down the interstate they found an open chain restaurant. He pulled into the parking lot. The place was nearly deserted. Most people were home with their families, he assumed. Or maybe they planned to eat later in the day. Either way, they'd have some privacy and more space for planning than crammed inside those motel rooms.

Otto pointed to a table in the corner where they could talk without being overheard. They ordered and when the waitress departed, got down to business.

For a tiny woman, Otto had no trouble taking charge. Branch liked that about her, even though he worried about the physics. It would be a simple matter for someone to overwhelm her if she didn't see him coming.

Branch said, "I made the call on the Rav 4. Maybe we'll have something on that shortly."

"Good," Villanueva said.

Branch nodded. "Maybe she's on her way to Disney World."

Villanueva grimaced. "Right."

Otto leveled her stare on Branch. "I want to know about Leo Abrams. The guy you said is on the ATF most wanted list. Who is he and what is he wanted for?"

Branch busied himself with his coffee. His days at ATF had included high-level security briefings with the Pentagon from time to time. He'd been privy to classified intel, including sensitive compartmented information. Simply acknowledging the existence of CCO intel would get him a long stretch in prison.

Branch figured Otto and Gaspar both had high-level security clearances, though, and, at this point, needed to know. Villanueva probably didn't have a current clearance, since he was retired, but this might not be the time to stand on protocol, at least for the broad strokes about Leo Abrams.

It was a risk either way.

Before he had a chance to begin, Otto reached into her pocket and pulled out her phone to read a text. She threw her napkin on the table. "Come on. Let's go."

"Go where?" Branch asked.

"We've located Duffy's car."

CHAPTER NINETEEN

Thursday, November 25
Abbot, Maine
12:32 p.m. Eastern Time

FORECAST AS THE WORST blizzard to hit Portland in three decades, radar placed the bulk of it still several hours to the southwest. The skies had already dropped three inches of heavy, wet snow in the past eight hours. Branch drove the SUV like a snowplow through the drifts across Route 1 following directions from the GPS.

There was scant traffic on the road. With all the snow, people must have either gotten a head start on their drives to their Thanksgiving dinner destinations or decided to stay home.

Otto was in the passenger seat scanning the road, turning her head from one side to the other. She looked like a child who had climbed into her daddy's oversized chair. Branch smiled to himself. He didn't dare say anything of the kind to her; their relationship was testy enough already.

"What are you doing?" he asked.

"Looking for wildlife. Deer, mostly. But wild turkeys, porcupines. Whatever." Her tone was serious.

He smiled. She looked like a child and being delighted with wildlife along the roadway seemed childlike to him, too.

"You don't have much wildlife bounding onto the roads in Houston, probably. But in places like this, they cause significant damage," she explained.

"Really?" He wasn't convinced.

"I know of two people who were killed when their cars hit deer on days like this. The snow muffles the sound of their approach." She paused and glanced at him. "The roads are slick. Drivers try to stop, only to swerve into oncoming traffic or off the road. Lots of things can happen."

Branch nodded and objected no further.

"Where did you say Duffy's vehicle is?" Villanueva asked from the back seat.

"They towed the Rav 4 to an impound lot, five miles south of Kennebunkport," Otto said. "The GPS history on it says it was coming north from Boston just before the accident."

"Any idea why Duffy was in Boston?" Gaspar asked.

Branch glanced at Villanueva in the rearview mirror. The old guy shook his head but didn't reply.

Branch turned off Route 1 and drove another two miles, following directions to the local police station. He parked out front. There was only one cruiser in the lot. He released his seatbelt and reached for the door handle.

Otto said, "Gaspar and I will go in. We've got active credentials. Fewer explanations will be required."

"Duffy's my partner." Branch opened the door and stepped out of the SUV. "You can come if you want. Or you can stay here." That was as much accommodation as he was willing to make, even though he knew she was probably right.

Otto climbed out of the seat and hopped down onto the pavement. Gaspar and Villanueva followed. All four doors of the SUV slammed in the unnaturally snow-muffled quiet.

Branch reached the front door of the station and pulled it open. Otto walked through, and the others followed like mallards trailing behind their mama.

The desk sergeant looked up when they came inside. "How can we help you folks?"

Otto pulled out her badge wallet. One glimpse was all any law enforcement officer needed to identify her as FBI. These small town cops shops could be refreshingly informal, too. "I'm Otto. This is Gaspar, Branch, Villanueva."

"Mik Brown. How can I help the FBI today?"

"We understand you folks impounded a white Toyota Rav 4 on Tuesday night. We need to have a look at it."

"Yeah, I think that's out back. There's a good bit of snow out there." Brown rummaged through a drawer in the desk and came up with a ring of keys. "Right this way."

Brown led the way through a locked door, down a long corridor to a steel door that led to the impound lot. He unlocked the steel exit door and held it open. The frigid wind blew snow inside. "You folks don't mind if I stay in here, do you? Keys are in the vehicle. I'll be here when you're done."

Otto led the way. There were three vehicles in the lot. Two old sedans and one badly mauled white Rav 4. It looked like the front bumper had slammed head-on into a brick building. The whole front end, from the bumper to the windshield, was a crumpled mess. The windshield was broken. The two front doors were jacked and wracked. The left side looked like it had landed in a ditch.

Otto pulled out her phone and began to take still shots and video of the wrecked vehicle.

Branch walked all the way around the Rav 4, looking in the windows. The front doors refused to open, but he lifted the handle on the back passenger door and yanked hard enough to free it. He leaned inside.

The stale air inside the cabin was infused with the combined stench of stale smoke, vomit, urine, feces, and blood, but no decayed human remains. After the first whiff, he held his breath.

The front seat, front dashboard, and most of the carpet was liberally splashed with dried blood. The front and side airbags had deployed and lay limp against the interior. The rearview mirror was gone. The side mirrors were cracked, and pieces were missing.

The back seat and the cargo area were also splattered with dried blood and deployed airbags and safety glass pebbles.

In the cargo area, four crumpled bags held the stinking remains of four fast food dinners.

What he didn't see inside was anything that he recognized as belonging to Duffy. And no bodies, dead or alive.

He moved outside and allowed himself to breathe again. Otto stepped around him and looked inside. She took a deep breath, held it, and shot stills and video of the inside of the vehicle.

When she pulled her head out, she moved upwind and took big gulps of air. He figured she was making every effort not to retch, as he was.

"See anything worth discussing at the moment?" Otto asked.

"Only that if Duffy was in this thing when it hit whatever blocked its path, she's going to be in a morgue somewhere." His words sounded a lot tougher than he felt.

"Local cops say the Rav 4 was stolen from a mall parking lot just north of Boston by a group of teens on Tuesday night," Gaspar said, reading from a text on his phone. "The four teens were drinking and speeding and ran off the road and hit a stand of trees."

"Fatalities?"

Gaspar replied, "The kids are in a Boston hospital, but they'll all be okay."

"Hard to believe." Branch shook his head, but the relief that washed over him was welcome. "Are we done here?"

"Almost," Otto said. "I've got everything we need except the odometer. Think you can get a look at it?"

"Yeah." He held out his palm, and she gave him the phone. He opened the passenger door again, held his breath, and leaned in until he could see the instrument panel. He snapped a few photos of all the instruments. He returned her phone.

Villanueva had walked around the entire vehicle. He knelt at the rear to wipe grime from the license plate. "Otto. Get a shot of this plate. We can run it."

"Something odd about it?" She walked to the back of the Rav 4 and snapped a few photos.

"It's a Virginia plate. Not Maine. Not even Massachusetts." Villanueva shrugged. "Common with rental companies for the plates to originate in various locations. But the plate could be stolen. We want to be thorough here."

They walked back into the station and asked Sergeant Brown a few questions, but he didn't know anything about the accident or the kids involved. He gave them a copy of the accident report and said they could call back on Monday and talk to the captain.

When they returned to the SUV, Branch entered the coordinates of the accident site into the GPS. "The crash took place about three miles further south. Let's go take a quick look at it."

Branch drove the SUV along the snowy route toward the scene.

"Any chance Duffy went shopping on Tuesday and that's why her Rav 4 was in that mall parking lot?" Otto turned her head to see into the back seat.

"Not a chance in hell," Villanueva replied. "I was with her in the morning. We had a bunch of things to accomplish, but shopping in Boston wasn't on the list."

Otto nodded.

Branch frowned and said nothing. The snowfall and drifting made driving along the side roads a full attention task. They reached the location after twenty minutes.

He didn't need to check the GPS. There was no mistaking the accident site, even under six inches of fresh snow. The trees were mangled, their newly jagged trunks poking up like fat, broken pencils. The ditch had begun to fill with clean snow, but deep ruts in the mud where the Rav 4 landed were still visible. Rescue vehicles had damaged the scene, too.

Villanueva handed the accident reports to Gaspar. "The report says one of the back seat passengers claimed the Rav 4 was sideswiped by another vehicle that took off. He said that's what shoved them off the road."

By spring, after the snow melted, the gouges in the landscape would be smoothed out, perhaps. But not yet. The damage was too fresh.

CHAPTER TWENTY

Thursday, November 25
Abbot, Maine
2:12 p.m.

GASPAR HANDED THE ACCIDENT report to Kim. She scanned it quickly. The crash occurred at three o'clock in the morning on Wednesday. "Villanueva? You saw Duffy last on Tuesday afternoon, right?"

"Around one o'clock, as I recall. We had lunch in Abbot. I dropped her off at the motel because I had to run back to Boston to pick up some surveillance equipment we needed." He paused in thought. "I had a couple of personal matters to attend to. When I returned to the motel around ten that night, Duffy's Rav 4 wasn't there, so I figured she wasn't back from her errands in Portland yet. We were supposed to meet up early on Wednesday morning, so I went to bed. Never saw her again."

Branch had reached the exit for the restaurant they'd found earlier. Kim glanced at her Seiko. Hunger gnawed her stomach.

"There's nothing open in Abbot today, and I need to eat at least one meal every twenty-four hours. Everybody okay with going back to the restaurant we bugged out of earlier?"

Hearing no objections, Branch took the exit and drove to the parking lot again. The restaurant was even less busy than it had been four hours ago. A fire burned in the fireplace. The room was warm and cozy.

Kim made a beeline for the same quiet table in the corner, and the others followed.

The waitress brought menus, water, and coffee. As she poured, she apologized. "Sorry to rush you, but we're closing at three. Everybody wants to get home before the blizzard keeps us stranded here overnight. You folks would be wise to do the same."

They ordered quickly, and she rushed off to put the orders in.

"Any chance your boss can get video of that Rav 4 crash from a satellite somewhere?" Villanueva asked.

"Maybe," Kim replied. "There were a lot of trees along that road. Visibility would be the issue. We might not be able to see anything useful. Snow all over. White Rav 4."

"I believe the passenger," Villanueva said. "I never worked in traffic, but I've done enough crime scene analysis to know that was no single-vehicle collision."

"What makes you say that?" Branch asked as if he might be testing his own conclusions.

"For one thing, there was a hell of a lot of damage done to that Rav 4 on the front and the left side. A lot of damage to those trees, too. More than I'd expect from a simple run off the road." Villanueva shook his head. "And it's just a little too convenient, don't you think?"

Kim agreed. Way too convenient. Duffy goes missing, and

her rental is stolen and destroyed, all in the span of less than twelve hours? She looked at Gaspar, and he nodded his agreement, too.

Villanueva looked pointedly at Branch. "What's going on with Duffy?"

"Meaning what?"

"She called me Sunday morning, four days ago, frantic about Teresa Justice. Did she talk to you about that?"

"I was in Mexico." Branch dipped his head and looked away from Villanueva's steady gaze. "I wish she had called me instead of you."

"Duffy trusts you. She'd tell you everything if she was here, I'm sure." Villanueva nodded as if he'd reached a decision about Branch. He looked at Kim and Gaspar. "And I need your help, so I have no choice but to trust you."

Branch said, "We understand each other."

Neither Kim nor Gaspar replied.

"Ten years ago, all three of us were DEA. All on the same team. Teresa, Duffy and me." Villanueva waited a moment as if still arguing with himself before he dipped his chin for a brief nod and continued. "We started an investigation into an LA drug ring that led us to the owner of that house, Abbot Cape. Duffy was lead on the case, and she screwed up. Our team got pulled off." He turned his gaze to Branch again. "But Duffy wouldn't give up. You know how she is."

Branch nodded slowly. He clenched his teeth. "Yeah, I know."

"So back then, she sent Teresa in undercover as a clerical worker in the owner's export/import operation. Off the books, you know?" He cleared his throat. "After a couple of days, Teresa disappeared. We tried to find her. No luck."

Gaspar frowned. "How many DEA agents followed Duffy into that madness?"

"Six of us, altogether."

Kim had read all of this in the files, which were incomplete at best. What Villanueva said was true, as far as it went. There were important bits he'd left out. "There were casualties. Agents died. Civilians, too."

"We were in way over our heads from the very beginning, we just didn't know how far. And we screwed up a lot more before all was said and done." Villanueva nodded. "Turned out Beck was involved with another guy. Named Quinn. A real badass from way back." He paused and lowered his voice. "Without Reacher, I doubt any of us would have survived."

"This was the case you worked with Reacher?" Kim's mouth dried up and her body began to vibrate.

"We were seven weeks into the situation when he showed up. I'm not sure how Duffy found him, but he was interested in Quinn. So we added him to our team." He cleared his throat again. Kim recognized it as a stress habit. "We put together a tactical operation to get Reacher inside Abbot Cape. Undercover. The point was to get Teresa out and then save our asses. Stay alive. Keep our jobs."

"And maybe you'd be heroes? I know how Duffy's mind works," Branch said. "That's what she's doing again, isn't it?"

"She was devastated about Teresa. And, yeah, she didn't want to get fired. DEA had been her whole life up to that time, and she was not ready to quit. None of us were." Villanueva paused. No one jumped in to fill the silence. "So we added Reacher to the mix and put our heads down and kept going."

"I've read the old files. And I know Duffy," Branch said. "When the dust settled, she made it look like a big win with limited collateral damage. Only three bodies recovered from inside the house and another one at Beck's warehouse. One agent and three bad guys."

"The reality was worse than that, wasn't it? Things got covered up," Kim guessed. Whatever Reacher was involved in always went south, left casualties, and his involvement got buried. Why should this time have been different?

"I don't really know the whole of it." Villanueva looked away, like a man who knew more than he was telling. "Reacher found Teresa and brought her out. Physically unharmed. But she was never the same after that."

"In what way?" Gaspar asked.

"Nine weeks in captivity. Closed in a damp basement cell most of the time. Sleeping on a filthy mattress on the floor." He shook his head and rubbed a flat palm over his face and around to the back of his neck. "They intended to sell her to some Arab sheik for ten thousand dollars, and she knew that the whole time."

The waitress brought their food, and they fell on it like a pack of hungry wolves. Kim heard sounds from the kitchen indicating they were closing up for the night and maybe for the weekend, depending on the blizzard.

"What happened after that?" Gaspar asked. "When the dust settled?"

"We all left DEA. Duffy went over to ATF." Villanueva looked at Branch. "Because of the big bust, you guys were glad to have her. I had enough years in for a government pension, so I retired early and went back home to Boston and joined Boston PD and later, retired again."

"And Teresa Justice? I know she was at ATF for a while and went through mandatory trauma counseling as all hostages are required to do," Branch said. "What happened to her after that?"

"She joined NYPD's Human Trafficking Unit. Her experience had imprinted deeply on her. She was determined to save other women held against their will and forced, well, forced to do anything they didn't want to do." Villanueva shook his head again and shrugged.

"Human trafficking is tough duty. Not many success stories," Kim said.

"Teresa worked NYPD undercover for a while." Villanueva cleared his throat. The habit could get annoying after a while. "She said the operation moved too slowly. Too mired in protocols and procedures. Too many victims got left behind. She felt stymied."

"So she washed out?" Gaspar asked.

"I don't know if she washed out or left voluntarily, but a couple years later, she was gone."

"And then what?" Branch asked.

"I heard from her from time to time because I was sort of a mentor to her when she first started out, I guess. She became a P.I. working with volunteer groups and nonprofit organizations, focused on human trafficking. She continued putting herself in terrible situations and somehow, every time, managing to get herself out." Villanueva closed his eyes and cleared his throat again. "She became more and more reckless. Had a couple of near misses. She was wounded more than once. I tried to talk to her about it, to get her more counseling, or whatever I could do. But she wouldn't listen. Kept sticking her neck out. It was like she was obsessed or something."

"Somehow, she got involved with something that led her back here, though," Branch said. "She's come full circle. And judging from what we saw today, those women in white, she's in way too deep." Branch shook his head. He took a breath and held it a moment longer than usual.

Kim asked, "How did Duffy get sucked into all of this again?"

Villanueva blew a long stream of air through his nose. "Teresa sent her a picture of that guy with the birthmark that Branch recognized. Duffy recognized him too. She was excited about it."

"Duffy thought if she could bring him down, she could save her career one more time," Gaspar said. "That about it?"

"Pretty much. Monday afternoon, while we were working out a plan to find Teresa, Duffy got a call from somebody about Otto and Gaspar." He nodded toward them. "She figured time was running out. She must've gone into the compound without me. It's the only thing I can figure. I've looked everywhere else. No luck. They moved her Rav 4 to that Boston shopping mall Tuesday while I was gone. Those kids must have stolen it right away. Bad luck for them because they destroyed the vehicle to keep it out of sight. They were willing to kill four teenagers to serve their own ends."

"And what happened with Reacher?" Kim said. "After the old operation was over?"

"I never saw him again."

"How about Duffy?" Gaspar asked. "Has she kept in touch with him?"

"I honestly don't know. I suggested that we call him, and she was, let's just say, not in favor of the suggestion." Villanueva flashed a sour grimace.

Branch laughed out loud.

Gaspar frowned. "What's so funny?"

"I've seen Duffy's temper only a handful of times," Branch

replied. "You do something she's opposed to and, well, let's just say she can be formidable."

Villanueva cleared his throat again. The habit was downright annoying. "We've got four trained agents on the outside and maybe two on the inside. Which is three more than we had before."

"Yeah, my fault for coming here. Violated the first rule of the Army." Branch shrugged. "Never volunteer."

Villanueva grinned. "Now you sound like Reacher."

Kim wanted to ask questions about Reacher but this was not the time. Her assignment was off the books and under the radar. She didn't know Branch, and she didn't trust him. And he didn't know Reacher or anything about him, either. She'd wait until Branch wasn't around to follow up with Villanueva.

"Duffy is our first priority. We find her, and we'll have more intel about Teresa and what's going on in the house," Villanueva said. "We can make another plan from there."

"No." Gaspar shook his head. "We find Duffy, get her out, interview her, and we are done."

Kim said, "Gaspar's right. After we get Duffy out, Branch calls ATF. They raid the place. They get Teresa Justice out of there. That's it. Game over."

"Where's your sense of adventure, Gaspar?" Branch asked, a grin widening his mouth all the way to the twinkle in his eyes.

"I can't afford adventure. I've got four kids with a fifth due any time and twenty years to go." Gaspar paused briefly. "You guys can die with your boots on if you want, but I've got to get back to Miami."

Nobody said anything for a few minutes while the waitress collected their plates and took Branch's credit card to pay the check.

Villanueva continued to negotiate, but he wasn't holding a strong hand. "The only person here who needs to get anything out of this mess is Duffy. So let's let her have what she needs. We find her and bring her out and let her decide what she wants to do about ATF and the rest."

"Villanueva," Gaspar said, looking the man straight in the eye. "We bring Duffy out of there, we're holding you to your promise about the Reacher files you say you have. And we want every ounce of information stored in your brain about the guy."

Villanueva didn't flinch. He didn't say yes, either.

"We're agreed," Branch said. "Get in, get out, nobody gets hurt. Everybody gets what they came for." He stood, and they walked outside into the storm.

CHAPTER TWENTY-ONE

Thursday, November 25
Abbot, Maine
3:05 p.m.

THE DIPLOMAT HADN'T SLEPT well or long enough. It had been a long day yesterday, and there were longer ones to follow. The next demonstration of his new weapon was scheduled in ten minutes. The last and most impressive demonstration would be tomorrow. After that, he would collect his money and send the visitors on their way with their women. He and Abrams would leave by the vessel which should be about five miles offshore.

Abrams had stepped outside for a cigar. The seven additional guests were arriving at the cape later, but they were gathered around their secure connections.

As before, the four screens had been set up for recording as well as viewing. This time, screen four focused on the target zone in the Indian Ocean, as far from active surveillance as possible.

While demonstrating the destruction of a tourist ship would

have been more effective, it also would have brought too much scrutiny and probably would have resulted in inconvenient changes to cruise industry security systems. His guests were unwilling to risk such changes.

While various international authorities had been warning against terrorist attacks on tourist ships for several years, security measures remained surprisingly relaxed. This, of course, was an opportunity his clients were keen to exploit.

The large cargo ship he had selected for the demonstration was transporting food and medical supplies to needy African nations. Their corrupt governments were not likely to distribute the drugs and groceries, so intense scrutiny of the lost ship was unlikely.

The big ship was 790 feet long with a gross tonnage of more than 31,000. Smaller than the largest passenger cruise ships, but the force of his weapon would be more than sufficient.

Screen three was the satellite photo of the cargo ship's current location and several nautical miles around it. The distance from the satellite to the ship made the ship appear tiny and insignificant. His volunteer notified them this morning that the ship's passenger list included twenty-nine members of the crew and no guests. Each crewmember would be a desperate man who needed the job. For no other reason would a man choose to cross the ocean on such a vessel. Sanitation would be absent. Meals disgustingly primitive. The Diplomat shivered involuntarily as he imagined the stench and vermin aboard. Eliminating the ship and its cargo and crew would be a service to humanity greater than its safe landing could possibly achieve.

The undulating sea was mesmerizing. It was like staring at a soothing blue screen. Fatigue almost overwhelmed him. He desperately wanted a nap.

Abrams walked in through the front door, and the Diplomat heard the metal detector alarm. He might have asked Abrams to leave his weapons in his room, but the request would have been futile and embarrassed them both.

The grandfather clock chimed the half-hour as Abrams entered the office and retook his seat. Five minutes to the deployment of the missile.

The Diplomat returned to his chair. He adjusted the volume of the narrator's monotone. No one else spoke, but all communication channels were open.

The weapon had never been tested against an oceangoing vessel. There was no recorded demonstration to substitute should the current test fail to deliver as required. Either the weapon performed or it did not. There was no backup plan this time.

Which meant he could relax and watch the demonstration along with his clients.

The thirty-second countdown began.

The Diplomat and Abrams watched the screen as the weapon deployed precisely as planned.

It struck the vessel midship, penetrated the exterior and exploded as expected.

White smoke followed quickly by billowing black clouds trailed from the surface into the sky.

When the camera zoomed in, the Diplomat could see that the vessel had been ripped in half. It looked like a child's toy that had been gripped on both ends and yanked apart by force.

The open centers of the two pieces canted downward into the cold, deep ocean, while the bow and stern protruded into the air.

Within ten minutes, the two halves sank completely out of sight. Abrams cackled with something close to glee. He raised his glass for a toast.

The Diplomat felt his mouth widen into an enormous smile. Had anyone other than Abrams been in the room, they would have thought he'd gone mad for sure.

The Diplomat signed off and left the remainder of the arrangements to his appropriate counterpart. The last and most significant demonstration would be tomorrow, once all of his guests arrived.

The Diplomat wasn't worried about his weapon. The weapon would do its job.

The problem was whether the insurgents could deploy it properly. He wasn't in the hand-holding business, however. He could sell them the hardware, but strategic implementation and hitting the target was not his concern.

His advisors would be on the ground with the insurgents to provide guidance. But in the end, they would succeed or fail based on their own efforts.

He closed down the screens and his computer and sauntered to the dining room.

A private Thanksgiving meal would be served this evening after Nathan returned with the limo carrying a guest and his bodyguard, and the Diplomat certainly felt thankful. Everything was in place. Soon, three years of work to bring this deal together would be completed. He would be leaving this godforsaken country and returning home. His reward for services rendered would be substantial. Wealth beyond his wildest dreams and a life of comfort for his remaining years. He would marry, perhaps. A young, sexy bride who would give him many children. Everything was within his reach.

CHAPTER TWENTY-TWO

Thursday, November 25
Abbot, Maine
3:40 p.m.

WHEN THEY RETURNED TO the Abbot Motel, they split up
for a quick pit stop in their rooms before meeting in Kim's room
to review the plan. She'd checked the Boss's cell phone but had
received no further communication from him.

She connected to the secure satellite feed of the Abbot Cape
compound on her laptop. It would be dusk in about thirty
minutes. She wanted as much video as possible in natural light
instead of night vision. Later, she'd pull up the video from the
past few hours to see what had been happening while they were
offline.

The video quality wasn't as clear as what they'd seen earlier
in the day. The snow clouds were heavier, although still
penetrable by the Boss's technology.

A limousine pulled into sight from the garage on the
northwest side of the house. It stopped at the gate, windows up,

engine idling. The driver was one of the big security guards. The same bald one who had been at the wheel each time. Exhaust smoke billowed from the tailpipe, visible in the cold air. The man who handled the gate left the gatehouse and approached the keypad on the granite wall. He punched in a code, and the gate opened.

The limousine rolled through the open gate, and the gate swung closed behind it. The huge guard returned to the gatehouse. Kim timed the entire process. From the time the limousine reached the gate until the gate swung closed behind, three minutes passed.

With the gateman standing there, it would be impossible to dash in or out while the gate was open. But, if he was disabled or not present, someone could probably get inside.

She pulled out her phone and called Gaspar. When he answered, she said, "Get Branch and Villanueva. We've got an opportunity. Someone's leaving the compound."

"10-4," he said, to be a smartass.

She grinned and disconnected.

The limousine had traveled through the open rocky beachfront before it entered the shelter of the woods. In Maine's late November, deciduous trees were not quite bare. Coupled with the salted pines, which retained their needles year-round, the trees and the cloud cover combined to make the road almost invisible to the satellite's surveillance.

Three sharp raps on her door and Gaspar pushed inside. Villanueva and Branch followed. All four gathered around the small laptop screen again. At this point, there wasn't much to see. She pushed the sliding frame reference to the left and showed the limousine traveling through the gate and into the woods.

"We can follow him and make a plan once he stops," Branch said. "Or, we can stop him before he gets wherever he's going. Either way is fine with me."

"What we want is to ride back into the compound in the trunk or something. We have no idea where he's going, how long he'll be gone, or when he'll come back. We may have another opportunity to drive in with another vehicle, too," Kim said. "So let's split up. Villanueva can stay here and watch the satellite feed. Gaspar and Branch can head out in our SUV. Gaspar drives. Follow the guy, see if there's a chance to ride back inside with him."

"And what are you going to do, Susie Wong?"

"I'm going to make some phone calls and see if I can figure out what's going on inside that compound. We may be overmatched here. I need to figure out what we can do about it. Branch, leave me your keys, just in case. If the limo is going too far, and we get another chance to go inside before you return, I'll call you."

Before they had a chance to implement the plan, Villanueva, who had taken his seat at the laptop, said, "Another vehicle coming out. This one looks like a catering truck or something. When did this guy go in?"

Kim walked over to get a better look at the screen. As before, the vehicle pulled up on the other side of the gate and waited until the gate was opened, passed through, and the gate closed.

This was a panel van, white with lettering on the side she couldn't read from her viewing angle. As it passed through the open space beyond the gate and before it disappeared into the trees, she said, "You two get going. I'll check this guy."

Gaspar said, "We have no idea who these people are. We

treat everyone inside the compound as armed and dangerous."

Branch nodded. "It's not likely these guys are nothing but civilians delivering a pizza."

"Agreed. Same with the limo driver," Kim said. "Maybe these caterers will be coming back with more food. We know there's more than thirty people inside. They've all got to eat, right? The two women we've been calling the cook and the maid surely can't be expected to feed them all. Stay in close touch, okay?"

"I'll stay alert here," Villanueva said. "This satellite feed is not bad for exterior surveillance. And I suspect it's supplemented sometimes with hacked feeds from the interior surveillance cameras. However it's being created, the video is better than we could do sitting inside with just the four of us. If anything significant happens, I'll let you know."

The other three left Villaneuva in the room and walked out into the cold.

Branch followed Gaspar to Gaspar's SUV rental and tossed his keys to Kim for the other one. She climbed into the seat, and he grinned. "Need a booster seat to see over the steering wheel?"

She glared at him and slammed the door, then started the engine and lowered the window.

Gaspar was saying, "Don't underestimate her. She's saved my ass more than once in the past three weeks. If you're in a situation where you need her to save yours, you want her to be inclined to do it."

Branch chuckled. "Yeah, right."

Gaspar grinned. "I'm telling you. She might be tiny, but she's a tiny stick of dynamite with a deadly aim. Watch yourself."

Kim rolled her eyes. "You two comedians get going. That

limo has at least a seven-minute head start. You've got to hustle to catch up." She raised the window and rolled out. Within minutes, Gaspar swept around her in the other SUV, running as fast as he could on the snow-covered road. Soon, she couldn't see his taillights.

Kim reached the intersection of Route 1 and the private road, Abbot Cape Drive. She peered down it as she passed it and saw no sign of the white caterer's van. She glanced at her Seiko. From the motel to here had consumed exactly seven minutes. The panel van would have to have been driving sixty miles an hour to have beaten her. Abbot Cape Drive was two lanes, nice blacktop from what she could tell from the surveillance, back when she could see it, but sixty miles an hour through snow and the woods didn't sound like a reasonable rate of speed, particularly for a panel van.

She fished in her pocket for her cell phone and called Villanueva. "Are you still looking at the video?"

"Yeah. Nothing exciting going on since the panel van left. Why?"

"Can you zoom out and see anything at all on the end of Abbot Cape Drive near the Route 1 intersection?"

"I can see you moving away from the intersection, but I don't see anything else."

The panel van was still passing through the woods, then. "Is there anywhere up ahead of me that I can stash this SUV out of sight while I'm waiting?"

"Not that I can tell from our eye-in-the-sky view."

"I'll get out ahead of it, then, and let him overtake me if he turns north on Route 1. Portland is closer than Boston, so he's probably turning north. I'm heading in that direction. Keep an eye out and let me know when you see him."

"Roger that. It won't take long. The road's only twelve miles and he passed through the gate seventeen minutes ago." Villanueva paused. "He could keep going west on Abbot Cape Drive until he hits the entrance to I-95, though."

"Roger that." She drove slowly northward on the almost empty road. She had driven almost five miles when her phone rang.

"The panel van came out and passed the intersection at Route 1. He entered I-95 North. I can see you and him. You're traveling almost parallel to each other, but he's moving faster. He's gonna pass you pretty soon."

"Is there another freeway entrance up this way?" The snowy conditions were worsening, and she worried about how long the surveillance video would be clear enough to see. She had the SUV in all-wheel drive, but so much snow covered the road that she could barely tell where it was in the expanse of white.

"You're not that far from Portland. I'll keep an eye on him," Villanueva said. "But you're going to have to drive straight north on Route 1. It looks like there's no entrance onto I-95 before Portland."

"Keep me posted." She gripped the wheel with both hands and stared straight ahead. She hadn't seen a single vehicle since Gaspar blew past her.

Her phone rang again fifteen minutes later. She was close to Portland.

"He took the Twelfth Avenue exit east and headed north on Route 1. He's a bit ahead of you. There are businesses on Route 1 once you get into the outskirts of town," Villanueva said. "There can't be that many catering companies open in Portland on Thanksgiving. Assuming these guys are really caterers."

"Can you read the name of the catering company on the side

of the truck and get me an address that I can punch into the GPS?"

"I still can't read it from this angle, but I'll let you know as soon as I get a clear view."

Kim continued to race north on Route 1 as fast as she dared. She began to notice signs of civilization. A few widely spaced houses surrounded by a sea of white at first, followed by a few small businesses.

Eventually, she passed the Twelfth Avenue intersection and called Villanueva again. "Do you still have eyes on him?"

"Yeah. He's still headed north on Route 1. Just approaching Fifth Street. He's turning right on Fifth, headed east. He keeps going, he's going to end up outside of town."

She turned on the speaker and tossed the phone onto the passenger seat. "Keep talking. Do you see me?"

"I do. You are about two blocks from Fifth Street. Turn right on Fifth. He's still going east. He's got to stop soon, or he's going to run into the water."

Kim blinked. She felt the stress in her shoulders and her forearms from her grip on the wheel. Her eyes were dry and gritty. She could barely touch the accelerator. She was perched as close to the front of the seat as she could be and the seatbelt pulled hard against her chest. She reached down and pushed the button to release the buckle. She'd take her chances.

"He's turning left into a parking lot. It's a little strip center," Villanueva said. "He's pulling around the back. You're close. Maybe another half a mile. On your left. You're almost there. Do you see it?"

She pulled into the parking lot of a small strip center containing not more than four storefronts. All of them were closed. On the far end was "Mac's Catering Company." She pulled around to the back and looked for the panel van. It had disappeared. Probably inside a loading dock. All four stores had roll-up garage doors, and all the garage doors were closed. Two old cars were parked nearby. Perhaps they belonged to the caterers.

She parked the SUV in plain sight because there was nowhere to hide it, and picked up the cell phone. "I'm going in, Villanueva. Keep this line open so you can hear what happens. But don't call me back if we get disconnected."

"Roger that."

"Have you heard from Gaspar and Branch?"

"Not yet." Villanueva paused. "I looked up this catering company, though. Be careful. Looks like they may be owned by Leo Abrams. Those guys are probably armed."

"Got it." She slipped out of the vehicle and closed the door. The cold wind pushed her back. The evening gloom was illuminated by parking lot lights, and she could see the snow falling softly around her.

She zipped her parka and moved forward. Trash littered the ground near the doors. Under the awnings, broken asphalt was slippery from snowfall and the ice underneath it.

She approached the back of Mac's Catering. Next to the roll-up garage door was a steel entry door. She tried the handle. It was locked.

She leaned close to the door but could hear nothing inside. She walked around the corner of the building and stood close to the wall and waited. Even inside the voluminous parka, she was cold. The wind was bone-chilling. She felt her toes and fingers begin to cramp. She wiggled her knees and moved in place for warmth.

After twenty minutes, she gave up. She was freezing. She

considered going back to the SUV and turning on the heat. She might lose the element of surprise if they came out and saw the monstrous SUV in the parking lot, but she wouldn't be frozen to an icicle at least.

As she approached the corner of the building, Mac's roll-up garage door began to lift. She heard two men talking. Doors on the van opened and closed. The van started. The door was partially up. She came around the corner and raised her gun. Soon, the driver would see her.

When the door was four feet off the ground, she ducked under and entered the building and cautiously approached the side of the van. The driver's head was turned toward the passenger.

She banged on the driver's window. The driver's head whipped around. His eyes widened in surprise. She screamed to be heard. "Turn off the ignition and get out."

He did as she asked. As if he was just a caterer and she was clearly a crazy woman.

"Give me the keys," she demanded, palm held out. He complied.

"Stand right there." She gestured toward the panel van. She pointed her gun across the driver's seat at the passenger, riveted to his seat. "You. Get out on this side."

He put both hands in the air, scrambled over the seats and climbed out the driver's side.

They looked like a couple of college kids to her, which probably meant she was getting a lot older than she admitted.

The driver said, "Lady, we don't have any money. We've got turkey dinner. That's it."

Which could be true. But it was a risk she couldn't afford to take. "Tell me, where are you taking that turkey dinner?"

"Down to Abbot Cape. We're due back there in less than an hour. If we don't get this food down there, our boss is gonna flip out, and we're not gonna get paid."

"Where's your boss?"

"He's at Abbot Cape already. Waiting for us to get back."

She reached into her pocket and pulled out the phone. She raised it to her ear. Villanueva said, "I heard. I'll call Branch. I'm not sure where they are. What do you want to do?"

"Ask them to pick up the SUV. I'll ride back your way with these two." She turned to the passenger. "How many seats are inside there?"

"Just the two. But I can sit on the floor. You can have mine."

"Good plan. You wait over here with me." She pointed the gun at the driver. She patted him down and removed a pistol from his pocket. She slipped it into her parka. "You back out. Slowly."

"Okay, lady. Don't shoot me. It's just turkey dinner. Cripes." He climbed into the driver's seat, restarted the van and backed out of the open doorway.

He put the van in park. Kim quickly patted down the second caterer. She removed a switchblade and a pistol from his jacket and slipped both into her bulging parka pockets. They walked around the front of the van and climbed in on the passenger side. He moved to the back and sat on the floor. She turned sideways in her seat and pointed the Glock at the driver. He pushed the remote to close the roll-up door.

"Let's go," Kim said.

The driver pulled out onto Fifth Street and then Route 1 to Twelfth, reversing his inbound route, and returned to the expressway. He exited at Abbot Cape Road, and when he reached the intersection at Route 1, Kim said, "Stop here."

She pulled out her phone and redialed Villanueva. "Where are we?"

"You got company arriving in that limo. Twenty minutes out, maybe. Branch and Gaspar are five minutes behind because they stopped to pick up your vehicle."

"Okay." She spoke to the driver again. "We're gonna drive around the block."

"Lady, what about my food? I got thirty people waiting for dinner. I've gotta go."

"Just turn south on Route 1 and drive."

He shook his head, but he turned right and drove toward Boston.

When her phone rang again, she lifted it to her ear. "Okay, the limousine is on Abbot Cape Road, headed toward the compound. You can turn around and come back. You should arrive right around the same time as Branch and Gaspar."

She left the line open and said to the driver. "Turn around and go back."

He shook his head and did what she ordered.

Ten minutes later, they were at the Abbot Cape Road intersection again. Branch and Gaspar were waiting. The limousine should have been almost to the gate and perhaps inside the compound already.

Branch stepped out of his SUV and left it running. He walked around to the passenger side of the van and opened the door.

Kim jumped down and left the door open.

Quietly, Branch said, "These guys are going back in with food. I ride in with them and find Duffy and get her out."

Kim was already shaking her head. "No."

"You got a better option?" Branch laid out the facts exactly as Kim had already analyzed them. "We've got two SUVs here. We can't leave them in the middle of the road. We've already let too much time pass. This food doesn't show up, someone is going to come out looking for it."

Everything he said was true. "It's too dangerous. You might find Duffy, but you might just die trying."

"That's a risk I'm willing to take. She's my partner."

"No. We'll call in ATF. Now. They can be here in a couple of hours, surely."

"Look. Let's be honest here. I'm the only one of the four of us who might be able to pull this off. If any of the rest of you go in with me, I'll be worried about you, watching out for you." He paused for breath. "We're more likely to get caught as a group than I am to get caught on my own."

"No," Kim said, again, but she could see she'd already lost the argument.

"I don't need your permission," Branch said. Which was completely true. "Come to that, I'm not a Federal agent anymore, either. I'm not bound by the same rules you are. I can do whatever it takes to get Duffy out of there. Frankly, we both know that you and Gaspar can't."

Short of shooting him, Kim could see no way to prevent him from going in alone, no matter how reckless that course of action was. *When there's only one choice, it's the right choice*, as her mother would say.

"These two guys might be okay," she said. "Or not. I can't really tell. All we know is their catering business is owned by Abrams. And it's not likely Abrams would leave anything to chance, including hiring civilian caterers he doesn't control. Once you get inside, you might want to disable them." She nodded as she stood aside.

"Roger that. Anything else?" Because that he'd won, Branch seemed more cooperative.

"You can't assume things will go smoothly. Villanueva is watching the video, but he can't see anything that happens on the road in the woods. If something goes wrong, if you have a problem in that no man's land, we won't be able to see you. You're on your own."

"Roger that. Anything else?" he asked again.

"We can't tell what's going on inside the buildings. We don't know exactly where Duffy is. If the basement cell still exists, Villanueva suggests you start there."

"Got it."

"Gaspar and I will wait under cover of the I-95 exit ramp. Don't stay gone too long." She paused again. "If we need to call reinforcements to come in and get you, give us some kind of signal from inside the compound that Villanueva can see. We'll do what we can."

"Roger that." He nodded. "I've gotta go. Now. The longer it takes these guys to get back, the more suspicious it seems."

"Take this. It's the driver's. Might come in handy." She gave him the pistol she'd removed from the driver's pocket. Then she moved aside, and he opened the van's door again. She looked at the passenger huddled in the back of the van behind the seats. "Climb out here."

The caterer did as instructed.

Branch swung up into the passenger seat. He bent at the waist and stepped into the back. Kim pointed her Glock at the caterer. "Get back in the passenger seat. Remember, we can see you. That's how we found you in the first place. Do what you're told and you'll be fine."

The caterer climbed into his seat. Branch had pulled out his weapon and showed it to both men. "I'm a good shot. It only takes two quick rounds for me to kill you anytime. Like the lady said, do what you're told and you'll be fine. Let's go."

Kim pushed the door closed. She slapped the door with her palm twice.

As the van pulled away and entered the twelve-mile stretch to Abbot Cape, Kim returned to Branch's SUV and both she and Gaspar headed back toward I-95.

CHAPTER TWENTY-THREE

Thursday, November 25
Abbot, Maine
5:35 p.m.

BRANCH SQUATTED IN THE space behind the two seats where he could see out of the windshield and also had a partial view of both rearview mirrors. He saw Otto standing behind the van as it pulled away and then she rolled out in his SUV. After that, he lost visual contact.

The road was mostly straight with a couple of bends. From the maps, he knew it led straight to the house. It was too dark outside to see beyond the areas illuminated by the van's headlights.

Branch had studied the satellite photos of the compound earlier. Twelve miles of road with nothing but rocky beaches and outcroppings on both sides closer to the gate. On this side of the rocky ground, the forest began. Plenty of trees for about the first eleven miles.

He spotted a few of the surveillance cameras on either side

of the road at regular intervals. The cameras might be on constantly, or they might be triggered by motion sensors or light sensors. He assumed there was other surveillance equipment that he couldn't see. There could be sensors in the road, too.

He hadn't seen any surveillance drones flying over the area, but the cameras posted at the gate and along the perimeter would do a fairly decent job of monitoring the entrance.

It would be possible to walk through the woods and approach the house, but it would be rough going and it would take a while. And he'd still need to get beyond the open area between the woods and the wall, and then somehow get through the gate. Despite the risks, it was probably better to ride all the way through the gate.

The van's back suspension was shot. He bounced around worse than riding in the back of a hay wagon. They covered the twelve miles to the gate in about twenty minutes. As they slowed for the approach to the gate, the giant exited the gatehouse, head down against the worsening blizzard, and pushed a code into the pad on the right pillar.

No one inside the van had done anything to signal their arrival. Which confirmed the gateman must have been watching the road from inside, probably had a perfect view from the surveillance cameras.

Branch ducked down out of visual range, and the caterer drove straight through the gate and around to the back of the house. He executed a three-point turn and backed toward the door, coming to a stop as close as he could get to the entrance. Branch saw a second catering van was also backed in near the rear entrance.

"Just do your job the way you plan to do it. Ignore me. Don't tell anyone that I hitched a ride with you. If I see *anything* that suggests *anybody* knows I'm here, I'm going to assume it ties back to you. And, well, we all know where that'll end." Both caterers nodded like bobble heads. It was a risk. But he didn't want to kill them if he didn't need to. And if he disabled them and left them in the van, he'd have the problem of attempting to deal with their continued absence. "If I need anything from you, I'll let you know. Leave your keys in the ignition and get going."

The two guys jumped down and went around to the back of the van and opened the back doors. They started unloading the food that had been tickling Branch's growling stomach for the past twenty minutes.

He climbed through to the passenger side and hopped out. A gale-force wind practically flattened Branch against the van's side. In front of the vehicle was rough, cold, churning, white-capped ocean.

He inched around to the back of the van and picked up a full chafing pan and followed the two guys into the house. As they filed through the back door, a metal detector beeped because they were carrying steel trays and serving dishes. In Branch's case, it was also because of the guns.

In the kitchen, Branch saw two more caterers and the two women—the cook and the maid. No one paid him the slightest attention. Everyone was too busy preparing what looked like dinner for at least forty in the big dining room. Which probably meant the twenty-eight women in white were included in tonight's party.

He quickly counted the others he'd seen in the compound. The four original security guards, the one at the gate, the limousine driver, Abrams, and the owner. Including Teresa Justice and Duffy, the total was thirty-eight.

Additional security must have arrived sometime in the night.

He'd seen more armed guards, including at least one woman, probably to guard what he'd been assuming were the virgins, but he didn't know the total number of security guards on site.

He spotted the door on a back passageway precisely where the floorplans he'd pulled from public records placed the basement entrance. Like a ghost, he moved down the hallway. He opened the door. The lights were already on down there. He pulled out his Glock, ducked inside and closed the door behind him.

He took the stairs quickly and reached the bottom without incident. The basement had been blasted out of solid rock. The walls were granite, patched here and there with concrete. It smelled damp and musty. Naked light bulbs hung in cages from the ceiling.

Several closed doors were set into the stone walls on either side of a large, open room set up as a home gym with workout equipment. Too many rooms to examine them all. But he didn't need to. When they'd looked at the floorplan back at the motel, Villanueva had pointed out which of the basement's corridors, warrens and cubbyholes were the two cells, and identified the one where Teresa Justice had been held nine years ago. Both cells were directly under the dining room.

Holding his Glock in front of him, Branch walked through the gym, past the washing machine, and turned the corner to a short corridor leading straight to the two cells. Both rooms were standing open. The door to the room next to them was closed.

A chair was toppled onto its side between the two cells. One of the big security guards was on the ground, his head at an odd angle like his fourth vertebra had been snapped. His glassy blue eyes stared as if his death had been a complete shock to him.

He started with the closed door, just in case. He stepped

around the dead guard and flattened himself against the wall. The door to the third room was locked, but the key protruded from the keyhole. He grabbed the key and turned it, grasped the handle with his left hand, and pushed the door open.

Nothing happened. The room was dark. He reached around the doorjamb and flipped a light switch. He waited for a second but heard nothing coming from inside the room. He stepped into the doorway and stared.

Stacked along the floor on raised pallets were demolition supplies. C-4, detonators, fuses. Serious charges, which he supposed they'd have to be to blast through the granite this basement had been carved into. Someone had expansion plans, obviously.

He closed and relocked the door, leaving the key in place. He turned his attention back to finding Duffy.

The keys still rested in the locks in the thick, heavy oak doors of the two cells. The dead security guard had probably refused to open the doors and paid the price for his unfortunate choice.

One cell was slightly larger than the other. Both were furnished like bedrooms. The smaller one was eight-by-ten, and immaculately clean. A metal cot with a rolled up mattress. A small but heavy chest of drawers against the chiseled rock wall. The air inside the room was damp, musty and stale.

The other cell was also furnished like a bedroom but had been recently occupied. Maybe ten-by-twelve. No windows. Solid rock walls and a cement floor, like the other two. A twin mattress on a cot, wrinkled white sheets, a tussled green blanket, and a single pillow. Tossed in a crumpled heap on the floor were a virginal white dress, white stockings, and white shoes.

Branch smelled stale food and something else that tickled his memory. He closed his eyes and identified the faint whiff of gardenia combined with musk. Unmistakably. He'd smelled it a million times over the past nine years. La Panthere perfume, Duffy's scent.

Duffy had been here. She'd been dressed like the other women, to join the others in whatever ritual Abrams and the others had planned. But she was gone. There was no way she'd broken that big dude's neck with her bare hands. He outweighed her by at least a hundred pounds. She was ferocious, and a trained federal agent, but the physics were wrong. In hand-to-hand, he'd have killed her immediately.

Someone helped her escape. That was the only logical answer. Where was she?

He made a quick check of all the rooms and spaces in the basement but didn't find her. Near the washing machine, he spied a telephone mounted on the wall. On a hunch, he raised the receiver to his ear. Nothing. No dial tone or line noise. The line could have been knocked out by the storm, or it could have been out for years. Easy enough to check, but Branch guessed this was the line Teresa Justice was using to call Duffy over the past couple of weeks. Until she'd been caught and someone terminated the line.

He climbed the stairs and slipped through into the hallway. The caterers and staff were still working to prepare dinner. He squared his shoulders and walked through the kitchen as if he had every right to be there. The two men who'd driven him into the compound stared at him, but he ignored them and walked outside. No one tried to stop him.

Outside, the floodlights from the wall illuminated the compound. It seemed to him that both the snowfall and cold wind were intensifying. He looked toward the gatehouse and the garage and the main house. Where was Duffy? Not in the main house, surely. The garage was dark. No light spilled from any of the windows. Which left the gatehouse. The only reasonable option.

A hulking man dressed in a pea coat stepped around the corner, head down against the blowing snow. A knit cap covered his head. Reddened ears lay flat against his skull. Both hands were shoved into his coat pockets, thrusting his elbows akimbo.

Branch saw him first, recognized him as the bald limo driver, one of Abrams' original five-man security team, a split second before he raised his head. The man's eyes widened.

Before he had a chance to pull his hands out of his pockets or settle his weight on both feet, Branch rushed forward with both hands in front of his chest, palms out. He delivered a sharp, hard strike with his cupped right hand, slamming fifty pounds of pressure to the man's left ear.

The man's eardrum burst, and he screamed. He raised his left hand to cover his destroyed ear, and Branch delivered a brutal palm strike under his chin, short, explosive and fast, shoving the man's head straight back. Branch heard a sickening crack and followed with his right fist to the man's throat, crushing his larynx before he dropped to the ground, floundering like a fish, fighting for breath.

Branch grabbed the man's ankles and pulled him into the shadows away from the back of the house, near the rocks. He was unconscious and would be dead in seven to fourteen seconds. No one entering or leaving by the kitchen door could see him in the dark.

Branch spent no time worrying about whether he might have disabled the guy instead of killing him. Without a doubt, the man would have killed him, given the chance. Branch knew enough about Abrams and his methods of operation to be certain.

Branch ducked his head into his jacket and walked along the back of the house, past the door to the kitchen, and around the driver's side of the caterer's panel van. The door pushed open. He heard his name from the front seat. "Branch!"

He frowned and turned his head toward the voice. He felt a grin plant itself on his mouth. "Good evening, Duffy."

Duffy whispered, "Get in. Come on."

Branch did as he was told. He jumped into the driver's seat while Duffy crouched down in the back.

"Where's Teresa?" he asked.

"I don't know. There's too many people here and too many places she could be. We need help. Let's go."

He fired up the engine and rolled slowly around the corner of the house, slowly around the carriage circle, and away from the house, toward the gate. It was a white van, and white snow covered everything, and slow-moving objects are less perceptible than fast moving objects. But he wanted to be seen.

He stopped at the gate. The big guard came outside, punched the code into the pad on the side of the wall, opened the gate and allowed the van to leave. Branch waved as he drove through the gate and watched in the rearview mirror as it closed behind him.

He drove across the open headland and into the pine forest. There, the road was sheltered from the storm, but even here at least four inches of snow covered everything. No matter the conditions, safer to assume the surveillance cameras were operational.

"How did you get out of that cell?" Branch asked. It was a risk to ask. Someone could have ears on them, too. Duffy must have been thinking the same thing because she put a finger over her lips and didn't respond. Neither spoke another word along the twelve long miles to Route 1.

CHAPTER TWENTY-FOUR

Thursday, November 25
Abbot, Maine
5:45 p.m.

KIM HAD PARKED THE second SUV behind Gaspar's under the overpass at the exit from the interstate and joined Gaspar in his vehicle. The engine was running, and the heat was on, which kept her from freezing to death. Under the overpass, they were somewhat protected from the wind and snow. The sun had not been visible at any point during the day, but nightfall was fast approaching.

"What happened when you followed the limousine?" she asked.

"He drove to Brisbee, a private airfield in Portland. He waited about twenty minutes. A Gulfstream 450 landed, and two passengers deplaned. They entered the limo, and he drove back." He pushed his seat back and stretched his right leg. His muscles must have been complaining from the forced captivity. "We would've intercepted, but you found the catering van. Seemed like a better option."

Reflexively, she asked, "Did you check the call letters on the plane?"

He flashed her a look of annoyance. "Sunshine, what you think?"

"What about the license plate on the limo?"

He glanced at her and raised one eyebrow.

"Have you heard anything back yet?"

"It's Thanksgiving. You haven't forgotten that, right? We'll get the info as soon as they have it, I'm sure." He pulled his phone out of his pocket and located photos he'd taken at the airport and passed the phone to her. "The plate on the limo, followed by the G-450 and head shots of the driver, the two passengers, and the pilot."

She looked at the photos and pushed a couple of buttons and sent them to herself in three places. She enlarged the picture of the license plate. "That looks like a diplomatic plate, doesn't it?"

She handed him the phone. He looked at the enlarged image. "I couldn't see the plate clearly before, but I think you're right."

He pressed a call back number and put the phone on speaker and waited for the pickup. "Any success on that plate?"

"Just came in," said a man's voice Kim didn't recognize. "The vehicle is registered to Viktor Sokol, a Russian Embassy attaché. A lower-level diplomat, ostensibly, but probably a spy and perhaps a criminal as well."

Gaspar continued to listen to his source, but once she had the name, Kim did a quick online search and found nothing in the public databases about Sokol. She ran the name through the FBI databases and was rewarded with a photo and a short biographical dossier marked confidential, but not classified.

"Hello, Viktor Sokol," she said, under her breath. She showed Gaspar the image on her phone of the well-dressed European they'd last seen in the photo standing in the front doorway at Abbot Cape.

According to the FBI bio, Sokol was forty-two years old and had been a member of the Russian diplomatic mission for three years. Because of his status, he was not restricted to the immediate vicinity of his New York embassy. He was allowed to travel, which meant he was not considered important enough to be a security risk or a threat.

The FBI file contained a few headshots and several candid photographs snapped by news outlets at formal events at the UN. Sokol was seen with various women on his arm. All were tall and lithe. Pale. And blonde.

The hair stood up on the back of Kim's neck. Were his escorts actually trafficking victims?

She called the Boss's cell phone.

He answered immediately. "I've got less than a minute. What do you want?"

"Everything you've got on a low-level Russian diplomat named Viktor Sokol. He might be involved in human trafficking, probably to the Middle East." Kim didn't know where the trafficking victims were being shipped, but their angelic, virginal appearance suggested Middle Eastern buyers.

"I'll check," the Boss replied, and then she was listening to dead air.

She held the phone out and looked at it as if she could will him to reappear. Nothing happened.

Gaspar frowned. "He's as charming as always."

She nodded and returned the phone to her pocket. "What did Branch tell you during your quality man-time on the road?"

Gaspar cocked his head as if he needed to think about her question. "He said he asked Villanueva to call Reacher, and the old guy admitted to him that he didn't have a clue where Reacher is."

"Not surprising."

"He also said Duffy would skin him alive if he tried to call Reacher. She specifically nixed the idea. Same thing he told you when you asked him."

Kim nodded. She was a careful person by nature. Confirmation of facts she'd been given was always a good thing. "Duffy's in way over her head. Wonder why she wouldn't want Reacher involved?"

Gaspar shrugged. "We got to the subject of Reacher and Villanueva when Branch asked me if *I* knew where Reacher was. After laughing for maybe ten minutes, I told him that if I did, I'd be home with my family on Thanksgiving instead of driving through this winter wonderland with the likes of him. He pressed me for what I *did* know about him, and I told him that Reacher lives so far off the grid even our boss can't dig him up. And that's saying something."

"What was Branch's response to that?"

"He said something like 'If Cooper can't find the guy with all the resources at his disposal, I guess we'll have to make do without Reacher.'"

Kim nodded. So Branch seemed to be clueless about Reacher. Which meant Duffy most definitely didn't tell him everything. All she'd learned beyond that was that Branch knew Cooper, somehow, and didn't much like him. Membership in that club was hardly exclusive. "Did Villanueva tell Branch anything else about Reacher?"

"Probably a lot more than he shared with me." Gaspar

stretched his neck and closed his eyes briefly like he was
thinking. "Branch said Villanueva had a high level of respect for
Reacher."

"We've run into that before." Strangely. Reacher had been a
military cop for a long time. But he wasn't a lawman anymore.
Not even close.

"Villanueva said Reacher had more grit than just about
anyone he's known and said he's known some bullheaded
characters in his life. So we've got that much in common."
Gaspar grinned at her, his implication clear. "Said none of us
would want to go up against Reacher in a dark alley, and not just
because he's about the size of all those guys in that compound
and strong as an ox. Said it would definitely help to have
Reacher on our side, and he was a little miffed because Duffy
refused to call."

"Anything else?"

Gaspar shook his head. "Nothing beyond the impression I
got that a lot of things were left out of the formal reports at the
time of that raid, and most of the omitted facts had to do with
Reacher."

They watched the snow fall on the vacant roads for a while.
Surveillance and stakeouts had to be the most boring part of any
cop job. Sometimes, it had to be done. But she didn't have to like
it.

She looked at her Seiko. Branch had been gone for more
than twenty minutes. She fished her cell phone out of her pocket
and called Villanueva. He picked up promptly. "See anything on
the satellite video at the compound?"

"The catering truck came out of the woods and drove to
the gate a couple of minutes ago. The gate guy let them
inside. They drove around to the back of the house. I can't

see anything that's going on back there. Angle's wrong."

She spent about three seconds thinking about it before she put the phone on speaker to allow Gaspar to hear and said to Villanueva, "You're the only one of us who has any experience with Reacher. Tell me."

"Tell you what?"

"Things I can't find out from looking at fifteen-year-old Army investigation files. And make it quick."

Villanueva had paused for a few moments before he said, "Reacher was a significant asset to us back then. I wasn't with him all the time because he was undercover. Embedded at the house with Beck's organization. He seemed professional, determined, and above all else, effective."

"What was his relationship with Duffy?"

"Relationship?" His voice had shot up a couple of octaves, which answered the question for Kim.

"They were lovers," she said.

She heard the shrug in his voice. "I never asked. Is it relevant?"

"It might be. Was he violent?"

"It was a violent situation."

"So that's a yes. Did he kill anybody?"

Villanueva paused a beat too long. "I can't recall."

"So that's a yes, too." She ran splayed fingers through her hair and quickly wrapped her low ponytail into a close chignon at the base of her neck. "I've seen the ATF files from that operation. Reacher is not mentioned. Not once. Why not?"

"I told you, the operation was off the books. We left him out of the reports." He paused and Kim waited him out. "He wanted Duffy to get the credit, anyway. And she did."

"So your story is that Reacher just showed up out of the

blue, got involved, killed at least one person and maybe more, in your presence, and he was not arrested or questioned and never even *mentioned* in the official records?"

Villanueva remained quiet.

"And you've never seen Reacher again?" Kim pressed.

Villanueva said nothing. The longest pause yet. She stared out at the snow falling and let him run his calculations, whatever they might be.

It was worth the wait.

"I think he's in the house," Villanueva said, finally. "I can't be sure. It's been a long time. But I might have recognized him in those photographs you showed me this morning."

Kim's body stiffened, and she took a few deep breaths. Maybe she should have anticipated Reacher showing up here, but it seemed unlikely. How did he get inside? When had he arrived? Not to mention that the Boss had the place under constant surveillance and had said nothing. He would have announced Reacher's presence if he'd known. Wouldn't he?

Whether Reacher was here or not, the Boss had stuck them in another situation where they might get killed, which wasn't in any way unusual. She ticked off the negatives in her head. Duffy and Justice missing. At least two known killers in that compound, Abrams and Reacher. And her tools were Branch, an old cop, a disabled agent, and her wits. *Dear God.*

Before she could ask another question, Villanueva said, "The caterer's van is coming around the back of the house, moving slowly. It's at the gate."

Gaspar said, "Can you zoom in on the driver?"

Like a play-by-play announcer he said, "It's Branch. Looks like he's alone. The gate's opening. He's outside the compound.

Everything seems okay. He's rolling along pretty well." A few seconds later, "He's disappeared into the trees."

Kim looked at her watch. "He should be coming out on this side in about twenty minutes.".

CHAPTER TWENTY-FIVE

GASPAR ASKED VILLANUEVA, "CAN you see the intersection at Route 1 and the entrance road, Abbot Cape Drive?"

"Not clearly. The snow is heavy and cloud cover is, too. But it's dark enough so I may see his headlights when he gets to the intersection."

"Was anyone in the van with him?" Kim asked.

"Passenger seat was empty."

That didn't mean he was alone. If Duffy and Justice were with him, they would probably be in the back and keeping out of sight. "Is anybody following him?"

"Not that I can tell. I didn't see anybody leave the compound after Branch drove the panel van out. But they could be watching him from the surveillance cameras along the road."

"Don't try to call him. Surveillance could include audio interception."

"Roger that."

She glanced at her Seiko. Branch had been gone for a total of ninety minutes. Twenty minutes to drive in, an hour inside, ten minutes so far on the drive out. "Keep watch as best you can, but focus mainly on the compound," Kim said. "If anyone else heads out in our direction, let us know right away."

"Roger that."

Maybe he'd have Duffy and Justice with him, and they could turn this situation over to ATF and get the hell back to civilization.

"When they get here, I'll take Duffy and Justice." Kim looked at Gaspar. "You and Branch get rid of the panel van and meet us back at the motel."

"10-4," he said, and she punched him in the bicep. He grinned.

She slipped out of the passenger door and stepped into a two-foot snowdrift. She stuffed her hands deep into the pockets of her parka and flipped the hood up. The driven snow whipped around her as if she were pushing into a wall of wind.

She slogged through the drifts on her way back to the second SUV, which was partially buried in snow.

She opened the driver's door and reached for the handhold to pull herself up into the cabin. She knocked the snow off her boots and closed the door. The key fob was still in her pocket, so she pushed the start button and flipped the heat and defrosters to high.

The bulky parka made it difficult to move inside the cabin, but the SUV was too cold yet to slip out of its warmth. She found her cell phone and called Villanueva. "Anything yet?"

"Not that I can see. Conditions are near whiteout and the cloud cover is too thick. I can barely see the ground. You're about three miles from that intersection. You might want to move closer to intercept him when the panel van emerges from the woods."

She pushed the conference button and dialed to add Gaspar's phone to the conversation.

"I'm here, Susie Wong. Your wish is my command."

"Villanueva's on with us. He says his visibility is near zero now. We need to move up. Intercept Branch as soon as he reaches the intersection at Route 1. If they see us through those surveillance cams, they see us. Nothing much we can do about it."

"10-4."

She grinned despite her best intentions to remain fierce. But he couldn't see her, so it didn't matter. "Villanueva, keep this line open. But don't talk unless you need to, just in case someone's listening. You have another phone there, right? If anything happens, call 911."

Villanueva paused briefly and said, "Will do."

She understood his hesitation. The call to emergency responders would be useless. No one would come out in this blizzard and even if they did, they'd arrive way too late to handle anything but the aftermath of any real emergency. But there was always the chance they might.

She tossed her phone onto the passenger seat, snugged up her seatbelt and scooted as close to the steering wheel as she could get. She pressed the toes of her left foot hard on the brake and moved the transmission into all-wheel-drive, first gear. "You lead, Chico. I'll follow."

She peered through the windshield into the near whiteout conditions. It was full dark outside. Headlights served mostly to illuminate the blowing snow and decrease real visibility. The road was completely covered. There was no way to tell the tarmac from the shoulders or the ditches beyond them.

Gaspar pulled into the traveled portion of the roadway and

moved forward slowly. His big, black SUV looked like a giant cockroach in a jar of marshmallow cream. She waited until he left the cover of the overpass to pull out behind him.

The windshield wipers flapped at high speed, pushing the heavy snow aside almost as fast as it accumulated.

Both vehicles plowed through the snow, moving slowly. They covered the three miles between the overpass and the intersection at Route 1 at ten miles per hour. Kim squinted and frowned in an effort to see more clearly. There were no streetlights along the road.

The oversized red stop sign at Route 1 came into view twenty-five yards ahead. Gaspar slowed and tapped his brakes. The taillights on his SUV flashed.

No one spoke.

When Gaspar reached the stop sign and rolled to a stop, Kim stopped twenty feet behind him.

Without releasing the steering wheel, she checked her Seiko. Branch should be arriving any minute, assuming he'd made it through. Her hands clenched the wheel at nine and three o'clock. Her forearms screamed with tension, and her shoulders ached from holding her body away from the seatbelt even as it pulled her back.

Gaspar turned off his headlights and left the parking lights on. Kim did the same to avoid confusion with the panel van's headlights when Branch approached. Assuming he made it through. Anything could have happened inside that dark tunnel. The only thing she could do was wait.

She had estimated Branch's arrival time, and he was three minutes past her estimate. The interior of her SUV had finally warmed up. Or maybe it was tension. Either way, she felt herself sweating inside the parka. Her palms were damp in her gloves.

She pried one stiff hand from the steering wheel and flipped the heat down.

Instant quiet. The only thing she heard was the soft rumble of the SUV's powerful engine.

Five more minutes passed. Both Route 1 and Abbot Cape Drive seemed deserted. No vehicles had passed them moving in any direction during the past hour.

Snowplows must have been busy in more populated areas. Out here, there would be no need to plow the road until after the snowfall ended. She guessed this was not a priority area for state or local services of any kind.

Kim knew how winter storms were handled in American small towns. She'd grown up on a farm about thirty miles north of Detroit. It was a small German farm town. A snowfall like this would block the main roads for days until the local farmers pulled out their personal tractors and plowed.

The house was located so far from civilization, it was unlikely to be connected to utilities and services in the usual ways. The compound at Abbot Cape probably had its own equipment for snow clearing. It likely had generators for electricity and maybe a propane or oil furnace, in addition to fireplaces, for heat.

Twelve minutes beyond the estimated time of arrival, she thought she saw the faint yellow glow of headlights in the distance. The blizzard camouflaged all ordinary light sources. There was no moon. No stars. What she saw through the blizzard and straight ahead must have been headlights.

"Do you see that, Cheech?"

"10-4."

White snow covered the land and everything on it. Even the salt pines were heavily flocked with blobs of white. White snow filled the air, falling like giant confetti dumps from the black clouds.

The white panel van blended invisibly with everything else. The headlights seemed alien as they approached, seemingly unattached.

Two minutes later, the panel van lurched from the tree-shrouded cocoon and slid across the intersection. Branch pulled up parallel to Gaspar's SUV. All three rolled down their windows.

"Any passengers?" Gaspar yelled into the howling wind.

Branch held up one finger. Gaspar stuck his left arm out the window and jerked his thumb back toward the second SUV. Branch flashed a thumbs up. Kim pressed the door release to unlock all the SUV's doors, which had automatically locked when she put the vehicle in gear.

The passenger door of the panel van opened, and someone climbed out. A tall woman dressed in running clothes. Her neon shoes sank into the knee-high snow.

Bent at the waist against the blizzard, she trudged around the front of the panel van and slogged her way to Kim's SUV. She opened the back door and climbed in and closed it behind her. Kim glanced into the rearview mirror and looked into Susan Duffy's sodden face.

Duffy's teeth were chattering, and her hair was wet with melting snow. She hugged herself and rubbed her arms to warm up. Kim flipped the heat to high again.

Still concerned about audio surveillance, no one said anything more.

Gaspar took his foot off the brake and pulled into the intersection, turning left on Route 1 toward Portland.

Kim rolled to the intersection and turned right toward the Abbot Motel.

Branch backed up the panel van and pulled in behind Gaspar.

Kim glanced up to see the panel van's taillights recede in her rearview mirror. They traveled five miles in silence before Kim said, "Villanueva are you still there?"

"I'm here. What's going on? I can't see you anymore."

"We're on our way back. I've got Duffy with me. Branch and Gaspar are on their way to deal with the van. What's going on out at that compound? Any sense of panic? Anybody following Branch?"

"Not that I can tell. I can't see much, but what I can see of the place looks like a cozy Dickens novel. The whole compound is blanketed in snow. No one has come in or out since Branch left."

Kim felt her shoulders relax slightly. Maybe they'd gotten away with this. For now. There was still the problem of what to do about the van and the caterers.

Duffy reached forward from the back seat, picked up Kim's phone, climbed over the console, and settled into the passenger seat. "Thanks for saving my ass, Otto. I owe you."

"Damn straight you owe me, and I plan to collect. You've chased us around in four states. We need to know everything you know about Reacher. Tonight." Kim glanced at her before turning her full attention to driving.

Duffy said nothing.

"Good to have you back, Duffy," Villanueva said.

"You're too good to me, Tony," Duffy replied, with a smile in her voice that seemed to break a little at the end.

"Damn straight." Villanueva laughed.

The Abbot Motel parking lot came into view. Kim pulled the SUV into the parking slot in front of her room. She slid the transmission into park and released her seatbelt and flopped backward. All the tension that had been holding her together seem to relax at once. As she exited the vehicle, her thoughts turned to Gaspar and Branch.

CHAPTER TWENTY-SIX

BRANCH FOLLOWED GASPAR FIVE miles north on Route 1 to a gas station. They pulled into the parking lot and around the back of the building. The station was closed, probably due to a combination of the holiday and the blizzard.

Branch shut off the ignition and jumped down into a snowdrift above his knees. He locked the door with the key and walked around to the back of the van. He pulled open the doors and stepped into the cargo compartment. He found a drip coffee maker, coffee, sugar, and cream. He also found what was probably meant to be dessert for dinner at Abbot Cape tonight. Pie, cake, and cookies. Not much of a Thanksgiving dinner, but better than anything they'd have back at the motel otherwise.

He loaded his bounty into the back of Gaspar's SUV, locked up the van, and climbed into the SUV's passenger seat. The cabin was warm and dry. Branch knocked the snow off his clothes and slammed the door.

Gaspar rolled the SUV over the snow onto Route 1 and headed south toward the motel. The wipers struggled valiantly to keep the snow off as it piled onto the windshield.

"I didn't find Teresa Justice," Branch said. "There were two cells in the basement, just like Villanueva said. But one was empty. Not much furniture, even."

"Wait and make your report to the group. You won't have to repeat yourself."

Gaspar paid strict attention to his driving. There were no other vehicles on the road. But the night was as black as pitch. The road was buried under at least eight inches of accumulation.

The SUV's four-wheel-drive and elevation from the road's surface made moving along the road at slow speeds barely possible. Ground speed was fifteen miles an hour, at best.

Headlights were useless on high beams. They illuminated the snow in the distance creating blinding glare. The SUV was equipped with high-performance fog lights, probably because driving in thick fog and heavy snow conditions was common.

The sky became darker, and visibility decreased with every passing mile. Gaspar was running the low beam headlights for distance and the fog lights to help see the edges of the road in the foreground. Branch estimated he could see about ninety feet ahead. At this rate, they wouldn't make it back to the motel for almost an hour.

"Want me to help with the driving?" Branch asked.

"I'm good for now." Gaspar resettled himself in the driver seat. He frequently grimaced as if he was in pain.

Branch had read Gaspar's file, which didn't contain a complete report of his injuries when he'd been shot. But he had observed Gaspar limping on his right leg. The damage to his muscles must have been extensive, and he probably didn't take painkillers stronger than Tylenol. Prescription painkillers would only add to his difficulties. Gaspar could barely do the job, Branch guessed. Under these conditions, Gaspar's pain undoubtedly dulled concentration and delayed reaction time.

Gaspar asked, "Did you see Reacher?"

"Reacher? You think he's inside that compound?"

Gaspar shrugged.

"Could have been, I guess," Branch replied. "I've never met the guy. I wouldn't know him if he bit me on the ankle."

"He'd be more likely to head-butt your face." Gaspard chuckled. "And believe me, if he did that, you'd know it."

They drove in silence for a while, making slow progress. Branch strained to see, keeping a lookout. He knew depth perception, color recognition, and peripheral vision were severely limited at night, but there was nothing much to see out there other than the relentlessly falling and blowing snow.

The road itself was impossible to identify. Gaspar was following the tire tracks they had laid down on the way to the gas station. The tracks had become filled with new snow in the past half-hour, and the blowing wind had wiped them out in many places.

There were ditches on either side of the road, but it was tough to tell where the roadway ended, and the slope toward the ditches began. A slide in the wrong direction and the SUV might be swallowed completely.

They crossed the intersection where a turn would lead them either west to I-95 or east to Abbot Cape. The intersection was identifiable only because the big stop signs still poked up above the snow mounds.

From this point onward, the only guide they had for the road's surface were Otto's tire tracks. She'd driven the second SUV back to the motel more than an hour ago, and her tracks had been covered in many places. This stretch of road had several wide bends, unmarked by guardrails on either side.

Gaspar stretched his neck and shoulders and shifted in his seat again. Branch said nothing.

"I'm driving by feel here," Gaspar said. "You see anything, say something. I need back up."

"Roger that." Branch had been watching already, but he redoubled his efforts. Gaspar turned the wheel on the big vehicle and followed a gentle forty-five-degree angle to the left. As he came around the stand of trees, an eight-point whitetail buck stood in the middle of the road staring directly at the SUV, glued to the spot by the oncoming lights like a statue.

Gaspard tapped the brakes, although he'd only been traveling about ten miles an hour as it was, and hit the horn.

The horn's blast startled the buck, and he jumped, but instead of running away from the SUV he ran toward them.

Gaspar pressed the brakes. The SUV carried enough momentum to fishtail. Its back end slid off the edge of the road, and still it slid on. Gaspar fought with the wheel, trying to right the vehicle on the slippery snow, flying blind without any understanding of where the pavement was.

The buck leaped into the air.

His front legs arched gracefully over the SUV's left front fender, but his rear hooves flew only halfway because the vehicle had continued moving under them. He scrambled onto the SUV's wide black hood as he struggled to get his footing, then his front legs slid off the other side of the vehicle, and his back legs followed over and then he was gone, out of sight.

Gaspar managed to straighten the vehicle and move up a few feet back onto the roadway before he slowed to a stop. He pushed the transmission into park and released his seatbelt.

"What the hell are you doing?" Branch asked.

"I'm going to check on the deer. Put him down if I need to. I can't let him lie there and suffer until he freezes to death."

"You get out there, you may not get back. Not to mention that another vehicle coming around that curve could slam into you. We can't stop here."

Gaspar looked at him briefly and then opened the door and stepped down beside the SUV. "You can help me, and this will go a little faster. Or you can wait here. Your choice."

Cold wind and snow whipped around him and shoved its way inside the cabin.

"Goddammit. Are you trying to get yourself killed? And all the rest of us with you?"

"Check the glove box for a flashlight. Bring it with you." Gaspar pressed the emergency flashers on and closed the door, leaving the engine running.

Muttering to himself, Branch rooted around in the SUV until he found a flashlight. He slipped out of the vehicle and walked around the back. Snow was calf-deep in places and drifted even deeper in others. This was lunacy. He couldn't tell where the road ended and the embankment began. There were too many shadows and too much snow and too much wind. He shined the flashlight beam ahead, sweeping back and forth, seeking the injured deer.

He swept the flashlight's beam across the snow, trudging deeper into the woods, when he heard the unmistakable gunshot, probably from Gaspar's Glock 17. He jerked his head toward the noise. A second shot followed the first. This time, he saw the flash of the shot in the dark.

He sent the flashlight beam toward the sound. Gaspar had turned away from the deer and struggled through the deep snow toward the road, a grim expression on his face. Tough situation. Nothing else could have been done tonight for the poor creature.

Branch turned to make his way back to the still-running SUV. Which was when he first heard the straining of a heavy equipment engine in the distance. "Do you hear that?" He listened intently until he identified its direction. He pointed north, toward the intersection they'd passed. The road to Abbot Cape.

"Anybody see you leave the compound with that van?" Gaspar asked.

Branch nodded. "We stopped at the gate. The big goon came out and punched the code so we could drive out."

Engine noise carried across the snow-covered silence. The big engine was moving slowly, west, away from the house.

"Sounds like a tractor of some kind. A snowplow, maybe," Gaspar said.

"Why would they be plowing snow tonight?" Branch asked. "Makes more sense to wait until morning when they can see the road, doesn't it?"

"Maybe they need to clear the road tonight for some reason," Gaspar replied. "Come on. We've got to get out of here. If they come south at that intersection, they'll be here in less than five minutes. We need to be somewhere else when that happens."

Without another word, Gaspar hurried back to the SUV. He climbed into the driver's seat and slammed the door. Branch followed. When they were seated again, Gaspar lowered all the windows and listened again. "I don't think that's a snowplow."

"You've heard so many snowplows in Miami that you can identify the engines, have you?" Branch was in no mood for nonsense.

Branch was cold to the bone and Gaspar's teeth were chattering. He reached over and flipped up the heat.

"I was in the army," Gaspar said. "I know what an off-road

vehicle sounds like. And even in Miami, we have farm tractors. Don't you have those in Houston?"

Branch cocked his head and listened over the rumble of the SUV's engine. A snowplow might have stopped and started. He might have heard the engine slip into reverse as it backed up or the transmission might have whined as it pushed snow to one side. But he heard none of those things. Just the steady westward march of the laboring engine moving silently through the snow.

"A snow cat?" Branch finally asked.

"That would be my guess. Call Villanueva. Ask him if he can see the vehicle from the satellite. Find out whether it's coming toward us." Gaspar didn't take his eyes off the snow-covered landscape ahead of the SUV while searching for a driveway to pull into to avoid discovery by the snow cat's driver.

They rode with the windows down to hear the big engine coming their way even as they made slow and steady progress away from the intersection.

Branch punched the number and held his cell phone to his ear. Villanueva answered. "Yeah?"

"You still watching the compound?"

"Can't see much."

"Did a snow cat pull away in the past fifteen minutes?"

"Maybe. There might have been headlights. Hard to say. The blowing snow is coming down hard and cloud cover is blocking the satellite images." Villanueva paused. "Why?"

"Something's going on. We think a big vehicle is coming toward us down Abbot Cape Drive. Keep an eye on the intersection. Call me if you see anything."

"Where are you?"

"About five miles out. But we won't pull into the motel lot if that snow cat heads this way." Branch looked at Gaspar and Gaspar nodded.

"Roger that." Villanueva hung up.

Gaspar strained to see the road ahead through the darkness in the blinding, wind-driven snow. The road was under the snow, somewhere, and all he could do was press forward. Branch kept a lookout and listened for the approaching snow cat. They made their way onward, slowly.

Branch's cell phone rang.

Villanueva said, "I see headlights emerging from the trees. The lights are weak and high off the ground. It's a big vehicle. Could be a snow cat, maybe a plow or another tractor. It's turning north. Away from us. Toward Portland."

"Keep watching. We'll be with you shortly." Branch felt his tense muscles relax. He relayed the intel to Gaspar. "They're preparing for something. Those women. The extra security. Sending a snow cat out in this weather. There's a reason for all that, and it's not trivial. Abrams is not a man to mess with."

"How long will it take to scramble ATF up here after you call them?" Gaspar asked.

"Good question," Branch said. "We need to give them as much lead time as we can."

Gaspar drove the rest of the way to the Abbot Motel without incident. He pulled the SUV into a parking spot between Villanueva's Town Car, almost buried in snow, and the other SUV, whose tires were already nearly covered, too. They would need shovels to get the vehicles free.

"I'm going to get a hot shower, and I'll meet you with the others," Gaspar said.

"Same here," Branch replied, although he planned to make a phone call to his ATF contact first.

CHAPTER TWENTY-SEVEN

Thursday, November 25
Abbot, Maine
5:15 p.m. Eastern Time

SOKOL, THE DIPLOMAT, WAS enjoying his cocktail hour
with Abrams and twenty-eight beautiful women. He'd been
expecting twenty-nine, but one—his unexpected addition to their
number—was late.

Earle entered the dining room and approached. He leaned
over and whispered, "I need a word."

They walked into Sokol's office. The big screens were black.
The next demonstration would take place tomorrow morning. He
intended to check the setup after dinner. His remaining guests
would be arriving throughout the rest of the evening and early
morning. The weather was proving to be inconvenient. Neither
the limousine nor the helicopters could get through the heavy
snow between Abbot Cape and the Brisbee airport where his
pilot, trained in Siberia, could land safely on the snow-covered
runway. The snow cat would be required.

Earle closed the door behind him and turned. He spoke softly. "The second jogger is gone."

"What do you mean? Gone where?" English was not his first language so he might have misunderstood.

Earle shook his head. "We're looking for her. She escaped from her cell."

Sokol frowned. "Escaped? How?"

"We aren't sure. The door was unlocked. The guard was disabled."

Sokol felt confused. The conversation made no sense to him. "Disabled? What does that mean?"

"He's dead. His neck is broken."

"I see." His confusion cleared. "When did this happen?"

"We're not sure. There's been a lot of activity around here today. Another member of my team is missing." Earle looked away. His voice weakened. "The maid said the jogger was there when she took her clothes to dress for dinner about two hours ago. So it happened within the past two hours."

Sokol felt heat rising in his chest. He'd known the woman was trouble from the start. He should have dealt with her the same way as the first one. A mistake. But not a mistake he wanted Abrams to hear about. He'd spent three years putting this deal together, and he didn't want that scrawny ATF bitch to mess things up.

"Find her. Be quick about it." He controlled his anger by projecting it into the future: When he located her, he knew precisely how to deal with her. "No one must know."

Earle glanced down at the floor, took a step back out of reach. "She may have left the compound."

"How is that possible? Is everyone on my security team incompetent? Good that we brought in more men." Sokol's anger was making it difficult to breathe evenly. He forced himself to take a deep, slow breath. And another. Better. "How did she get past the gate and the gateman?"

"One of the catering vans left the compound right around the same time that she escaped her cell. She wasn't driving. But he didn't search the van."

Sokol's breathing ceased so that his next words came out in a croak. "And the gold?"

"Untouched. I checked. Personally."

All right. A breath. Another. Still, Sokol's rage mounted. He couldn't afford to lose control. If she escaped in that van and contacted ATF, how much time would he have before they would raid this place again, as they had done nine years ago? He'd chosen Abbot Cape because he believed it would be off the government's radar. He had convinced himself that they would surely not imagine illegal activity would be occurring here again. Who would be so brazen as to attempt it? Surely not the mild-mannered, mid-level Russian diplomat who had purchased the place with easily verifiable family funds and so loved to entertain his friends here. But, with the woman's escape, they would know otherwise.

"Find her. Be quick about it." He was pleased to find himself abnormally calm. "Say nothing to anyone."

Sokol turned and left Earle standing alone to solve the problem his incompetent security staff had created.

He'd intended to eliminate the compound's entire staff eventually. Now, he had no choice. He was required to kill them on Sunday before he escaped. That skinny bitch had negated his alternatives. Earle would find her and deal with her if she was still within the compound. If she wasn't inside the gate, blood would be on her hands. The thought cheered him. At some point, she would know. She would be mortified. He smiled and returned to his companions with good cheer restored.

"Everything all right?" Abrams asked when Sokol rejoined him.

"Yes, of course. Technical issues with one of the screens we will need in the morning. We will have it running smoothly. No problem."

"Excellent. Shall we eat?"

"I believe food will be ready in a few moments. First, I must reassure our new guests. Please excuse me." He was impatient to conclude the meal. Twenty-eight women who had been instructed not to speak unless spoken to seemed overwhelmingly annoying at the moment.

He joined two Arabs standing amid four of the women. Muslims were so tiresome because they didn't drink. At least their tempers were not spiked with alcohol. Russians, on the other hand, had famously short fuses. It was certainly true of himself, and of Abrams, a fact Sokol never allowed himself to forget.

There were plenty of civil wars raging around the world. He had no difficulty finding potential customers. In addition to the Arabs, there were two from China, two from India and two from Africa arriving in the next few hours.

He planned the final demonstration to take place live, on the monitors in real time. There were ten chairs set up in the screening room. The timetable was, as always, exact. Very soon, Grand Ocean Airways Flight 86 carrying 279 passengers would be destroyed before their eyes.

After that, they would be more than willing to deliver the gold wherever he chose in exchange for his weapons.

He smiled and decided to refill his vodka. Why not? The

remainder of the evening would proceed as planned. The storm had become increasingly violent throughout the day and evening. Because it had been forecast hours in advance, he'd made preparations. The caterers and the women had been provided rooms above the garage to separate them from his guests. No one would leave the compound tonight.

If the skinny bitch had left the compound, if she had contacted ATF, if ATF returned—none of that would happen before the deal was concluded and Sokol was well on his way. Sokol had lived in Siberia. He understood snow and storms. He knew how to navigate them. A skinny bitch ATF agent from Houston would be no match for him. He would be long gone before anything she could set in motion could bother him, and anyone and anything left behind at Abbot Cape would be dealt with.

With more vodka and a bit of logical thought, his good humor had completely returned. All was well.

CHAPTER TWENTY-EIGHT

HALF AN HOUR LATER, Branch and the others were gathered in Otto's room again. Her laptop was still connected to the satellite, but the compound was barely visible through the blizzard, even on the views that came from the hacked security cams. He wondered about infrared aimed at the compound to locate the people inside, but it might have the same limitations under these conditions.

The laptop was probably open for Cooper's benefit. Hacking it was an easy way for him to watch and listen to what went on in the room.

Branch tapped Villanueva on the shoulder. "Give me a hand, will you?"

Villanueva followed Branch to the SUV. They collected the items Branch had liberated from the caterer's van and brought them inside. They had coffee brewing in short order and food, such as it was, ready to eat.

Duffy said, "This might be the best Thanksgiving meal I've ever had."

"Are you ready to call ATF? Let them take over in the

morning?" Otto glanced at Duffy and Branch between bites of chocolate cupcake. "We need a couple of hours with Duffy and Villanueva tonight. To debrief. Nobody's leaving here. Roads are impassable. Helicopters can't fly. Commercial planes can't land. Tomorrow, we could wrap this thing up and head out."

Branch said nothing. He had accomplished his mission. He'd come here for Duffy. He'd take her back to Houston with him tomorrow. The others were running separate agendas that he didn't want to get sucked into, particularly if they involved some war between Reacher and Cooper. He simply munched sweets and sipped coffee.

No one else replied to Otto's question, either.

"We can't leave Teresa," Villanueva said as he brought the coffee pot around and refilled everyone's cup. No one agreed or disagreed. He touched Duffy's shoulder when he passed by, like a signal of some kind. "Why did you go inside there when you did?"

"I didn't intend to go inside the compound Wednesday morning. My plan was simply to drive as close as I could get and then take a look at the place. I wanted to see how it had changed, how we might get in. To find Teresa." Duffy was sitting on the end of the bed. She had finished a third cookie, and after Villanueva had refilled her coffee, she nodded, but she didn't speak immediately.

Gaspar said, "You were inside the place nine years ago. Why did you need another look?"

"There were no cameras on the entrance road back then, so I didn't think there was much of a risk in running up to the gate to take a look." She shook her head. "I drove the RAV 4 partway along, and I saw the surveillance cameras. Probably start about twenty feet in from the intersection at Route 1. And then about every fifty feet or so after the first ones."

"That's right," Branch said. "Easily visible all the way along Abbot Cape Road, even at night. It's like they want you to know you're being watched."

Villanueva said, "We could see a few of the cameras on the satellite images before the whiteout. In better weather conditions, they can probably see the intersection with Route 1, at least. Maybe farther, depending on the angles."

"I pulled deeper into the woods and parked the RAV 4 and jogged the rest of the way. When I got to the gate, the surveillance cameras posted there must have announced me." Duffy took a deep breath. "A huge man came out from the gatehouse and asked me what I wanted. I told him I was a tourist. I said I'd seen the road and it looked inviting. I told him I thought I'd be able to jog all the way to the ocean. I said I wasn't expecting to find the estate or a gate on the road. I asked him if I could pass through the compound to see the ocean."

"That guy is huge," Branch said, nodding. "Let me guess. He said no. Stay out."

"I wish." Duffy grinned, rubbing her knees with both hands. "Actually, he was almost friendly. He said there was a lovely view of the ocean on the other side of the house, and I should come take a look at it. Of course, I should've known better. He opened the gate, and I went inside."

She stopped a moment. Another deep breath. "He tackled me and knocked me to the ground. Really banged up my knees. I'm surprised I didn't break something. He's huge, did I mention that?"

"Yeah, we've seen him on the video," Gaspar said.

"I thought later that Teresa must have put up a hell of a fight, and he wasn't willing to risk me doing the same." She paused. "Otherwise, there was no reason for him to tackle me like that."

"Seems reasonable." Otto nodded. "So then what?"

"He used a cell phone to call someone out of the house. Another big man. The first guy held me captive, and the other one gave me some kind of drug. Probably Rohypnol, if I had to guess. I don't remember anything after that for several hours." She took a deep breath and finished her coffee. "That was Wednesday morning. When I woke up, I was in a cell in the basement of that house. I was still wearing my jogging clothes, and I had been asleep on a thin mattress on a metal cot."

"What happened after that?" Villanueva asked. "Did you see Teresa?"

She shook her head. "They brought me food and left me there until a few hours ago. Thursday afternoon." She looked at Villanueva and then Branch. "A woman, I think she was a domestic or something, brought me clean clothes, soap and water, and towels. She told me to clean myself up and put the clothes on because I would be joining everyone for Thanksgiving dinner."

"What kind of clothes?" Gaspar asked.

"White dress. It was long and flowing, like a nightgown, in a way. White stockings and white shoes. She specifically told me not to wear any makeup. I didn't have any with me, so that wasn't a problem. She told me to wait, and she would come back to take me to dinner."

"And did she do that?" Otto wanted to know.

Duffy looked at Branch and grinned. "I left before she had a chance."

"How did you escape that basement cell?" Gaspar asked.

"The maid turned her back on me. I knocked her out and

overpowered the security guard when he came in to check on her," Duffy said.

Branch covered his surprise with another bite of cupcake and waited.

Gaspar raised his right eyebrow. Otto raised both of hers.

"I'm a lot tougher than I look," Duffy said.

Branch had seen the dead security guard, and he'd seen the maid walking around in the kitchen. He knew Duffy was lying. But he said nothing to contradict her story. Duffy was his partner. If she didn't want to explain herself in front of the others, she had good reasons. He would respect that. For now. He'd find out what her reasons were before he contradicted her.

Villanueva asked, "You didn't see Teresa?"

"No. But I believe she's there."

"Why?"

"Teresa told me she was going inside the compound a few days ago. And the maid who brought me the clothes said she would take me and my friend to join the others for dinner. I told her I didn't have any friends with me. And she got flustered and said she'd made a mistake." Duffy paused for a deep breath as if to steady her nerves. "But I thought she meant Teresa. I'm sure of it."

Otto's eyes narrowed, and her nostrils flared. She turned to Branch. "Besides Duffy, what else did you find while you were inside?" Otto looked at him as if she could see all the way through to his conscience this time. "Anything useful?"

"There's quite a few people in that house. I saw four caterers, the two in the van that I rode in with, and two more. There's another van as well. It looked like they had enough food for at least forty." Branch pretended to think back. "I heard men talking. The dining room was set up for a big crowd."

"Probably the women from the helicopter and the other personnel we saw on the video cams," Villanueva said.

"And the two guys that came in the limo from the airport tonight," Gaspar said.

"They've added more security, too." Branch nodded. He considered mentioning the second dead security guard but waited until he had a chance to debrief Duffy first. There was an underlying vibe between the others that he didn't yet understand. Instead, he said, "Something was going on in the room that looks like an office on the layout drawings. I heard cheers a couple of times from behind the closed door."

"Did you see Abrams?" Otto asked.

Duffy shook her head and so did Branch.

Duffy said, "Are you sure Abrams is still in there?"

Branch shrugged. "We saw him this morning, and we haven't seen him leave."

Otto stood and stretched and refilled her coffee. "Time to call ATF. Let's turn this thing over to them and let them find Teresa Justice. Handle Abrams. Do whatever they're going to do with Sokol." She looked at Duffy and Villanueva. "We'll talk with both of you. Get what we need. And we're done here."

"Who is Sokol?" Branch asked. Otto filled them in on the little they knew about the Russian diplomat they had earlier believed to be the owner of Abbot Cape.

Branch and Duffy exchanged glances. Duffy nodded.

"What is it?" Gaspar asked.

CHAPTER TWENTY-NINE

BRANCH TOOK A DEEP breath and looked at Villanueva. "You might be the only one here who was around at the time. But during the Reagan administration, a defense system formally known as the Strategic Defense Initiative was conceived. It's still on the books. Still in the budget. Know anything about that?"

"Are you kidding?" Villanueva grinned. "Everybody knew. We called it Star Wars."

"Exactly." Branch nodded and sipped the coffee, which he knew was stalling. The intel was classified. Villanueva wasn't authorized, for sure. And Otto and Gaspar might not be. Simply acknowledging its existence could land them all in prison. He tread carefully. "Well, Reagan's idea wasn't stupid. It was just ahead of its time. What he wanted to do wasn't possible back in the '80s. We've been working on it for thirty-some years, and it's still not possible. But we can achieve some of its goals by other means."

"Meaning what, exactly?" Gaspar asked.

"We can deflect incoming weapons from the air from great distances," Duffy replied. "We can destroy them long before they get close enough to harm us. In essence, that's what Reagan's Star Wars was supposed to do."

"That's not exactly a state secret," Otto said.

"No." Branch cleared his throat. Abrams was inside that compound, and they deserved to know what they were up against. He nodded. "What is a closely guarded secret, need to know only, is how good our defense systems actually are. How far they can travel. How easy it is to deploy them. How amazingly accurate they are."

"You think the guys in that house are involved in something related to the Star Wars program?" Gaspar asked.

"Not exactly." Branch lowered his voice. Cooper could probably hear him anyway through the laptop's microphone. "We don't know for sure. What we think, as I told you earlier, is that Leo Abrams is Russian mafia. We've speculated that Abrams is also unofficially working with Moscow to secure their less politically correct objectives."

"Seriously?" Villanueva said.

"Sokol's presence here suggests we're right about that. My new employer, BlueRiver, believes the Russians are acquiring our defense systems, including certain long-range missiles, and selling them to shadowy dealers like Abrams, who will then sell them to insurgent groups in locations that are strategically important to Moscow." His throat was dry. He paused and sipped the coffee again. "The insurgent groups use the weapons against their enemies, but also in terrorist attacks against civilian non-combatants. As a way to discourage attacks against themselves. And also as a show of power. To persuade their enemies to surrender."

"Can you prove any of that?" Otto asked.

"We can't prove it yet, but we're close. That's why I was in

Mexico when Duffy first went missing. Abrams had been operating from there not long ago." He shook his head. "Our intel is very good. There have been some casualties around the world that can't be satisfactorily explained otherwise. Makes sense."

"The Cold War comes full circle," Villanueva whispered under his breath.

"Something like that," Branch said, and then tried to cover his ass. "All of this is currently a working theory, you understand."

All five sat quietly with their thoughts for a few moments.

"That can't be the whole story, though," Villanueva said, shaking his head. "Teresa was working on breaking up a human trafficking ring. Those women were dressed like virgins. Hell, maybe they are virgins. Maybe the women are being sold, too. Maybe Abrams will use them for payments or enticements or bonuses or some other crap like that."

Duffy nodded. "Teresa was convinced that the guy who currently owns Abbot Cape would help her with a human trafficking ring," she said. "She thought that organization was backed by the Russian mafia, but she didn't know about Abrams, specifically. She must have known Sokol was a Russian diplomat, though. She said the guy who owned the house had the right contacts to put a stop to things. Teresa has been accumulating gold because we all know the Russians want it. They use it to fund terrorism all over the world. She thought Sokol would facilitate a deal where she could buy the trafficked women with that gold."

"So she miscalculated, but only slightly," Otto said.

"What do you mean?" Duffy asked.

"Teresa was probably right about the human trafficking.

Those pale blond women dressed in white are perfect for Middle Eastern buyers," Otto said. "But she misconstrued the role Sokol plays in the operation."

"Roger that," Villanueva nodded. "Seems like Sokol's on the inside of the crime, not the outside."

"All the more reason to call the ATF tonight and get them out here in the morning. Or the FBI. Or BlueRiver. Or maybe all three," Gaspar said.

It was not a question. Branch supplied no answer. "I didn't even know Abrams was inside that house until today. I doubt the ATF knows he's there. And we sure as hell don't know what he's doing in there."

"We have to get Teresa out of there first. Before we call in the agencies." Villanueva said, shaking his head. "And you know how the agencies work. The bureaucracy alone will take a month to organize. The whole thing could be over by the time the good guys show up."

Duffy said, "Tony's right. They'll never get organized for a raid like that in time."

"In time for what?" Gaspar asked.

"I don't know. But whatever it is, they plan to do it this weekend. The maid said they've got more people arriving tonight. And then something big is supposed to happen tomorrow." Duffy cleared her throat. "They told me I'd be leaving on Saturday."

Branch knew Duffy well. He figured there was more to this story than she was telling. Maybe she was concealing intel because she didn't trust Otto and Gaspar. But he was long past worrying about them.

"There's something else," Branch said. He'd been leaning against the wall, but he pushed away and began to pace. "One of the things we've known for a while is that payments for the missiles are made in gold."

"Gold? Isn't that tough to transport to third-world countries?" Gaspar said. "I thought bitcoins were all the rage with criminals these days."

"The gold is stored all over the world. Both BlueRiver and ATF believe Abrams has been stockpiling significant quantities." Branch grinned. "And bitcoin is illegal in Russia. Not that the Russian mob and the likes of Abrams care about the law, but they do like to have control of their assets."

Otto stared at him. "And you think maybe there's a significant stockpile of gold inside that house."

"Traffickers need to get paid, and gold is a good way to handle payment," Villanueva said. "If Teresa thought they were interested in gold, that's proof enough for me."

Branch nodded. "And there are places in the world where gold is prized simply for itself. As a symbol of wealth." He was thinking about those five gold coins he'd found in Duffy's bedroom safe. Each from a different country. Each country a place where the population valued and desired gold. Duffy didn't volunteer any information about the coins, but she didn't know he'd found them, either. This was another thing he'd ask her about when they were alone.

Otto said, "But it's cumbersome. Unless criminals need to use gold, lots of other options would be a hell of a lot easier."

"Gold is acceptable currency anywhere," Villanueva said.

"You're a gold expert, are you?" Gaspar asked.

Villanueva glanced around the room. "More than anyone else here. Absolutely."

CHAPTER THIRTY

KIM HAD NEVER INVESTED in gold. Her work as an accountant before she joined the FBI had dealt with client investments, but on an entirely different level. Gold futures and similar paper transactions made sense to her. They showed up on income statements and balance sheets and tax returns. Especially tax returns. She loved tax returns. Some of the best reading in the world. But gold bars? Gold coins? She'd assumed gold investments were the favorites of crazy people. Survivalists. Nutters. And apparently gold was also the darling of certain criminals.

"Stockpiling gold coins and gold bars seems incredibly awkward, doesn't it? Like Gaspar said, the metal is heavy," Kim said. "Moving it from one location to another isn't as easy as clicking a few buttons on a computer keyboard."

Branch gave Duffy some kind of meaningful look. Duffy cleared her throat. "It's not as awkward as you think. The coins have value around the globe that's well beyond their face amounts, which is substantial to begin with. When Teresa first contacted me about this, I bought a few. They're in my safe back in Houston. Set me back a bundle, I can tell you."

Kim nodded. An FBI bulletin she'd reviewed more than a year ago said the country possessing the most gold was China. Gold smuggling was big in India and Africa, too. Wealthy Middle Eastern moguls drove gold cars and transported them everywhere at significant expense, even to London. Teresa Justice's theory made sense.

With Russia's ascendancy as a world power again, perhaps gold was the go-to method of exchange wherever Russian criminals did business.

Offshore banks were less secret than they once were. If nothing else, the Panama papers had proved that. The Swiss reported taxable transactions to foreign governments these days instead of keeping deposits confidential. It wasn't easy to hide wealth in banks anymore. All of those changes had made gold more viable.

"So tell us what you know about buying and selling gold." She nodded toward Villanueva.

He settled on the foot of the bed, opposite Duffy, and spoke quietly. "Gold investing has its skeptics. And maybe more than a few nuts are involved. But smart investors are in the game. Try explaining something like a bitcoin to a poor kid in the street in India. Can't be done. Toss a merchant in a Third World country a gold coin, you can buy just about anything you want, and lots of it."

"Some places," Branch nodded, "Gold is even more desirable for criminal enterprises than for legitimate ones."

"But how do you get gold in and out of this country?" Gaspar asked. "Gold is a heavy metal. It's gonna show up on any kind of scanner going through any port of entry or any kind of checkpoint."

"So you avoid government checkpoints. An import export business can hide the gold." Branch ticked off the ways. "A courier with a diplomatic passport, like Sokol, will not be searched. Private jet travel is pretty much a license to transport anything and everything. Private yachts, too, although they're a bit more cumbersome. Those are the main ways of smuggling gold as far as I know. I've never worked that side of Treasury, though. There's probably more ways to do it effectively."

"No one is going anywhere else tonight. We're stuck here, whether we like it or not." Duffy stood and stretched. "I'm exhausted. I need some sleep. In the morning, I'm going back for Teresa."

"I'm in," Villanueva said.

"Me, too," Branch added.

"We need to talk, Duffy," Kim said. "You, too, Villanueva. Tonight."

"Tomorrow. After you help us find Teresa." Duffy left. Branch and Villanueva followed her out.

"You up for that plan, Susie Wong?" Gaspar lifted himself off the bed and stretched.

"I guess I could tackle them both and tie them to the bed. Otherwise, do we have a choice?" she replied sourly.

CHAPTER THIRTY-ONE

Friday, November 26
Abbot, Maine
6:30 a.m.

SOKOL ROSE BEFORE SUNRISE and joined Abrams and his guests for breakfast. Arrivals had been delayed slightly because of the storm, but the snow cats had collected everyone, and they were back on site.

Each guest had deposited payment with trusted bankers in their home countries where the weapons would be delivered. Deposits had been verified.

The caterers were short the supplies that had left with the second van, but earlier in the week, the cook had been worried about food quantities on hand and had overstocked. The caterers assisted with preparation and breakfast went smoothly.

Afterward, Sokol led his guests to the screening room, and Abrams helped with the setup. Sokol activated a large screen in the front of the room to demonstrate the plan for taking down Grand Ocean Airways Flight 86.

He nodded toward the two gentlemen from Africa, who had won the lottery drawn last week. They had acquired the right to claim responsibility for destroying the jet and the 279 souls aboard. The gold they'd brought with them covered the purchase price.

Sokol was mildly concerned that none of the insurgents to whom these dealers would ultimately deliver his weapons could execute a successful attack on their own. Still, he had not contracted for training and implementation and did not intend to do so.

The screening room appeared the same as any typical business meeting. His guests were dressed in Western suits and ties. The Arabs wore traditional *keffiyeh* on their heads, but the others might have been sitting in a boardroom in New York or London or Delhi or Beijing or anywhere else in the world where multimillion dollar deals, legitimate or otherwise, are conceived and concluded.

Sokol stood in the front of the room with a laser pointer. He displayed the first graphic on the big screen to his right. "This is a rendering of a Boeing 777-200ER passenger jet. It is identical to the target we will destroy later in the morning demonstration."

The Africans smiled. The others nodded.

"It's important to know that you will have some room for error. The missile doesn't need to strike the jet." He aimed the laser pointer's red beam to the sky. "It need only explode close enough to cause the plane to break up in midair."

There were no questions raised. Abrams stood and made his way quietly to the exit. He'd seen it all before. While the demonstration continued, he slipped quietly out of the room.

Sokol wondered where Abrams was headed, but he did not pause his presentation. He pointed to the next image, a large land area marked inside a red box. "The missile can be fired from somewhere within about 320 kilometers, making it less likely that the launch area will be accurately pinpointed."

The India delegation nodded.

"Our target will not issue a distress call because there will be no advance warning." The next image was a photo of a cockpit with the pilot and crew in place. They seemed unconcerned. "The target will be flying at 33,000 feet, which is just above closed airspace in this region of civil unrest, where fighting has been continuous for the past year."

The Africans smiled again. This was their region. They were well aware of the wars being waged there.

"The plane will be leaving the airport and flying over the target zone in two hours, local time." An image of the airport and a digital clock filled the screen. "The first notice ground control will have is when the plane loses contact after we launch the weapon."

The Chinese delegation whispered among themselves. Their airspace was heavily monitored. Surprise was difficult to achieve. They were pleased that they would not need to attempt stealth or secrecy.

A new rendering of the Boeing 777-200ER flying through clear air consumed the screen. "The crash will be caused by the detonation of the warhead whether or not it strikes the airliner. We will attempt to explode about four meters above the tip of the airplane's nose on the left of the cockpit." His laser pointer placed a red dot in the precise spot.

"This will shower the plane with fragments of the warhead." A series of new graphics appeared with each sentence that followed. "The forward section of the plane will be penetrated by hundreds of high-energy objects from the warhead which will kill the crew and cause the plane to break up in stages. First, the cockpit will break away."

He paused a moment. "After a short time the wingtips will come off, and the rear of the plane will break away. The tail section will separate further."

Another short pause as an animation image showed the falling jet. "And the body of the plane will crash to the ground, landing upside down."

Sokol waited until he saw comprehension in the eyes of every man present before he continued. "Elapsed time after the cockpit comes off before the aircraft hits the ground should be sixty to ninety seconds."

One of the Africans gasped. "Such a short time."

"Could be longer," Sokol hid a satisfied smile, "but not much."

He waited for the murmured expressions of approval to die down.

The final image was a montage of actual photographs of another plane that had landed precisely as Sokol described. "Debris should be distributed over an area of about fifty kilometers."

The men murmured among themselves, raising a low conversational hum in the room. Sokol waited like a proud maestro while they expressed their awe and admiration to each other.

"The passenger list contains 279 names, including the crew," Sokol continued. "We do not expect survivors."

The next image was a flight map showing multiple planes flying over the busy area on a typical Friday morning. "We could easily isolate and destroy our target from this heavy air traffic, but we have chosen instead to make tactical use of it, for redundancy's sake. We expect multiple jets to fly this same general vicinity in the relevant timeframe, and have identified three potential commercial airliners that could be impacted should there be any sort of glitch with our target."

Their quiet conversations buzzed a bit louder. They were excited at the randomness of the kills. Dead civilians advanced their causes. The more, the better.

"As you know, the gentlemen from Africa won our lottery to fund this demonstration and to claim responsibility for it." He nodded toward the African delegation. They smiled. "We have carefully drafted the press release approved by the African delegation. We will distribute that release from the appropriate location in Africa immediately following the demonstration."

Hearty applause broke out around the table. Sokol waited for it to subside.

"Are there any questions?" He looked around the room and saw nods, smiles and body language suggesting a desire to applaud again and he was pleased.

After this demonstration, Sokol's fame would spread exponentially. This was the last such meeting he should need to conduct until he acquired an even better weapon for which he could demand even higher prices.

"Gentlemen, please make yourselves comfortable. Visit your rooms. We will have coffee and tea available here for you. Please return and be seated no later than thirty minutes from now." Sokol stood aside, gesturing toward the door. "In approximately one hour, we will begin our celebration."

CHAPTER THIRTY-TWO

THEY LEFT THE ABBOT Motel well before sunrise. Duffy's idea had been to leave even earlier. She wanted plenty of time to search the outbuildings for Teresa. But the worsening blizzard had made that impossible.

The blizzard had finally ended, but snowplows had not been through the area yet.

They left the motel together in all three vehicles, Otto and Gaspar in the lead. Villanueva's Town Car was lower to the ground than the SUVs, but he was experienced with snow, and its big engine powered the heavy vehicle through Gaspar's SUV tracks. The going was slow and treacherous, but they pressed steadily onward until they reached the first stop.

Villanueva parked under the I-95 overpass. Branch left the SUV there, too. The five piled into Gaspar's SUV and drove further north along Route 1.

The snow cat they'd heard last night had traveled this way. Its tracks had been covered by new snow, but they were faintly visible, providing a guide, of sorts, all the way to the gas station where Gaspar and Branch had left the panel van a few hours ago.

The snow cat's tracks continued toward Portland, and the return tracks were also discernable. Wherever the driver had traveled to last night, he'd returned this way as well.

During their preparations last night, they had argued about which vehicle to drive into the compound along Abbot Cape Drive. Duffy had insisted the panel van was the best choice because it was the least likely to be noticed on the surveillance cameras. She'd argued that if the van was noticed, it might be allowed to pass along the road to the gate anyway. There was a slim chance that the gateman didn't know she had escaped last night.

Very slim, Kim thought. She didn't like it. She thought there was no chance. Surely the original security team and the added security that came later were fully aware of Duffy's escape by this time. Particularly since at least one member of the original security detail had died in the process. After the escape, they'd had plenty of time to search for her. They were all on full alert most likely. Beyond that, the van did not have all-wheel-drive and maneuvered less well in the snow. Driving it along the entrance road and into the compound presented a significant risk of failure to arrive at the compound at all.

But the van had the advantage of being white, affording at least the possibility of a small element of surprise the other three vehicles—all black—couldn't match after the blizzard. And if they knew Duffy had used the van to escape, they certainly wouldn't be expecting her to come back inside. They might not think the van was really a Trojan Horse. No, the big gateman would most likely assume the van to be just another delivery from the catering company—or if he didn't, they could still count on him to let them enter and then try to contain them once they were inside. He'd believe his advantage was greater than anything Duffy could have mustered up in the past few hours during the blizzard. Given the additional security teams and superior firepower inside, Kim would agree with him. If he seemed suspicious of them, they'd need to move on him quickly after they were in—subdue or kill him, if they had to—before he had the chance to act on those suspicions. Four trained agents with guns should be at least an equal match for one oversized street fighter who tackled women from behind. She hoped.

Gaspar pulled the SUV around to the back of the gas station, and they all piled into the van, which could easily have stored sides of beef, it was so cold after the night parked outside.

Branch had been in the driver's seat when the van left the compound last night, so it made sense to put him in the driver's seat on the way back in. It was a brazen plan. But Branch might have been one of the caterers. He might have gone out last night for more food and returned this morning with breakfast. A new face in the driver's seat would almost certainly eliminate that element of doubt. Or so they'd allowed themselves to believe.

Gaspar took the passenger seat. Kim, Duffy, and Villanueva sat on the icy floor in the back, out of sight.

The wind gusts had subsided, but the combination of heavy snowfall on the road and the panel van's unstable top heaviness made driving treacherous. The van slid off the road several times before they reached the Abbot Cape Drive intersection, but it was heavy enough to get traction without them having to pile out and push it back onto the road.

Carefully, Branch turned left onto the entrance road. He drove slowly. Not only because the white van in a sea of white would be less visible at slow speed, but also because the road was snow-covered and difficult to see in the early morning light.

As they traveled closer to the compound, snow accumulation

on the road diminished, because the dense trees had protected the road from the worst snowfall and drifting.

Branch noticed snow tracks on the road similar to tracks made in the sand by tanks. "That was a snow cat we heard last night, all right. Duffy, did you see one inside the compound?"

"I didn't have a chance to thoroughly search the garages. There's more than one, and they're a good distance from the house," Duffy said. "There's the big garage that was once a stable. The second floor of that one is guest rooms. That must be where they've housed the women you saw delivered by helicopter. The main house doesn't have enough bedrooms to sleep that many."

"Where's the second garage?" Gaspar asked.

"On the north side of the guest house," Duffy replied. "You can't see it from the driveway or those video views you downloaded from the satellite. But it's there."

Branch continued to drive straight toward the compound. This was the third time he had traveled the road. He anticipated the curves this time, which also helped him to keep the top-heavy van between the ditches.

They kept their voices low in case the surveillance along the road also captured sound. They'd gone over everything several times back at the motel, so there wasn't much to talk about anyway.

They had ridden about nine miles in silence before they saw the open land ahead. They'd be leaving the protective cover of the salt pines and emerging into the open headlands. The vehicle would be totally exposed for about three minutes before it reached the gate. In three minutes, anything could happen.

"Everybody ready?" Kim murmured as she pulled her Glock from its holster. Duffy had acquired a Glock from Villanueva earlier, and did the same. Gaspar and Branch held their weapons ready and out of sight.

Villanueva had a Mossberg M500 Persuader. A Cruiser model. No shoulder stock. Just a pistol grip. It was a paramilitary weapon Kim didn't see often.

"Interesting choice," Kim whispered.

"You should try it sometime," Villanueva grinned. "Moves like silk on skin and clicks like a Nikon. Seven Brenneke Magnum slugs in this baby. Punch a hole in a cinderblock wall big enough to crawl through."

Kim nodded. "That may come in handy."

Branch rolled the van slowly through the last of the headlands, past the beaches, and stopped at the gate.

For the first time, the bulky security guard did not come out of the gatehouse when the van approached.

Kim gripped her Glock. Shooting the guard was not the best option, but if he attacked them first, she was prepared to do whatever was necessary. She saw Duffy and Villanueva ready their weapons, too.

Branch waited, the van's engine running. He lowered the window. For a moment, Kim worried that he'd tap the horn the way an unsuspecting caterer might.

"Now what?" Gaspar whispered.

They'd discussed and rejected all of the options for blasting into the compound and agreed: To rescue Teresa Justice and get out alive, they needed to breach the gate without drawing undue attention to themselves.

"Let's see what's going on." Branch pushed the transmission into park and opened the door. He stepped down into the snow and walked ten feet to the gate, in full view of the surveillance camera. He stood tall and raised his hands and shoulders in a "What gives?" gesture, as an unsuspecting visitor would.

He was fully exposed. No opportunity for cover. If the gateman or one of the other security guards wanted to take Branch out, they had an easy target.

Kim kept her Glock in position, just in case their first shot missed.

After two full minutes, the iron gate swung open, slowly. The big man must have released it remotely, from inside the gatehouse. Perhaps he'd done so before. They hadn't been watching him around the clock.

Gooseflesh rose along her arms. This felt too easy. Too good to be true. She didn't like it.

Duffy seemed too relaxed about the gate opening. Villanueva, too, for that matter. Kim's awareness of her team and their behaviors was on high alert.

Branch waved and said, "Thanks!" toward the camera, and returned to the van. He climbed into the driver's seat and engaged the transmission. When the gate had swung fully open, Branch took his foot off the brake and rolled easily inside the compound.

They had discussed this part at length.

They could travel freely in and out of the compound, even on foot, as long as the gate wasn't closed and locked.

Villanueva wanted to leave the van at the threshold in the driveway to block the gate open. The problem with that was that one of the security team or one of the guests was bound to notice. The big man responsible for ingress and egress would investigate, and no one wanted that.

In the end, they'd agreed to return the van to the back of the house, near the kitchen—the same spot Branch had stolen it from the evening before—and solve the problem of reopening the gate when the time came.

Hardly ideal, but no better alternative presented itself.

When the van cleared the gate, it swung closed. No one spoke. No one asked why the gateman had stayed inside instead of punching in the code on the keypad on the outside pillar as they'd seen him do before. Nothing she could do about that now. They were inside. One hurdle completed.

Branch rolled the van slowly along the driveway, through the carriage circle, and around behind the house. He completed a three-point turn and backed the van into its place. The cargo doors would be closest to the kitchen, exactly as the first panel van next to it was parked. Exactly where this panel van was sitting when he stole it last night.

Kim looked at her watch. How much time did they have to find Teresa Justice and get the hell out of here? Also not knowable, though sooner was definitely preferable to later.

Duffy and Branch had been in the compound before. The others had studied the video and public blueprints of the compound and the structures within. As Duffy had said, there were three large buildings. The main house, the gatehouse, and the garage.

Duffy and Branch were convinced that Teresa Justice was not in the main house last night, but that didn't mean she wasn't there now. Kim and Villanueva would search the basement and the remainder of the main house.

Duffy would begin the search of the gatehouse. Branch would search the garage and the guest rooms and then assist Duffy.

Gaspar moved into the driver's seat. He'd be ready to get the hell out of here the moment they all returned.

"Remember, we agreed," Kim said. "Twenty minutes. No more. We meet back at the van and go, whether we've found Teresa or not. We don't even know if she ever came here. We don't know if she's still here. We can't risk staying too long, no matter what."

Duffy nodded. Branch flashed a thumbs up. Villanueva said, "Roger that."

The four piled out of the van and peeled off.

CHAPTER THIRTY-THREE

BRANCH DUCKED INTO THE shadows between the main house and the ocean. Deep snow covered the rocks, creating an unstable walking path. The cloud cover had lifted overnight. The morning's pale sky barely illuminated trampled snow that must have been traveled by the women last night and pointed him toward the old stable.

The morning was unnaturally quiet. Deep snow muffled sound. But the ocean continued its normal rhythms, big waves crashing against the rocks and receding like a hypnotic metronome. He glanced ahead, south and east, where two shelves of granite met, a deep V between them. The gray ocean water washed into the V with every incoming wave and then returned to its source.

Must be a hell of a riptide here. The ocean was deep, dark, cold. Sharks. Crabs. Who knew what other creatures were out there. If Teresa Justice had been sneaking around back here, if she'd slipped on these rocks, fallen into the riptide—certainly, she'd never be seen again. An involuntary shudder ran the length of his body. *What a horrible way to die.*

Branch turned his head away from the wind and ducked into his jacket. He stuffed both hands in his pockets and was reassured by the feel of his weapon against his side. He trudged, one foot in front of the other, along the rocky path. Stepping carefully. Just in case.

The path eventually ended at the old stable, out on its own inside a small, walled courtyard. The blueprints he'd seen showed granite cobblestones in front and a vented cupola on the roof, originally to let the horse stench escape. Since the second story had been added, the cupola was purely decorative.

At the time of the earlier ATF raid, nine years ago, the stalls had been knocked together and four garages created. Those four garages were still here, but the hayloft had since been removed and the second-floor guest rooms added.

The four garages had separate doors, but all opened with electronic lifts controlled from somewhere inside. Branch followed the trampled snow to the south end of the building where he found a steel entrance door. He reached for the handle and turned.

To his initial surprise, the door opened. But then he realized leaving the door unlocked presented very little risk. Assuming they wanted to escape, if one or more of the virgins left the dormitory above the garage, how far could they go?

Teresa Justice was tougher and better trained than the others, probably. She might have escaped. He hoped she had.

He stepped through the doorway and closed the door softly behind him. If it was equipped with an alarm, he heard no evidence of one. The entrance was six-by-six square. A door led into the garage. A staircase led to the second level. Emergency lighting cast a pale glow over bare walls and vinyl flooring.

He allowed his eyes to adjust.

He paused a moment longer, listening for movement overhead, but heard none.

He quietly knocked the snow off his boots and tread lightly up the staircase.

At the top, he entered a long corridor that ran the length of the former stables. He counted eight closed doors on either side. Again, the emergency lighting seemed bright by comparison to the blackness outside. He blinked several times to adjust his pupils.

Eight doors on each side. Sixteen rooms. Twenty-eight women. Probably meant two women in each room, with the caterers or security staff bunking in the extras. At this hour, he hoped they were all still sleeping.

Was Teresa Justice among them? Only one way to find out.

Weapon raised, he walked softly to the first door and eased it open. The door swung inward, silently, on well-oiled hinges. The darkened interior was quiet.

He directed his micro-beam light to the ground and swept it low across the floor. An open doorway on the right probably led to a bathroom. Two straight-backed chairs flanked the two full-sized beds. The beds were occupied, one still form in each. He imagined their even breathing.

He crept toward the narrow opening between the beds. He paused at the foot of the beds, held his breath, raised his weapon, and briefly flashed the microbeam across the two heads on the pillows. They didn't stir.

It had been several years since he'd seen Teresa Justice in person. She'd looked fragile and pale back then. Too young for her age. Too inexperienced for her job. But she'd been through a lot since then, and her experiences must have aged her, probably well beyond her years. Even in sleep's repose, her face could not possibly look as young as these two angelic faces asleep on the pillows.

They were kids. Eighteen, maybe. Twenty, at the most. And they didn't stir so much as a quickening breath. They must have been drugged. That was the only reason he could think of for their total oblivion, given these strange surroundings and their uncertain situation.

He backed slowly out of the first room and moved on to the next. Again, he slipped inside. Again, he prepared for resistance. Again, he found sleeping girls. Young and practically comatose.

All along the corridor, he repeated the process. At the end of the corridor, he turned and headed back toward the exit. Every room and its occupants were eerily the same.

After fourteen doors, he felt like he was embedded in a recurring dream. He'd spent fifteen of the twenty minutes they'd agreed upon, and he hadn't found Teresa.

Only two rooms left to check. If Teresa was inside one of them, she'd probably been drugged as well, but he could scoop her up and run her outside. Pile in the van, gather the others, solve the problem of their exit through the damn gate, and get out of Dodge. The ATF would rescue the others when they arrived in a few hours.

Branch felt the tension in his limbs and his shoulders. He stretched his neck, took a deep breath, raised his weapon, and pushed the fifteenth door open.

The familiar darkness greeted him. He swept his micro-beam across the floor to identify two beds.

One bed was occupied by a snoring man.

The other one was empty.

He noticed a thin line of light at the bottom of the bathroom door. Someone was inside.

He ran the micro-beam across the snoring man's face. It was the caterer. The one who had been driving the van. He might get lucky. The guy in the bathroom should be the second caterer. Neither should be armed.

He backed up quietly and left the caterers' room before he was discovered.

Branch stood in front of the last door. He was more likely to walk directly into well-trained security guards than a slumbering Teresa Justice on the other side of it. But he'd come this far, and she could be there. He had to check.

One last time, he raised his weapon. He clasped and turned the doorknob. He pushed the door inward, prepared to shoot.

Quickly, he absorbed the scene.

The bathroom door was open. Bright light spilled out, illuminating the room.

Two beds.

One unused. A man's jeans, shirt, socks, underwear, and jacket were thrown across it. Next to the jacket were two weapons. One Beretta, essentially the civilian equivalent of the U.S. Military M9, and one MP5K, a short, futuristic-looking Heckler & Koch submachine gun.

His mind whirred. The Beretta made sense. It functioned in extreme heat and extreme cold, after submersion in salt water, even after being buried in sand, mud, and snow, or dropped on concrete. It was a reliable pistol. Branch held one exactly like it in his right hand.

But what the hell was the H&K needed for?

The second bed was currently unoccupied. Wrinkled bedclothes had been tossed across when the sleeper left its warmth.

Branch heard the bathroom shower running. Steam wafted

through the open doorway. He grinned. At least the guy would be unarmed.

He closed the door behind him, flipped on the lights, and crossed the room. He picked up the Beretta from the bed and slipped it into his pocket.

He stepped into the bathroom, his Beretta pointed directly at the billowing shower curtain. He reached around and flipped off the light switch.

"What the hell?" The man in the shower turned off the water.

Scraping metal on metal as he pushed the shower curtain aside.

Branch flipped the light switch on again.

Standing in the tub, soaking wet, hair plastered to his head, eyes wide, mouth open, was Harvey Walter Earle. Sokol's head of security. Branch grinned. He didn't spend a moment wondering why in the hell Earle had bunked over the garage last night. Why would he? He'd hit the jackpot.

"At this distance, I can't possibly miss." Branch pointed the Beretta at Earle's stomach, below his navel. He'd be blown in half. "Where is Teresa Justice?"

Earle scowled. "I have no idea who you're talking about."

Branch figured the statement was half-true. "Teresa Justice. She came into this compound nine days ago."

Recognition flickered in Earle's eyes. He smirked. "She's no longer with us."

Branch understood exactly what he meant. He tossed a towel toward Earle, who caught it with one hand. "Let's go."

"Go where?" He used the towel to dry his body without covering his face. He was watching closely. Probably for a chance to overpower Branch. Fat chance.

"Let's go. You've got two minutes to talk me out of throwing your sorry ass off those rocks out there." Branch held the Beretta steadily aimed at the same center spot on Earle's abdomen. "Or I can shoot you and save myself a lot of trouble. I don't think anybody in the main house would hear the gunshots all the way out here and nobody else in this building would care."

Earle scowled again, wrapped the damp towel around his waist, and stepped out of the tub.

Prodding him with the Beretta, Branch encouraged Earle to leave the room, enter the hallway, and walk to the stairs. When they reached the landing, Branch gave Earle a hearty shove between the shoulder blades.

The blow was unexpected. Earle tumbled violently down the stairs, making an impressive variety of unpleasant sounds before coming to a sudden, messy stop at the bottom, his limbs a tangle of odd angles. He might have been dead. Or unconscious. Branch couldn't bring himself to care.

Branch ducked back to the room and snagged the MP5K. The last thing he needed was one of the caterers to find it. Then he hurried down the stairs.

At the bottom, he checked Earle's carotid pulse. Against all odds, still alive. He opened the garage door and pulled Earle into the big, cold space. A quick survey of the closest workbench yielded several rolls of gray duct tape. He used one of them to bind Earle's battered, twisted wrists and ankles, forearms and calves. Then he wrapped two layers around his head to cover his mouth and used the last of the roll to create a diaper, binding his short and curlies with the sticky adhesive, simply to make him cringe when he removed it, should he survive. The bastard.

He left Earle lying naked on the cold cement floor.

CHAPTER THIRTY-FOUR

AFTER THEY HAD JUMPED from the van, Kim led the way to the back door of the main house, and Villanueva followed. There were only two entrance doors. The other was in the front of the house. Too risky. They might have tried to climb in through a window, but that would have taken too much time. The kitchen entrance was the best of the bad choices.

A snowdrift blocked the storm door on the kitchen porch, which probably meant no one had left through the kitchen in the past few hours. Kim's heartbeat quickened. How many people were inside the house? No way to know for sure. They'd seen at least a dozen people milling around at various times, not including the virgins.

Villanueva kicked away the snow and pulled the storm door open. Its hinges protested. The sound of screaming metal seemed extraordinarily loud in the snow-muffled morning.

Lights were on in the kitchen. She heard bustling activity inside. Pots, pans and metal utensils clanged together. After a couple of moments listening, she heard two female voices and three males. Kim readied her Glock and Villanueva raised the Persuader.

Carefully, as quietly as possible, she turned the handle and pushed the door open into the kitchen.

Before she stepped through, Villanueva put a hand on her arm. He gestured to the doorframe. He mouthed "metal detector."

Kim stepped back and pulled the door closed. She watched through the window until both women carried food into another room and the caterers seemed occupied with cooking, with their backs toward the door.

Now or never.

She opened the door, knelt down, and laid her Glock on the floor. Carefully, she pushed it through into the kitchen along the dead spot at the bottom of the metal detector. She did the same with the two spare magazines she carried in her pocket. She stood and walked through the door and picked up her weapon and the two magazines. The caterers were intent on their work and didn't seem to notice. Or maybe they did notice and had seen so many people coming and going the past few hours that they were unconcerned with two more.

She turned back and gestured to Villanueva to follow her lead. The Persuader was a bigger weapon than her Glock. It might have been too big to pass through the dead spot. She held her breath and kept her Glock ready until he was safely inside. He closed the door again.

They stood inside the kitchen to orient themselves a moment before Kim sent Villanueva ahead of her toward the back hallway. When she reached the archway, she ducked inside. Their feet were quiet on the thick carpet. She could hear the buzz of conversation from the dining room. The pitch was low as if there were no women speaking.

Villanueva walked past a door to the room that had once

been a parlor. He glanced inside and kept going to the stairs and went up, quick and quiet. Kim reached the open door a moment later and looked inside.

The space was set up like a conference room. Seating for ten. Five big screen TVs on the walls. Water glasses and pitchers were placed on the tables at each chair. She wondered what Sokol had planned, and whether the ATF would get here in time to stop him. Her makeshift band wasn't up to the task. Sokol's security team was heavily armed and outnumbered them, for starters.

Villanueva reached the second floor and peeled off to check the rooms behind the closed doors. Kim continued up the stairs to the third floor. There were only four rooms off the common hallway. She checked each one quickly. Three were in use, but the guests who occupied them must have been in the dining room downstairs. Teresa Justice was not here.

She moved quietly along the carpet to the fourth room. It was plain, square, oak-paneled. Like the others, it was furnished with dark, old furniture. A bed and an armoire, because there was no closet. A small bedside table. One straight-backed chair. The room had one window facing due east. At this point, she had to be standing fifty feet above the rocky shoreline. She imagined an amazing view of the ocean in the daylight.

Across the room, on the left, another door stood open. She heard a toilet flush. Abrams walked into the room. His eyes widened. He reached into his jacket with his right hand.

She raised her weapon. "Stop. Get your hands up."

He stopped, but he didn't remove his hand from his jacket.

"Hands up." She had boxed herself in.

She couldn't shoot him without alerting Sokol's security team. She wasn't close enough to disable him. Her only advantage was superior knowledge. She knew who he was. He'd never seen her before.

"Who are you?" she demanded. "Why are you in this room?"

He didn't raise his hands, but the tension in his body visibly relaxed, and he removed his hand from his jacket. "You don't know who I am?"

"No." She didn't lower her weapon. No halfway decent security guard would have. "I was told to secure the rooms on this floor, which should be unoccupied. Our guests expect us to ensure their privacy and the security of their possessions."

"Of course. I was merely interested in the view. This is the highest point in the house. The room was, as you say, unoccupied." He gestured toward the window where dawn peeked above the horizon. "Thank you for your diligence. I'll rejoin the others."

He moved two steps forward, toward the door. Her choices were limited. She stepped into the corridor to allow him to pass. Just as he fully entered the hall, his weight distributed on his leading foot, she stepped forward and shoved him down the corridor ahead of her. Fast. Hard. Using her entire bodyweight.

Already off balance, he slammed onto his right side, pinning his gun arm beneath his body. She kicked him in the temple, one of the softest places on the human skull.

The carpet absorbed some of the impact on the other side of his head. She said a little thank-you prayer for that. ATF wouldn't schlep all the way out here today if their most wanted suspect was already dead.

She searched him, removed his cell phone and a pistol from his jacket pocket and another pistol from an ankle holster. His trouser pockets held a knife and a handful of mismatched gold coins. His wallet rested in his left breast pocket. She pulled those, too.

With considerable difficulty she dragged him back into the bedroom and spied the room's key lying on the bedside table, ready for the room's next guest to lock the door on his way out.

She rushed to the window and looked outside. She'd believed Abrams when he said he'd come to this room because it was the highest point in the house. But what could he have been looking for? It was still dark. The ocean was a black hole of nothingness beyond the rocky shoreline.

She squinted and scanned the area near the shore until she found it. Lights. Maybe a quarter mile out. A boat. Waiting.

Waiting for what? For Abrams? Did he intend to leave the compound by boat when Sokol's meetings concluded? Maybe so. Much easier to smuggle gold out of the country that way, if that was his plan.

Time was short. She turned, grabbed the key, and stepped into the hallway.

She locked the door from the outside. He'd be unconscious for a while. By the time they found him, her team would be gone. She'd report the boat to the ATF. Boats were slow. One of the agencies would be able to run it down from the air.

She stuffed Abrams' possessions into the pockets of her parka. She'd dump them somewhere else in the house, first chance she got.

Kim hurried down the stairs.

Villanueva was waiting at the second-floor landing. He shook his head. He hadn't found Teresa or a stash of gold, either.

They returned to the first floor. The door to the conference room was closed, and people were milling around inside. She couldn't hear the conversation. She felt like a ghost and an eavesdropper at the same time.

Villanueva walked past the conference room and led the way to the basement door. He raised his palms in question.

Kim glanced at her Seiko. They'd made good use of their time but only five minutes remained to return to the panel van. Duffy had been held captive in one of the basement cells. Teresa could be there. She nodded.

He opened the door and crossed the threshold. Kim was five steps behind.

She followed Villanueva down the stairs, past the laundry, through the gym and toward the room that had been Duffy's cell. The door was wide open.

Villanueva stood like a statue looking into the room.

Kim came up behind him. She stopped abruptly and stared.

"Were you in the army, Otto?" Villanueva asked.

"No, but I've had quite a bit of anti-terrorism training."

"That will work," he said. "Terrorists use C-4 as effectively as the army. What you're looking at is C-4 explosive packaged as standard-sized M112 demolition charges, manufactured into the M183 demolition charge assembly, which includes the priming assembly. Add a detonator on a timer, like that one," he pointed, "and you've got a powerful bomb."

She asked, but only to confirm. "In plain English, what does that mean?"

"It means there's enough explosive there to blow this building sky high."

She nodded. Just as she'd thought. "How much time do we have before it detonates?"

"The timer's display window has been sprayed over with black paint. It's there, and I can make out that it's running down, but we can't read it. In the movies, they set these things with hours-long lead times, but most guys don't hit 'Go' until they're almost ready for it to blast. Minutes, not hours. Otherwise, someone might find it. Disarm it, maybe." His voice was remarkably steady.

"Can you disarm it?"

"No. Can you?"

"No. Do I have time to run back upstairs?" She was thinking of Abrams. She'd left him locked in that room on the third floor.

Villanueva shook his head. "No way to tell. But since we know Teresa's not in this house, my preference would be to—"

"Get the hell out of here," she said along with him. She turned and ran back the way they'd come, with Villanueva close behind her. She stopped briefly at the laundry and dumped Abrams' cell phone and weapons and wallet and mismatched gold coins into the washing machine.

Villanueva gave her a questioning glance. "What's that?"

"I'll explain later," she said over her shoulder as she dashed up the stairs.

When they reached the kitchen, all of the staff had disappeared. The dining room was empty, too. For a moment, she wondered where they'd all gone. Far from the house, she hoped. She'd warn any of the household staff she encountered, but that was it. If she ran through the house shouting warnings, Sokol and his crew wouldn't believe her. She'd get herself, her team, and probably everyone else killed.

They hurried out the back door. The metal detector beeped when Kim went through and again when Villanueva followed. No one came running, but that didn't mean they wouldn't. Lucky for them if they did. At least it would get them out of the house and away from the bomb.

Gaspar was alone in the van. Kim hopped into the passenger seat, and Villanueva jumped into the back through the cargo doors. "Where's Branch and Duffy?" Kim asked. "We've got to go. Somebody's got this house rigged to explode."

"Explode? What the hell are you talking about?"

CHAPTER THIRTY-FIVE

BEFORE SHE COULD RESPOND to the question, Branch popped in through the cargo doors. He'd heard her instructions to Gaspar. He'd seen the bombing supplies first-hand last night. He had no need to ask for clarification. "Where's Duffy? Anybody seen her?"

Gaspar said, "She went into the gatehouse when you all fanned out twenty minutes ago. She hasn't come out."

"Drive over to the gatehouse. We'll find her and get away from here."

Gaspar started the van and pulled away.

"Branch?" Kim said. "You want to call ATF? That building goes up, Abrams and Sokol and everyone in it is going to die."

Branch asked, "How long have we got?"

Villanueva shook his head. "No way to tell. The detonator is set. It's on a timer but the remaining time has been obscured. Can't read it. You go back in there, you might not get out."

Gaspar rolled toward the front gate, which was closed. "Why

would Sokol want to blow up his house and everyone in it?"

"Can't see Sokol or his team setting that bomb," Villanueva said. "The way it's rigged. Looks like someone with U.S. military training to me."

Branch said, "There's a hell of a lot of explosives in that basement. I saw them in the room next to Duffy's cell last night. Once that first bomb goes, more are likely to follow. The big garage is far enough from the house. Those virgins are likely to be okay, as long as they stay where they are."

"Could we get them out?" Kim asked.

Branch shook his head. "No chance. They're all drugged. We'd have to pick each one up and carry them all to waiting vehicles of some kind. Do we have time for that?"

"No." Villanueva's tone was final.

They'd reached the gatehouse. No time for more speculation.

"Keep the engine running," Kim said. "Villanueva, can you figure out how to open the gate?"

He grinned and held up the Persuader. "I think this'll do the job on the locking mechanism."

"Perfect." She turned to Branch. "You go in the front door, and I'll run around to the garage. Be careful of the big guard. He didn't come out before, but he could have been on the toilet or something. He'll see you this time. From what I've seen, he'd only need to land one punch to kill you."

"Roger that," Branch said, climbing after Villanueva out the back door.

Kim left the van and stayed in the shadows and made her way around to the back of the gatehouse as quickly as she dared through the heavy snow.

At the garage were two entrance doors. One was a double-wide roll-up. Tractor marks ran under the door, suggesting the snow cat was inside. A standard thirty-six-inch steel entry door was next to the garage door. Hers were the only footprints in the snow anywhere near either of the doors.

She tried the handle on the steel entry door. It was unlocked. With the security staff and systems flooding this compound, they felt no need to lock doors, apparently.

She slipped inside.

The cavernous garage housed only two vehicles. The black limousine with the diplomatic license plate was parked closest to the house. Next to it was the snow cat. On the other side of the snow cat were what looked like two storage rooms. The door to one was closed.

The second door was open. A padlock hung from a hasp that had broken open when the door was splintered by what must have been a ferocious blow. Maybe a sledgehammer wielded by a powerful arm. Duffy couldn't have done it, for sure.

The light was on, but Kim heard no noises from inside the room. Her heart pounded, and her breathing was shallow. Blood thrummed in her ears. She held her Glock ready and crept around the vehicles, crouched low.

The last ten feet between the snow cat and the open storage room door was completely exposed. There was no way to cross the space without being seen.

She scanned the entire garage again and found no one. The big gate guard could have been watching her on surveillance cameras from inside. He could be on his way to deal with her. A chance she'd have to take. *When you have only one choice, it's the right choice.*

She dashed across the open space and flattened her back to the wall left of the open doorway. She craned her neck and looked inside.

Duffy stood with her back to Kim before a white chest freezer about seven feet wide that filled most of the room. The freezer lid was open. A padlock and hasp just like the one on the door had secured the freezer lid until recently. The padlock remained secured but worthless. This hasp, too, had been sheared as if someone had hit it with a sledgehammer. The padlock was still closed.

Duffy stood totally still, staring not into the freezer, but at the floor.

A black body bag lay at her feet.

The bag was unzipped and pushed open.

Inside the bag was a frozen corpse.

Kim walked into the room and stood next to Duffy.

She had never met Teresa Justice but recognized her all the same. Her eyes were closed. She might have been sleeping peacefully. In the photo Kim had seen of her from nine years ago, she'd looked innocent. Younger even than she was. The years had not been kind to her.

Duffy knelt next to her. Her friend was dead. Murdered, almost certainly. Duffy would blame herself. She'd been too late to save Teresa.

Kim touched Duffy's shoulder and spoke softly. "Come on. We've got to go."

"I can't leave her here."

"We can't take her with us. We'll come back. ATF will come back. But we can't carry her."

Duffy didn't move. Kim took hold of her by one bicep and pulled her to her feet. Gave her a little shake. "Come on. We've got to go. Now."

Still, Duffy didn't move.

The first shots came from inside the gatehouse.

After that, three loud explosions from Villanueva's Persuader at the gate.

She jerked Duffy's arm and said, "Come on."

Maybe it was the gunfire that woke her up. Duffy finally began to move.

Kim led the way.

CHAPTER THIRTY-SIX

SOKOL'S GUESTS HAD RETURNED to the conference room when he heard the first gunshots. The old house was like a fortress, but the snow muffled all ambient noise and amplified sounds inside the compound. Even so, a less experienced man, one who had never seen combat, might not have recognized the sound of gunfire from the gatehouse.

The India delegation was the first to react. He saw the alarm in their eyes.

The Africans' concern was laced with consternation, perhaps because they feared the mass destruction they'd paid for today would be interrupted.

"Gentlemen, please do not concern yourselves," Sokol said as if he were soothing irrational fears instead of valid ones. "My security team will investigate and resolve matters outside. We have only a few minutes left on our countdown. The weapon will launch. The plane will be destroyed. Please remain seated. We'll be showing the images of Grand Ocean Airways Flight 86 shortly."

No sooner had he calmed them when he heard three shotgun

explosions at the gate, each powerful enough to knock a hole in the eight-foot granite wall surrounding the compound.

The first shotgun round sent nervous comments through his guests. The second shot pushed half of them to their feet. The third round raised the remaining members of the delegation and sent them like a herd of warriors toward the front of the house.

Only Sokol and the Africans remained, looking at the big screens, glowering. "Will the weapon deploy? We've paid already. We're expecting success."

"Of course. Everything is in place. Please remain here." Sokol had the gold already. He didn't need to tell them the truth. The weapon would not be released toward the target unless he sent the signal. Which he would not do unless everyone returned to their seats. He wanted more than the Africans' gold. He wanted the gold promised by the others as well. Discipline was required. A man was only as good as his word.

The Chinese had led the herd from the conference room to the front of the house. The Arabs and the Indians had followed.

Where were Abrams and Earle? It was their job to maintain order. To ensure everything went smoothly. Earle should be outside, dealing with the gunshots. But Abrams should be here, dealing with the buyers.

Sokol nodded toward the Africans. "You stay here and watch the plane go down. I'll be right back."

He left the conference room. When he walked through the front of the house, Abrams was not there yet. Where the hell was he? Sokol had told Moscow never to trust the thug, and he felt justified.

The buyers and their bodyguards had drawn arms. As they passed through the front door into the carriage circle, the metal detector alarmed in one long, piercing shriek. More gunfire had erupted outside.

Sokol raised his palms to cover his ears.

Through the big front windows, he saw the additional security staff, along with his usual team, had armed and moved into the carriage circle from various points on the compound. He didn't see Earle or Abrams. Neither had arrived.

Sokol's only option was to escape. While he still could. He couldn't wait until the appointed time.

He hurried through the dining room and into the kitchen.

He pulled his cell phone out of his pocket and sent the signal to the captain on board the waiting ship anchored a few hundred yards offshore. A speedboat would be dispatched to meet him at the base of the rocks behind the house.

Sokol hurried to the back corridor and down the basement stairs. Through the laundry, through the gym, on his way to the escape tunnel he'd built into the renovated house when he acquired the property.

The tunnel was inside the unused cell. Next to the skinny bitch's cell.

He was almost there. He heard the gunfire outside intensify, like an army invasion.

He rushed toward the tunnel's entrance. When he reached the open door to the skinny bitch's cell, he glanced inside.

He stopped moving.

Sokol knew precisely what he saw. His breath came painfully as his heart slammed in his chest. His eyes widened.

He saw the detonator. He saw the timer, but he couldn't read it.

He backed away from the bomb.

Every nerve in his body said he had mere seconds to escape.

No time to run back upstairs and away from the explosives.

If he could run through the tunnel and out to the ocean before detonation, he might survive. And get away. It was the only way.

He ran into the second room. Cold sweat bathed his neck and face. He struggled to move the heavy old chest away from the tunnel's entrance.

He yanked a gold chain from around his neck containing the key to the three padlocks, the same manufacturer and indestructible style as the two he'd used to secure the dead woman in the freezer in the gatehouse.

The gold chain broke.

The key flew away from his palsied, sweaty hands and skidded across the cement floor, sliding under the empty cot on the opposite wall.

He fell to his hands and knees, scrambling after it in what he suddenly realized with horror was almost certain pointlessness.

CHAPTER THIRTY-SEVEN

DUFFY AND KIM RAN across the garage and through the steel exit door to the interior of the gatehouse. A long corridor led to the front of the building. Running full out, Kim reached the open living space, and before she could stop, she tripped over the body of a huge dead man with a broken neck and a giant hole in the middle of his back sprawled in the middle of the floor.

She slipped on his pooled blood and landed on all fours, inches from his head.

There was absolutely no question. He was dead. His hands and arms were a mutilated mess like he'd been steamrolled. No life-saving techniques could possibly resurrect him.

Duffy seemed unconcerned by the mutilated body as if she'd expected to find it there.

Gunfire. From the direction of the main house.

Duffy pulled Kim away. "Come on!"

Kim scrambled to her feet and followed Duffy out the front door.

More shots were fired before they reached the van at the front gate.

Four security guards were thrashing from the main house through the deep snow covering the driveway, firing handguns as they came closer.

Villanueva and Branch were already inside the van.

Kim pushed Duffy through the rear cargo doors, jumped in after her, and pulled the doors closed.

Gaspar stepped on the accelerator. The van lurched and fishtailed. He backed off the gas until the tires found purchase on the snowy driveway, and then they shot through the gate.

Kim perched between the two front seats and looked back using the side mirrors as Gaspar drove as fast as he dared away from the compound. At least half a dozen men had already run from the front door toward the gate, and what felt like an endless parade of armed shooters followed.

The images receded as Gaspar continued to race away.

Before the van crossed the open beaches and reached the cover of the salt pine trees, the C-4 bomb in the basement detonated. The big house exploded, sending a fireball like a nuclear mushroom cloud high into the morning sky.

Debris from the explosion flew everywhere.

Bodies between the house and the gate flew like rag dolls and landed awkwardly in the snow.

Gaspar kept going.

What seemed like an hour later, when they finally entered the cover of the pines, Kim reached into her pocket and pulled out the Boss's phone. She auto-dialed his number, heard the familiar ring at the other end of the line.

He picked up.

Breathlessly, she said, "Did you see that?"

"What the hell happened?" he asked. Followed quickly by, "Is Reacher dead?"

She hung up.

Villanueva scowled, knowing full well by now who'd been on that line. "Charles Cooper," he muttered. "I wouldn't trust that viper if he was the man bringing my last meal on death row."

"Amen to that," Branch and Duffy said simultaneously.

Gaspar said nothing but Kim could hear his "I told you so" ringing in her ears anyway. He'd never trusted the Boss. But she had. In the beginning.

CHAPTER THIRTY-EIGHT

KIM HAD SPENT THE past hour uploading her private reports to her personal server. Paying her insurance premium, she called it. Just in case. She was packing the last of her electronics when Duffy walked in with two black coffees and offered one to Kim.

"Branch is warming up the SUV. I wanted to say goodbye and thank you again. And I promised you answers." Duffy cleared her throat and seemed to struggle with her emotions. "When you helped me with Teresa."

Kim took the coffee. She sat on the edge of the bed and waved Duffy to the only chair. She seemed a bit fragile this morning. Which was understandable. She'd been through a harrowing experience the past few days.

"How did you escape that cell in the basement?" Kim asked, warming up to her real questions. "You didn't manage that by yourself, did you?"

Duffy looked down at her hands, one holding the coffee, the other flat on her thigh. She looked like a woman in need of a drink much stronger than caffeine. "I owe you, Otto. I know you didn't have to come after me, and I know I might not have made it out without your help."

Kim nodded to acknowledge the truth. "Reacher freed you from that basement cell, didn't he?"

"That's an old house, but it's a sturdy one. There was no way to break free of that room without a key. There was no keyhole, and there was no window and no means of escape. Someone had to come in from the outside." She looked steadily into Kim's eyes. "Reacher did what needed to be done."

"So when Branch arrived, you were already free. Branch did not kill that bodyguard. Reacher did." Kim was affirming the facts for herself as much as for Duffy. "What did the two of you do next, before Branch arrived?"

"We searched for Teresa. Sokol and Abrams were busy with other matters in the dining room. A cocktail party or something for the arms buyers they'd brought in. They barely paid any attention to the rest of us. Maybe they thought we were with the catering staff or something." She drank her coffee and rubbed her palm along her jeans. "We searched the rest of the basement and the house. Teresa wasn't there. We went outside. Reacher took the gatehouse. Before I could search the garage, I saw Branch. I didn't want him to hang around, and the weather was getting worse, and Reacher wanted us to go."

"Why?"

"I think it was because he wanted time to set up that explosion." She shrugged. "At the time, he didn't say, and I didn't ask. I told him we'd be back for Teresa, and I'd wait for Branch in the van. Reacher said he would look for Teresa while I was gone. He had met Teresa last time, and he knew her."

Kim had her own ideas about Reacher's motives, but she didn't argue. "You had some time to talk with Reacher. What did you talk about?"

"I asked him why Charles Cooper is looking for him." Duffy paused. "Cooper is a dangerous man. He's not someone I want to be on the wrong side of. I told Reacher that."

"What did he say?"

"He said it was old scores to settle. He told me he'd settle them when the time is right." She paused. "Unless Cooper gets to him first, was my answer. Reacher said he's not ready to deal with Cooper yet."

"You know we're doing a background check for the SPTF. We need to fill in the blanks," Kim said. "Why did you warn us away from looking in the FBI files for mentions of Reacher when we saw you in D.C.?"

"Reacher has been a friend to law enforcement in the past. He's worked with the FBI and other agencies. Always unauthorized. Always off the books. Of course, there *should* be information about him in the files." She paused, maybe to be sure Kim paid attention, before she stressed, "There's nothing there, and nothing will ever be there. Stop looking."

Kim shook her head. "Why would anyone remove all references to Reacher from the files?"

"I don't know. What I do know is that you're drawing the wrong kind of attention to him. And to yourselves, understand?" She looked hard into Kim's eyes. "It's dangerous for you and for Gaspar to keep searching those files. Stop."

"Roger that," Kim said to acknowledge, but not to agree. "Is Reacher CIA?"

"He's the farthest thing from covert that any man could possibly be." Duffy laughed. "He's a freelancer. Works when he feels like it and not when he doesn't. But you're thinking in the right direction. He's definitely a ghost."

"What did he tell you about Lamont Finlay?"

"Finlay? Special Assistant to the President for Strategy? The guy who's one heartbeat away from the President? Nothing." Duffy looked bewildered. "You think Reacher knows the guy? He's pretty high up the ladder. Reacher is more likely to know Finlay's doorman."

Kim thought for a minute. She had a willing witness sitting in front of her. What did she need to know? "Reacher couldn't have just shown up here out of the blue. Someone must have contacted him. Was that you?"

"Not exactly. I've never known how to contact him. He says he doesn't want to be tethered to anything."

"So how did he know you were here?"

"You already know that I helped him in D.C. and again in Virginia. I didn't see him in Virginia, so we didn't talk then. But when I saw him in D.C., I told him about Teresa." She paused again, as if to gather her thoughts, but probably she was considering what to leave in, what to leave out. "I told him she'd been in a bad way for the past nine years. I told him she was working human trafficking as a PI and that she was looking at the current resident of Abbot Cape. I said she probably would need help soon, and if she called, I planned to help her."

Kim thought about the answer. How would Cooper have known that Duffy told Reacher where to find Teresa? He might have listened in on that conversation in D.C., either at the time or to the recording later, although that seemed unlikely. He didn't have the time to listen to every conversation floating around in the air. Maybe it was something simpler, though. "Does Reacher have a cell phone?"

"No." Duffy smiled. "But he uses burners and pay phones. He's not a total Luddite."

"So Reacher called you. He asked about Teresa," Kim guessed. Cooper had to be monitoring Duffy's calls. That's how he'd known she was headed to Abbot Cape and why she'd come here. "You told him Teresa had disappeared. Told him you were headed this way."

Duffy said nothing, which Kim took as an affirmative.

"Why is Reacher hiding from us? From Cooper?"

"Reacher isn't hiding." Duffy threw back her head and laughed out loud. "It would be impossible for him to hide. He's too, well, let's say distinctive, to hide anywhere for very long. Hiding is not what he does."

"Susan, I like you. You're a practical woman, and I respect that. You're ambitious and driven and hard-working and exceptionally competent. I respect all of that, too." Kim took a breath. "What I don't understand is your connection to Reacher. Why would a woman like you be involved with a guy like that?"

"A guy like what? A stone cold killer, you're thinking?" Duffy cocked her head. "Reacher's got his...charms. He likes to see the right thing done. Like me, and I suspect, like you. He's practical and pragmatic, too. No drama."

Kim waited.

"He has certain skills which can be put to good use and that's no doubt why Cooper and Finlay are interested in him." Duffy folded her hands in her lap and seemed to relax a bit. "Let's just for a moment assume that you actually *are* completing a background check for the Special Personnel Task Force." She paused, and Kim thought she might actually wink, but she didn't. "What you want to know is whether Reacher is physically, mentally, emotionally, and financially fit for the job.

What I can say is this. I've been in serious trouble more than once, and Reacher has been on my side. I can't begin to tell you how glad I've been about that. He doesn't play by the rules, and his methods are a little unorthodox. But if you're ever in trouble, you'll want him on your side, too."

Kim could ask Duffy questions for a week. But neither one of them had the time. And Duffy was only going to reveal what Reacher had given her permission to say, no matter how long the interview lasted.

"Do you think he got the virgins out? Maybe he survived that explosion, too?" Kim had her doubts. The entire house had been destroyed, along with a lot of its rocky foundation.

Duffy shrugged and lowered her head, but not before Kim noticed the tears that pooled in her eyes. Which answered another question. Reacher and Duffy had definitely been lovers.

Whatever else he was, whether it made any sense to Kim or not, Reacher definitely had some kind of appeal to women who carry guns and should be more than capable of taking care of themselves. They were beyond loyal to him. And he seemed loyal to them, too, in his own peculiar way.

Kim moved on to a different set of questions. "Does Reacher know he might have a daughter?"

Duffy's eyes widened to the size of gold coins. "I, uh, have no idea. What makes you say that?"

"I met a girl. She's the right age. Her mother was at the right place at the right time." She paused. "The girl has the right look and the right attitude."

Duffy shook her head slowly. "I knew Reacher for a short time a long time ago. If he has any family at all, he never mentioned it to me. Our relationship, if you can call it that, wasn't long chats in the moonlight."

"You knew him well enough. Better than I do." Kim paused. "If he found out about the girl, would he try to find her? Meet her?"

"He told me a story once. About challenging a subordinate who accused him of having feelings. It was a funny story, and I'm not sure he's as detached as he claims, but you get the point." Duffy was silent for a long time. Finally, she shrugged. "I really can't answer your question any better than that."

A sharp knock on the door was followed by Branch poking his head in. "Time to go."

"I'll be right there," Duffy said, and Branch ducked out again.

"Where are you going? In case I need to call you?"

"It's hard to say. I'm leaving ATF. I'm joining BlueRiver with Branch. We're on our way to Mexico. I don't know where I'll be next week." She paused briefly. "But I've told you all I can. Just know this: When he's ready, Reacher will find you. That's what he told me to tell you."

"Even if Reacher survived that explosion back there..." Kim shook her head. "Cooper's not going to accept that answer."

"The guy's had more than nine lives already. He almost died in that house years ago, but he survived." Duffy shrugged again. "And whatever Cooper wants Reacher to do is between them. Reacher will do it only if he wants to. Cooper knows that already."

"And what about Finlay?"

"I know nothing about Finlay. Sorry."

"One last thing." Kim nodded, accepting, finally, that Duffy might be telling the truth, or at least, most of it. "Why is Reacher living so far off the grid?"

"Because he can." Duffy stood and smiled and extended her

hand. They shook hands and then Duffy hugged her, like old friends. When she stood back, she looked sincerely into Kim's eyes. "It's as complicated and as simple as that."

After Duffy left, Kim collected her remaining possessions and slipped into the parka. It was still incredibly cold outside and not likely to be any warmer when she landed in Detroit.

She left her room at the Abbot Motel for the last time, and she wasn't sorry to close the door behind her.

Branch and Duffy were already gone. Villanueva had said his goodbyes earlier and headed back to Boston.

Gaspar had the SUV running to warm up. Kim tossed her stuff into the back and settled into the passenger seat. One advantage to the parka's hood was that it kept the shoulder harness off her neck. She didn't bother fishing out the alligator clamp.

"The roads are still a mess," Gaspar said, "but I-95 to Boston is likely to be our best option if we want to arrive before my unborn son goes off to college." He was grinning, probably just happy to be headed home to Miami.

"Make it so."

Kim was thinking about Reacher and the women she'd met who were so loyal to him. Reacher's file, such as it was, revealed a violent and brutal man who cared little for the rule of law and was exceptionally competent in all aspects of personal warfare. He was a fighting machine, no question. He had nothing to lose and killed without an ounce of remorse. Psychiatrists would label him a psychopath.

And yet, he was much more complicated than that.

Which only made him a more dangerous enemy.

She thought about Cooper, too. And Finlay. The three men were powerful in their own ways. They were engaged in some kind of elaborate game that she didn't yet understand. And she'd begun to wonder which side she should be on.

"Earth to Suzie Wong," Gaspar said. She looked over. He grinned. "Your phone's ringing."

She'd slipped the Boss's phone into the pocket of the parka. She couldn't feel it vibrating inside that big pillow. She pulled it out. "Otto."

"Everything at the Abbot Cape house is under control. Change of plans for you," Cooper said. "I can't talk now. I texted revised flight info. New files in the secure server. I'll call you."

Once again, she was holding dead air.

THE END

FROM LEE CHILD
THE REACHER REPORT:
March 2nd, 2012

THE OTHER BIG NEWS is Diane Capri—a friend of mine—wrote a book revisiting the events of KILLING FLOOR in Margrave, Georgia. She imagines an FBI team tasked to trace Reacher's current-day whereabouts. They begin by interviewing people who knew him—starting out with Roscoe and Finlay. Check out this review: "Oh heck yes! I am in love with this book. I'm a huge Jack Reacher fan. If you don't know Jack (pun intended!) then get thee to the bookstore/wherever you buy your fix and pick up one of the many Jack Reacher books by Lee Child. Heck, pick up all of them. In particular, read Killing Floor. Then come back and read Don't Know Jack. This story picks up the other from the point of view of Kim and Gaspar, FBI agents assigned to build a file on Jack Reacher. The problem is, as anyone who knows Reacher can attest, he lives completely off the grid. No cell phone, no house, no car…he's not tied down. A pretty daunting task, then, wouldn't you say?

First lines: "Just the facts. And not many of them, either. Jack Reacher's file was too stale and too thin to be credible. No human could be as invisible as Reacher appeared to be, whether he was currently above the ground or under it. Either the file had been sanitized, or Reacher was the most off-the-grid paranoid Kim Otto had ever heard of." Right away, I'm sensing who Kim Otto is and I'm delighted that I know something she doesn't. You see, I DO know Jack. And I know he's not paranoid. Not really. I know why he lives as he does, and I know what kind of man he is. I loved having that over Kim and Gaspar. If you haven't read any Reacher novels, then this will feel like a good, solid story in its own right. If you have...oh if you have, then you, too, will feel like you have a one-up on the FBI. It's a fun feeling!

"Kim and Gaspar are sent to Margrave by a mysterious boss who reminds me of Charlie, in Charlie's Angels. You never see him...you hear him. He never gives them all the facts. So they are left with a big pile of nothing. They end up embroiled in a murder case that seems connected to Reacher somehow, but they can't see how. Suffice to say the efforts to find the murderer and Reacher, and not lose their own heads in the process, makes for an entertaining read.

"I love the way the author handled the entire story. The pacing is dead on (ok another pun intended), the story is full of twists and turns like a Reacher novel would be, but it's another viewpoint of a Reacher story. It's an outside-in approach to Reacher.

"You might be asking, do they find him? Do they finally meet the infamous Jack Reacher?

"Go...read...now...find out!"

Sounds great, right? Check out *Don't Know Jack*, and let me know what you think.

So that's it for now...again, thanks for reading THE AFFAIR, and I hope you'll like A WANTED MAN just as much in September.

Lee Child

ABOUT THE AUTHOR

Diane Capri is an award-winning *New York Times*, *USA Today*, and worldwide bestselling author.

She's a recovering lawyer and snowbird who divides her time between Florida and Michigan. An active member of Mystery Writers of America, Author's Guild, International Thriller Writers, Alliance of Independent Authors, and Sisters in Crime, she loves to hear from readers and is hard at work on her next novel.

If you would like to be kept up to date with infrequent email including release dates for Diane Capri books, free offers, gifts, and general information for members only, please sign up for our Diane Capri Crowd mailing list. We don't want to leave you out! Sign up here: http://dianecapri.com/contact/

Please connect with her online:

http://www.DianeCapri.com

Twitter: http://twitter.com/@DianeCapri

Facebook: http://www.facebook.com/Diane.Capri1

http://www.facebook.com/DianeCapriBooks

Made in the USA
Coppell, TX
24 May 2021